"Do you want the truth?"

"Yes, please," Sheila answered.

"All right." Running a hand through his already untidy hair, Tony began to pace the small room. "I've never been in love. Thirty-four years old. Never." He stopped, turned to face her. "Have you?"

"No." She thought she saw a flicker of relief in his eyes before he resumed his pacing.

"I've never wanted to be. I've watched so many people *think* they are, *feel* they are, *know* they are. Then, in weeks or months, a year or two, it's gone. I don't want to make promises I can't keep. So I've never made any." He moved to her, close, very close, his breath warm on her cheeks. "Then you came along, only a short month ago. And you've ruined it for me."

Dear Reader,

Spellbinders! That's what we're striving for. The editors at Silhouette are determined to capture your imagination and win your heart with every single book we publish. Each month, six Special Editions are chosen with *you* in mind.

Our authors are our inspiration. Writers such as Nora Roberts, Tracy Sinclair, Kathleen Eagle, Carole Halston and Linda Howard—to name but a few—are masters at creating endearing characters and heartrending love stories. Their characters are everyday people—just like you and me—whose lives have been touched by love, whose dreams and desires suddenly come true!

So find a cozy, quiet place to read, and create your own special moment with a Silhouette Special Edition.

Sincerely,

The Editors
SILHOUETTE BOOKS

PAT WARREN
Final Verdict

Silhouette Special Edition

Published by Silhouette Books New York

America's Publisher of Contemporary Romance

To my mother,
Isabel O'Reilly,
who always believed in me.

SILHOUETTE BOOKS
300 East 42nd St., New York, N.Y. 10017

Books by Pat Warren

Silhouette Special Edition

With This Ring #375
Final Verdict #410

PAT WARREN

is a woman of many talents, including a fluency in Hungarian. She has worked as a newspaper columnist, a real estate broker and for a major airline. Growing up as an only child in Akron, Ohio, she learned early to entertain herself by reading books. Now she enjoys writing them. A mother of four—two boys and two girls—Pat lives in Arizona with her husband, a travel agent. She and her husband have traveled extensively throughout the United States, Canada, Mexico, Europe, Israel, Jordan and the Caribbean. She also enjoys tennis, swimming and theater, and visits New York City often.

Chapter One

Pulling around the cul-de-sac, Sheila North stopped her purple Volkswagen in front of 9193 Seminola Avenue and studied the small wrought-iron sign hanging from the front-yard lamppost. Adams, Blair and Adams, Attorneys at Law. Glancing down at the newspaper she held, she read the circled ad.

Efficiency office for rent; 550 sq. ft.; $315/mo. includes utilities, secretarial and janitorial services, private lav and kitchen privileges; good Indian Village location; prefer young, new attorney; lease; call 555-3090 for appointment.

Her eyes skimmed the three-story English Tudor building, once a stately home in this genteel section on the east side of Detroit, recently renovated and converted to offices with what appeared to be a loving touch. It looked every day of fifty years old, she decided, yet the structure was *House & Garden* perfect in the morning summer sun, with its newly mowed grass and freshly clipped hedges. Yes, this had to be the place the no-nonsense secretary, Rosemary Norris, had described to her on the phone yesterday afternoon. Fleetingly she wondered if the building's owner would consider twenty-seven young enough and three years' law experience new enough for rental purposes.

Sheila certainly hoped so, because she was tired of looking for an office. By next week she had to decide whether or not to take the Morgan case, so she had to find a place quickly. This one seemed ideal, close to her apartment, attractive, reasonable. Now if only the landlord turned out to be reasonable as well. She'd met only one of the partners, Jed Blair, a tall man with black hair and smiling brown eyes that effectively camouflaged one of the shrewdest legal minds she'd ever encountered.

Angling the rearview mirror, she glanced at her image, running a slender hand through her wind-tossed blond hair. There was a lot to be said for convertibles, but neatness was not one of the pluses. Oh, well, she was only here to look at an office, not interview for a job, she told herself. Never again, hopefully, would she have to go job hunting.

Reaching into the small box of raisins on the seat beside her, she scooped the final few into her mouth and tossed the empty container into her cluttered purse. Chewing her breakfast thoughtfully, she wondered why she was nervous about meeting Tony Adams. Now that she was a defense attorney out on her own and not a junior flunky in the corporate scheme of things, perhaps it was Tony's reputation as one of the rising stars in the prosecutor's office that had her slightly intimidated before she'd ever laid eyes on him. Though she'd never seen him at work in a courtroom, she knew he was very intense, extremely intelligent and often ruthless. And devastatingly handsome, or so she'd heard. Which had absolutely nothing to do with her renting an office in his building, Sheila reminded herself as she let up on the clutch.

Easing her car onto the gravel driveway, she drove around back, parking in the designated area. A vintage Mustang, a sleek white Corvette and a red Mercedes sat gleaming in front of a wide garage. Not bad, Sheila thought as she reached for her shoulder bag and stepped out. Her ancient Volkswagen looked a shade out of place alongside those three, but she loved it anyway.

Since it was Saturday, Rosemary had instructed her to take the back stairway to the secretary's main-floor office. The snow-white gravel crunched underfoot as she walked, admiring the house's old-world charm. Rough-hewn dark wood, beige stucco, sloping gabled roof, many oddly shaped windows. Her father would appreciate this place, Sheila decided as she approached the walk. And her father really knew houses. Maybe, if she rented the office, the next time he and her mother were in town, they'd...

The rattle of cans and the sound of breaking glass made Sheila turn toward the cement apron in front of the wide garage along the fence line. A tall man with sun-bronzed hair stood with his back to her, holding high a black trash bag with a gaping hole at the bottom. A final empty Scotch bottle plunked from its dark folds and rolled, landing noisily at Sheila's foot.

"Damn," he muttered, viewing the mess. Having emerged from the garage's side door, he hadn't seen her approach. As he turned, his gaze followed the trail of trash to Sheila and moved slowly up the length of her. Deep gray eyes registered annoyance, then surprise and finally appreciation as he looked at her.

She was stunning, Tony thought, with the pale, almost translucent skin of a true blonde and dusky brown eyes crinkling at the corners as she smiled.

Bending, Sheila picked up the bottle near her foot and walked toward him. "Party last night?" she asked.

"Sort of," he answered, pulling a cardboard box toward him. Stooping, he picked up a few of the larger items as he continued to study her. She wore a nubby-knit brown cotton sweater and ivory linen slacks, the top of her head not quite reaching his shoulder. Nice—she was nicely put together. He straightened, facing her. "It was a welcome-home party for the senator."

Of course, Sheila thought. Senator Maxwell T. Adams, recently retired, was coming back to the law practice that Jed Blair had been handling alone since Tony Adams had joined the prosecutor's office. She tossed the bottle into the box. "Looks like a good time was had by all," she commented as she mentally counted the number of scattered liquor bottles. She scooped up several empty peanut jars and threw them in also.

"I can manage," he told her. "You'll get all dirty." He saw her blink, her long lashes dark against her face, and wondered what she was thinking.

She was thinking she was decidedly overreacting to this handyman. Perhaps she'd been concentrating too much on her career lately and not giving her personal life much thought. Why else had her mouth gone dry as those solemn gray eyes had examined every inch of her?

He was attractive—but she ran across attractive men daily. He was slim-hipped, the sleeves of his checkered shirt rolled high on muscular arms, his shoulders broad. He looked to be a man in control, his thick auburn hair the only thing about him that didn't obey him, sticking up at the whim of the wind, curling along his neck. Appealing certainly, but when was the last time an appealing man had caused her to stare so?

"It's all right," she said to cover her nervousness. "Hands are washable." She glanced at him and saw his eyes had moved from boldly appraising to contemplative.

She couldn't help wondering why a man like this was doing ordinary labor. "Are you the one who just cut the grass?" she asked, her voice a shade on the husky side.

"Yes," he answered with a sudden smile, wondering why such a thing would matter to her. Then it struck him. She thought he was the gardener. For an instant, he toyed with the idea of correcting her quick assumption, then decided to let the scene play out. Both as an attorney and as a man, Tony Adams knew that it gave you an advantage over your opponents if you retained a piece of knowledge they'd not yet discovered.

His whole face changes when he smiles, Sheila noted, watching humor touch his eyes. What an oddly fascinating man, she thought, deciding not to examine her reactions to him right now. Some people just appeal to you more than others, that's all. Turning toward the small back lawn, Sheila dusted off her hands and inhaled deeply. "Mmm, I love that smell. Don't you wish someone would bottle it, and we could uncap it in the middle of winter?"

Lovely and fanciful—she was both. The fragrance that drifted to him from her had the grass beat two to one, he thought. Lightly floral, drenched in the summer sunshine, warm and inviting. Who was this woman? he wondered. "Are you looking for someone?"

"I have an appointment with Rosemary Norris about renting the upper-floor office." On impulse she thrust her hand toward him. "Sheila North," she said.

Wiping his hand on the faded denim of his jeans, he took her slender palm in his. "Are you an attorney?"

"Yes. I'm just setting up my own practice after three years with Babcock, Aimes and Whitney. They're a corporate law firm in the Penobscot Building. Downtown."

She was babbling, Sheila thought. Irritation with herself moved color into her face. Why was she telling this yardman, who hadn't even offered his name, all about herself? And why was her hand trembling in his?

An attorney who assumes too quickly and jumps readily to conclusions, Tony thought. Well, well. He couldn't resist teasing her a bit. "Yes, I've heard the Penobscot Building is downtown."

Chagrined, she felt a full blush flood her face. It'd been a long while since she'd acted quite so nitwitty. Buried beneath Sheila North's somewhat breathless facade and often impish grin was a native intelligence, a smart business head and an I.Q. that had surprised educators since her childhood. But Sheila knew that wasn't the impression she sometimes gave. Raised in a large, boisterous family, she sometimes came across as down-home friendly, which usually put people at ease. Today, much to her embarrassment, she seemed tongue-tied.

Pulling her hand from his, she stammered an apology. "I—I'm sorry. I'm a little distracted this morning. I'm not usually so... Oh!" She took back the hand she'd just released, examining it. "You've got a cut on your finger."

"It's nothing," he said, glancing at it.

Unzipping the purse that hung from her shoulder, she shook her head. "You probably cut it on one of those open cans or broken bottles," she said, rummaging in her large bag. "Have you had a tetanus shot lately?"

"I don't remember," he said, trying valiantly to suppress a grin. He also couldn't remember the last time that someone had fussed over him quite so appealingly. He found he liked it.

"Here we go," Sheila told him, extracting several items. "My sister's a nurse, and she's always stuffing home remedies into my purse. I've got a Band-Aid and an antiseptic pad to cleanse the cut."

"You don't have to bother, really," he protested halfheartedly, knowing his words wouldn't stop little Miss Florence Nightingale on her mission of mercy.

"Of course I do," Sheila told him, dabbing at the jagged cut with a moist pad. His hand was deeply tanned, his fingers long, lean, hard and oddly uncallused for a man who worked outdoors. "There's no point in risking infection."

Tony watched her brisk, efficient movements, admiring her small, ringless hands, enjoying the touch of her soft skin. "You look like you do this often."

"Fairly often. I have several nieces and nephews. Someone's always getting scraped."

No wedding ring, no children—interesting. "Do you live around here?"

"Not far. On Sequoia. There," she said as she tucked the Band-Aid around his finger, "that should do it."

Raising his left eyebrow quizzically, he took her hand and turned it over to study the back. Smooth, unpolished, well-manicured nails. Except the smallest finger. Chewed down nearly to the quick. He rubbed the rough end with his thumb, his eyes wrinkling at the corners as he swung them to hers questioningly.

She shrugged, grinning. "Nobody's perfect. I've been trying to quit biting my nails forever. Nine down, one to go. I keep it for emergency crises."

He returned her smile. It'd been years since he'd met such a natural woman. "Looks like you've had a recent one."

Sheila thought of her struggles over deciding to leave the security of her position with a respected and established law firm for the tenuous stability of her own law practice. "You could say that." She pulled her hand from his. Something about his touch made her lose track of her thoughts. "And I'm going to have another if I'm late for my appointment with Rosemary Norris."

"Rosemary's flexible. You'll like working here."

As a female, Rosemary was probably equally susceptible to this man's silver gaze, Sheila decided. It would indeed be interesting to have his 'janitorial services' available, as the ad had promised. "I'm sure I will," she said, zippering her bag closed as she turned toward the stairs.

"Thank you, Sheila," his deep voice called after her.

Halfway up, her hand on the railing, she glanced down at him.

He waved his bandaged finger in the air as he smiled up at her. "For fixing me up."

With a bright smile and a quick nod, Sheila hurried up, moving inside. Her eyes adjusting to the dimness, she saw that the broad hallway was wide and the walls richly paneled, with the front door opposite where she'd entered. Walking across the slate floor, she caught the glint of the sun filtering through the narrow twin leaded-glass windows edging the heavy, carved door.

An archway off to her left led into a reception area decorated in warm browns, a soft peach and touches of rich ivory. A small marble fireplace was tucked into a wall opposite a trio of bay windows bordered by an inviting cushioned seat. Two high-backed wing chairs flanked a low table holding a cut-glass vase from which the aroma of early-summer flowers drifted pleasantly into the air. The wallpaper was a conservative stripe, the carpeting thick and muted and the atmosphere one of understated elegance. It would seem our eminent prosecutor has style, Sheila thought.

The short woman standing on tiptoe watering a massive hanging philodendron turned and smiled a friendly welcome.

"You must be Sheila North," she said, offering her outstretched hand. "I've been expecting you."

"Nice to meet you, Mrs. Norris," Sheila said, shaking hands.

"Call me Rosemary, please," she said, setting down her watering can and moving behind her large mahogany desk to study its cluttered top. She patted her salt-and-pepper hair, then adjusted her pale blue shirtwaist dress over her ample bosom with one small hand while she searched for something with the other. At last she found a ring of keys and nodded. "Let me take you on a quick tour and then we'll talk."

Briskly she led the way into the hall and up the carpeted stairway, whose dark balustrade glowed with polish and tender loving care.

"I'm very impressed with this building," Sheila said with utter honesty. "It's lovely."

Huffing a bit with the climb, Rosemary nodded agreement. "It is, isn't it? Only two walls had to be removed, and it has all original hardwood flooring. When Tony bought this place, they'd had this tacky old carpeting everywhere. He took it all out and scraped and sanded and worked his buns off, I can tell you. He recarpeted only the reception area—for sound control, you know—and left the rest natural."

"He did all the work himself?"

"Oh, yes. Wouldn't trust anyone else with it." Reaching the top landing, Rosemary tried the door and found it unlocked. "I wasn't sure," she confided, "but I guess Tony's been up to air out the place a bit."

Their heels echoed on the bare wood in the emptiness. The room was a good size, yet somehow managed to look cozy. A small fireplace with an ornate wooden mantel was on one side, triple built-in bookcases that looked like solid oak along the opposite wall. The wallpaper was white-on-white, silk and newly hung. Three long, arched windows, open to the summer air, looked out on green treetops and a blue sky. Rosemary was rushing to open another door.

"And you have a private bath here," she went on. "The tenant gets a choice of window coverings, within reason, of course," she added with a small smile. "Let me show you the only other room up here." Trailing out the door, she headed toward another. "This is the law library Jed uses. And Tony when he's not downtown."

Fantastic—an oriental rug in shades of blue on the polished floor. East exposure from the sun, two round tables, comfortable leather chairs. Floor-to-ceiling bookcases on three sides, artfully arranged yet stuffed to overflowing. In twenty years she couldn't hope to accumulate this fine a collection, Sheila thought, running her hand over some of the smooth bindings.

"Beautiful," Sheila murmured.

"Yes," Rosemary agreed, her blue eyes roaming over the younger woman from top to bottom. "Tony likes to surround himself with classically beautiful things."

Sheila swung her gaze to the secretary, wondering at the protective note she'd caught in her voice. "How long have you worked for Tony Adams?" she asked, turning to face Rosemary.

"I was a court stenographer when Tony asked me to join him seven years ago. Four years downtown and three years here. Of course, he's been with the pro cutor's office the last two years, but he still stops in nearly every day, and maybe soon... You've never met him?"

Sheila shook her blond head.

Rosemary jingled her keys, warming to the conversation. "Tony's a fine man and a brilliant lawyer. Jed's good, too—been with the firm four years. Like brothers, the two of them."

"I've known Jed casually for some time, and I like him," said Sheila, moving down the stairs beside the loquacious secretary. "And now the senator's back?"

A small, pinched look about the lips told Sheila more about Rosemary's opinion of the senator than her answer. "Yes, he is," she commented heavily. "Starting next week."

"He's been gone a long time?"

"Four years. I'd hoped... Well, voters are fickle."

They entered the reception area. "Tony's office is there," Rosemary said, pointing to the nearest door.

"Jed's is the next one, and the senator will be taking the suite across the hall. There're two conference rooms over there as well, and we have another lav, a small kitchen and a storage room downstairs, plus an apartment that no one ever uses anymore."

At the raising of Sheila's eyebrow, she went on to explain. "Tony lived there for a while, during the renovation, but he's since moved to a lovely apartment nearer town—Riverfront West." She smiled, and her face looked warm and motherly. "I'm afraid I'm partially responsible for that. He was working too hard, at it all the time. I told him he needed some distance from his work, more time to relax. For once he listened to me."

From the scuttlebutt she'd heard, Tony Adams had definitely not spent every waking moment working, Sheila thought. But then, his secretary probably knew very little about his many rumored romances. And wouldn't say if she did.

"If you lease the space, secretarial services are included in the rent. That's me, unless you'd prefer other arrangements." Rosemary pointed to a utility desk in the far corner. "We've a young lady, Doris Hanson, who sits over there and does typing and filing. And I understand the senator's bringing his own secretary." A quick look of disapproval passed over her features as she scooted around and sat down at her desk. "Tony's around here somewhere if you want to talk to him. And Jed comes and goes on Saturdays."

"It's all right," Sheila told her. "I really don't need to talk with them."

"Well, I've a bit of work to do yet," Rosemary said, moving behind her desk. "If you want to wander around before deciding, feel free. I'll be happy to answer any questions you may have."

She was back to her no-nonsense tone.

"Thank you. I'd like that."

Sheila strolled from floor to floor, inspecting, examining, considering. Finally she found herself back in the office that would be hers. It wasn't difficult picturing her distressed cherrywood desk there, where her back would be to the window light. And her antique filing cabinet, a gift from her father, would go just there. And by the fireplace, her favorite chair, the one with needlepoint work done by her mother. She'd need a couple of low tables, maybe a settee, a painting or two. Yes, it would do. It would more than do. It was classical beauty, as Rosemary'd said.

Standing at the window, Sheila watched the high maple swaying in the breeze and inhaled the clean, fresh scent of summer sunshine mingled with rich wood polish. Peering through the leaves, she saw the dark-headed handyman sweeping off the back walk. A red cardinal, brazen in his unabashed beauty, landed on a branch and cocked his perky head at her. "Good-luck birds" was what her mother called them. Carmella North loved birds. Sheila smiled at the cardinal as he trilled a short tune in her direction, then flew off.

Yes, good luck, Sheila thought, deciding to take the bird's visit as an omen of things to come. Quickly she moved down the stairs, anxious to read and sign the lease before someone drifted in and snatched this charming office out from under her.

By seven that evening, Sheila had signed the lease, written the check, hired a small van and had two husky young men haul most of her things into her second-floor office. As they left, she sat at her desk in her walnut-based Queen Anne chair with the delicate lilac cushion and sighed tiredly. Finished for the day, she thought. And so, very nearly, was she.

Her stomach growled, reminding her that she hadn't taken the time to eat. Scrounging about in her bag, she found another box of raisins and opened it. Munching, she eyed the boxes of books waiting in front of the bookcases to be sorted and put away. Not tonight, she decided. Perhaps tomorrow she'd return in the afternoon, do that and finish filling her desk drawers. Next week she'd try to find a good area rug and a few other pieces she needed. And talk to the landlord about window treatments.

The landlord. Sheila shifted her gaze out the window at the gathering dusk. Tony Adams hadn't shown his face, though she'd been in and out of his building several times today. She'd run into Jed briefly, and they'd shared a quick cup of coffee in the compact little kitchen. She liked Jed, finding him easy to talk with and to be around. They'd reminisced about the six months they'd both worked in the state attorney's office.

Sheila'd been fresh out of law school and had acquired the position on the recommendation of one of her University of Michigan professors. Though she'd done little more than research briefs and act as an all-round 'gofer,' the experience had been worth it, for she'd learned what she *didn't* want to do. Her years at Babcock, Aimes and Whitney had been valuable, too, but again not the right choice for her. A law career, like life, was a process of elimination, she'd decided. Finding out what you *don't* want and, hopefully, learning and growing and discovering the things you *do* want.

Jed had spent four years in the air force, thereby getting a late start on his law career. He, too, had moved on shortly after she'd left, joining a large firm, then leaving that to join with Tony Adams in a diversified law practice, which he'd been handling alone since Tony had moved downtown. The senator had started the practice years ago, but had gotten sidetracked into politics. He'd hoped to make a career of that, Jed revealed, but the voters had decided otherwise. Sheila'd been surprised to hear a note of derision in Jed's voice when he'd spoken of the senior Mr. Adams, much the same tone she'd caught earlier in Rosemary's voice. It would seem the ex-senator's return was not a cause for celebration, despite the party remnants she'd seen. She wondered how Tony Adams felt about his father being back.

"Need any help?" a deep voice asked.

Glancing up, Sheila met the gray-eyed gaze of the handyman as he leaned casually against the door frame. He looked larger to her here inside, out of his element, his tall, lean body filling the doorway.

"You work long hours," she observed, wondering how long he'd been lounging there, watching her. Giving him a polite smile, she tossed her crumpled container into her purse. She'd have to see about getting a wastebasket.

"So do you," he said, pushing away from the frame, entering and looking about. He might have known she'd have excellent taste from the way she dressed, the proud way she carried herself, Tony thought. Not much furniture, but good pieces with quality and style. "Nice. This is very nice."

Turning to face her, he saw that she still didn't know who he was. Just as well, for now. He'd always enjoyed stretching out the moment. He'd been watching her for long minutes as she'd sat there chewing on raisins. Funny, he'd have thought she'd prefer Brie and imported crackers. She was classically lovely, with an oval face, a small nose, her mouth full and feminine and barely tinted pink, her chin hinting at determination. A light breeze from the open window lifted strands of her shoulder-length hair and playfully dragged it across her cheek. Inexplicably, his fingers suddenly twitched, wanting to do the same.

She looked tired, he could see, but her eyes were alert, thoughtful, planning. No doubt a sharp, busy brain lay behind those reflective brown eyes. Not the simple, impulsive woman he'd first thought her to be. Perhaps he, too, was guilty of judging too quickly. Catching her unaware and seeing her surrounded by her choice of things, he felt a sudden urge to discover more about Sheila North.

"Thank you," she said. "How's the finger?"

Stepping closer, he smiled and held up the finger, which was still wearing a slightly smudged Band-Aid. "Fine." He turned toward the boxes of books. "Would you like me to put those up for you?"

She shook her head and tucked a fall of hair behind one ear. "No, thanks. I'll do it tomorrow," she said, her eyes studying him. Up close, his face had a raw-boned look, lean and angular, yet oddly hinting at an aristocratic background. His nose had a slight bump, giving him a rugged look, and his mouth was full, suggesting pleasure. She wondered why his nearness made her feel a shade uncomfortable. Rising, she arched her back and stretched, catlike, easing tired muscles.

Tony saw the edge of her sweater creep up with her movement, revealing a flash of creamy skin at her midriff. Her scent drifted to him again, something warm and a little wild. The desire to touch her surprised him. Automatically he reached to his shirt pocket to pat the cigarettes he always kept there, then swore to himself at the sudden craving.

Needing to move around, he picked up a paperweight from her desk and hefted it in his hands as he circled the room. He made an effort to keep his voice level. "You work on Sundays, too? Are you a workaholic?" Upending the glass weight, he watched snow fall on Santa Claus and his sleigh. Her laugh sent a quick shiver up his spine. This woman and his responses to her were beginning to fascinate him.

"No, far from it. But I have to see a client Monday, and I'd like to be settled in by then."

Coming back to lean against the edge of the desk, he set down the piece and folded his arms across his chest. She stood, and the setting sun's rays streaked her hair with gold. Lovely, Tony thought, watching her gather notes and pens and put them into her oversized purse. "A client already, and you've just begun your practice?"

"Mmm. Actually, he's not my client yet. His mother's my hairdresser, and she's asked me to see if I could help him. So I'm going to meet with him to hear his side."

"What's the charge?"

"Kidnapping. I—" Stopping herself, Sheila slowly raised her head to look up at him. What was she doing discussing her case with the handyman? Lord, she must be more tired than she'd thought. Intelligent gray eyes or not, this is ridiculous. "I've got to go."

Watching her expressive face, Tony hid a smile. She was going to be livid when she learned his name and figured out he'd deliberately avoided introducing himself to her. "Are you sure there's nothing I can do to help before you go?"

Sheila settled her purse on her shoulder and nodded. "I'm sure."

"You have a set of keys?"

"Yes, Rosemary took care of that." She moved toward the door. "Are you leaving?"

"No, I've got a couple of things to finish up yet. I'll lock up, don't worry."

"I'm not in the least bit worried," she told him. The man was truly the boldest handyman she'd ever run across. Even now, his eyes were challenging, flirtatious and somehow secretive. As if he knew something she didn't, and the joke was on her. "Good night," Sheila said, and left him watching her walk away.

She shook her head as she descended the stairs. Occupational hazard this business of always trying to figure out the motivation of others. She'd have to stop being so overanalytical. He was probably an ordinary man doing ordinary work and fascinated with law cases, thinking them all filled with murder and mayhem like Perry Ma-son. If only he knew how tedious and commonplace many aspects of the law were, she thought.

Pulling open the back door, she nearly collided with Jed Blair.

"Hello again, Sheila," Jed said with a friendly smile. He wore a dark business suit, but he'd pulled his tie loose and opened the two top buttons of his shirt. It was a warm evening. "All moved in?"

"Not quite, but getting there. You're working awfully late for a Saturday."

He held up a bulging file. "Yeah, the Thornton case. I just spent three hours over there talking with the help. Everyone from the cook to the gardener. Slow going."

Sheila remembered reading about the case. The elder Thornton had made a fortune in the auto industry—the papers had labeled him a near genius. He'd died recently at seventy-two, seemingly of natural causes. Only there was a youngish third wife, two separate wills of questionable validity found, and four children demanding exhumation of the body and hurling accusations of coercion. A tangled mess, complicated by the presence of money, power and position.

"Whew, you're handling that? I don't envy you."

Jed smiled, and it reached his eyes, making him look younger than the thirty-four Sheila knew him to be. "I don't envy me tonight, either. I'm hot, hungry and tired, and I've got a wife waiting at home for me with a dinner that's probably ruined. But such is the life of an up-and-coming whiz kid, right?"

"I imagine Tanya's used to it," Sheila answered. They'd met once at a banquet, and she'd immediately taken to Jed's soft-spoken wife.

"That she is," Jed said, moving past her and heading for his office. "Have you talked to Tony yet?"

"No, he hasn't shown up."

Jed wrinkled his brow. "Odd. His Mercedes is parked out back."

Sheila shrugged. "I'm sure I'll see him Monday. Good night."

"Have a good weekend, what's left of it."

Outside, Sheila flung her heavy bag onto the passenger seat, climbed behind the wheel and started the Volkswagen. Her gaze drifted to the shiny red Mercedes. So Tony Adams drove that—classic beauty again, but with a flash of color. Interesting.

Dusky shadows from the trees overhead trailed across the lawn. She watched the streetlights pop on as she shifted into gear. On impulse, she looked up to the third-floor windows of her office.

He stood there, clearly outlined in the lamplight, a tall man with coppery hair. She could picture those gray eyes, though she was too far away to see them. Catching her face turned upward, he waved. Though she felt a little silly, Sheila waved back as she stepped on the gas.

On the drive home, she thought about her day. The office was a great find, out of the ordinary, a quality place with charm. She liked Jed, and Rosemary seemed nice. Now if only her absent landlord would make an appearance soon and turn out to be equally accommodating.

It would be nice working among people who were pleasant right down to the yardman. Unbidden, silvery gray eyes and a slow smile came to mind. Just who was this enigmatic handyman whose name she didn't even know, and why had he unnerved her so? she wondered.

Giving herself a mental shake, Sheila decided to concentrate on the questions she wanted to ask her would-be client, Jimmy Lee Morgan, on Monday morning.

Chapter Two

Parking for the state courthouse was underneath the building, a cavernous concrete facility with color-coded levels and a maze of winding, twisting ramps. With a quick glance at her watch, Sheila grabbed her jacket, purse and briefcase and headed for the elevators. She had twenty minutes to spare, but rushed anyway. She hated being late.

Shrugging into her navy linen suit jacket, she waited a shade impatiently for the elevator, her mind already on the eighteen-year-old boy she'd come to see. Jimmy Lee Morgan's mother, Sophie, had literally begged Sheila to help her son, her dark expressive eyes damp and red from tears and strain. Sheila fervently hoped she could. She'd spent some time last week going over the police report and listening to Sophie's version of Jimmy Lee's problems.

A widow for years, Sophie ran a small beauty shop on Detroit's east side in a neighborhood that was gently resisting change. She had a married daughter and a son in his mid-twenties who was an electrician. Jimmy Lee, her youngest, was clearly her favorite. Not the best student, Jimmy Lee studied hard and was a good boy who'd never been in trouble with the law before. While still in high school, at a local dance, he'd met Kim Tremaine, small, blond and from the wealthier side of the tracks. According to Sophie, they'd fallen madly in love.

But J. D. Tremaine, Kim's industrialist father, didn't want his only daughter involved with a poor boy who he'd predicted would have a limited future. The kids dated on the sly when they could, but after Kim's graduation, her father'd sent her upstate, away to college and away from Jimmy Lee. He'd gone so far as to forbid her to correspond with or accept phone calls from him. And he felt his tactics had worked until last month when Jimmy Lee'd driven up to Kim's dorm and kidnapped her. Not my Jimmy Lee, Sophie'd sobbed. We'll see, Sheila thought, stepping into the elevator at last.

Hurrying along the hallway leading to the conference room where they'd be bringing Jimmy Lee to meet with her at ten, Sheila shifted her briefcase to her other hand and shook back her hair. It'd been stifling hot in the underground garage. She welcomed the courthouse air-conditioning, feeling as though her pale lilac silk blouse was already sticking to her, thanks to Michigan's humid June air.

Engrossed in her thoughts, she rounded the bend and glanced up, surprise nearly stopping her in her tracks. Standing beside an open office door, involved in a conversation with two other men, was the handyman from her building, wearing an expensive three-piece suit, a paisley tie and the same reserved smile she'd seen on him Saturday morning.

What on earth was he doing here? she wondered, slowing her pace as she passed him and his companions in the wide hallway. Of course, he could be here waiting to testify in a case, or perhaps he was otherwise involved in a lawsuit. He looked unreasonably handsome, his unruly auburn hair still damp from his efforts at taming it and his shoulders appearing even broader in more formal clothes.

She was almost past the small group, looking over her shoulder, when he turned and caught her eye. His smile of recognition was slow and warm, with just a hint of mischief. Swiveling toward her, he held up his index finger, still wearing a bandage, and moved his face into an open grin. Sheila nodded, then turned, frowning. There was something very disturbing about that man.

Tony watched her stroll off, liking the contrast between her fair hair and her dark business suit. She had a nice walk, a long-legged yet immensely feminine stride. She'd looked honestly puzzled and confused to see him here. Soon now, she'd discover who he was. And he'd discover whether she did a slow burn when she was angry or turned into a spitfire. He liked passion in women, in bed and out, and he'd already decided Sheila North showed promise. Turning back, Tony smiled. Soon, things would start getting interesting.

Moments later, as Sheila sat down at the conference table, she pushed all thoughts save those concerning her client from her mind. She'd found working at Babcock, Aimes and Whitney dull and without challenge. It had never led her here. This was the place where they separated the men from the boys, the law clerks from those in the winning circle. Swallowing a small, nervous lump, she hoped she would measure up.

For all the professional polish of the justice halls, this room had an institutional look, a tired shabbiness in its faded yellow walls and plain tiled floor. How many frightened defendants had sat in that orange plastic chair across the scarred wooden table, wondering about their freedom? And, Sheila thought, how many anxious attorneys had sat where she was, also filled with doubts

and questions? Removing the Morgan file from her briefcase, she placed it next to her pad and pen with a sigh.

At the sound of the lock clicking, Sheila looked toward
the heavy door. The guard nodded and brushed two fingers to his hat in greeting, then closed the door as Jimmy
Lee Morgan shuffled in. Avoiding her eyes, he slumped
into the chair. Close in height to her own five feet seven
inches, thin, with dark curly hair and a feathery, youthful
mustache, his eyes were hooded and his hands drummed
nervously on the table.

Her own hands crossed on the table in front of her,
Sheila waited. At last, he risked a furtive glance into her
eyes. Then another, longer one. It was hard to tell what he
was looking for or what he saw there, but finally he took
a deep breath and sat back a bit. Eyes almost black stared
back at her, wary but with a definite vulnerable edge.

"Hello, Jimmy Lee. I'm Sheila North, an attorney. Your
mother asked me to talk with you."

"Yeah, she told me." A surprisingly deep voice. "You—
you got a cigarette? They took mine and I—I could really
use one."

"No, I'm sorry. I don't smoke."

He swore under his breath. The finger-thrumming
resumed. His dark eyes shot to hers as she pulled the pad
in front of her and picked up her pen. "You think you can
get me outa here? I'm going crazy. Is my mom okay?" He
ran a shaky hand through his thick hair. "Can you find
out for me if Kim's all right? Man, why'd they take away
my smokes? Think I'd burn this cement joint down, or
what?"

He was frustrated, nervous and worried. But for his
mother and Kim, more than for himself. Something here,
Sheila told herself.

"I think the usual procedure here is that I ask you the
questions. Tell me what happened on the weekend beginning May sixth."

An angry fire moved across his face. "No. You answer my questions *first*."

Slowly Sheila ran her fingers along the pen and held his gaze without flinching. "Compromise, Jimmy Lee. I'll answer one of yours, if you answer one of mine. Okay?"

Reluctantly the boy nodded.

"Your mother's health is fine, but she's worried about you, naturally. Now tell me what happened on the weekend beginning May sixth."

"That's not a question."

Sheila slapped the pen down atop the wooden desk with a clatter and stood, scraping back her chair. She saw the sudden shock move into his face, but at this point she didn't give a damn. "You want to play games, play them alone, young man. Your mother's a good woman and a friend of mine. I agreed to come here for *her*, not you. You want to be big man on campus, find another audience."

Eyes dark and angry, Sheila reached for his file. A strong, thin hand stopped her.

"Okay," he said, his deep voice softer. "I was out of line. What do you wanna know?"

She sat down, shoving her trembling hands into her lap. It had worked—this time. "Tell me, Jimmy Lee, about that weekend."

According to Jimmy Lee, it hadn't happened quite the way Mr. Tremaine had stated. He and Kim had been corresponding and talking on the phone for months. Finally neither could stand the separation any longer, and they'd agreed on a date when Jimmy Lee would drive up and Kim would sneak out of the dorm, meet him, and they'd find a justice of the peace to marry them. Only they hadn't counted on Kim's roommate calling Mr. Tremaine and reporting Kim missing. And they hadn't counted on her angry father calling the state police, who'd located them before they'd found someone who'd marry them.

Sheila studied his handsome young face. Was Jimmy Lee an accomplished liar, an impatient opportunist or just a boy in love? she wondered. "You said that you and Kim planned this whole wedding, that she went with you willingly?" Sheila asked.

"Yeah, sure. You think I'd force her? I *love* her!"

"Are you going to school now, or do you work?" She knew some of these answers, from his file and from his mother. She wanted to hear his version.

"Both. I work days at Long's Drugs and take evening classes at Wayne State. Or I did until they locked me up."

"What are you studying?"

"I've worked for Mr. Long on and off since the eighth grade. Everything from stocking shelves to delivering prescriptions to helping with the books. I want to be a pharmacist, like him."

He looked a little embarrassed, as though she might laugh at a young man's dreams. The boy didn't lack ambition, Mr. Tremaine, Sheila thought, just a silver spoon.

She gave him an encouraging smile. "What is Kim's roommate's name?"

"Sara. Sara Hendrix."

"Are they friends from before or new friends? Did Kim trust her?"

"They met up there. Kim didn't mention Sara much."

"Have you and Kim been intimate?"

He'd been twirling an empty ashtray with shaky fingers. Suddenly his hands stopped and his hooded eyes raised to hers, but he didn't answer.

"Do you understand my question, Jimmy Lee?"

"Yeah. What business is it of anybody's?"

She had her answer, but he probably didn't realize it, Sheila thought. "Would you rather answer on the witness stand?"

He thought that over, then dropped his gaze. "Yeah, we've made love."

She liked the way he'd rephrased her words. Sheila couldn't decide if she was gullible or inexperienced, but she was beginning to believe her client. "For how long now?"

"A while. Why do you want to know this?"

"Because the prosecution will surely bring it up. Is she pregnant? Is that why you decided to run away and marry?"

"No! I hadn't touched her in months until . . . until . . ."

Her eyes held his in their firm grip. "Until the night you and she left the dorm." She watched the sure knowledge skitter across his young features before he could disguise the truth. "Right?"

He nodded, dropping his head. Sheila knew he had to be feeling rotten about now, but she hid her sympathy. Sympathy wouldn't get Jimmy Lee out of jail.

Taking a deep breath, Sheila brought out some big guns. "Does Kim love you?"

"Yes!"

"Then why do you think she didn't tell the same story you did to the police, Jimmy Lee? Why'd she agree with her father's version?"

Anger at the injustice was a crimson stain that crept up his neck and moved onto his thin cheeks. "She's scared, that's why. That bastard's got her scared to death. I don't know what he's holding over her head, but it's something. Kim loves me. I *know* it. He got to her somehow."

Maybe, Sheila thought. But how? Jimmy Lee sat slumped in his chair looking defeated. He'd had enough for one day, and she certainly had plenty to work on next week. She began to put her things away.

"In answer to your other questions, I don't know if I can get you out of here. I do know I believe your story, and I'll try my best. I also don't know how Kim is, but I'll find out for you by our next visit."

Looking up at her, his eyes were wide with disbelief mingled with hope, making him look impossibly young. Sheila swallowed another lump.

"You really believe me?" he asked, his voice quivering.

"Yes, I do. But don't ever lie to me, not about one single detail. Not if you want me to help you." Snapping her briefcase closed, she picked it up and moved to the door. Turning back to him, she raised a questioning brow. "*Do* you want me to help you, Jimmy Lee, to be your counsel?"

For a moment, he almost smiled. "Hell, yes. My mom, she's a pretty good judge of character."

Sheila did smile. "Yes, I think she is, too. And she believes in you. I'll go to the newsstand now and drop off some cigarettes with the guard for you. I'll be in touch, Jimmy Lee."

"Thanks. Thanks a lot. No filters, okay?"

Nodding, she signaled the guard that they were finished. After delivering the boy's cigarettes, Sheila strolled back down the long corridor, stopping for a moment to chat with Mike Delaney, a police officer who'd been transferred to court duty recently. He'd worked for years in Records when she'd been researching in the other building, and she'd often listened to his sad meanderings after his wife of thirty years had died.

Chuckling at something Mike told her, Sheila looked up just in time to see her handyman again, walking out of a courtroom and talking with Jed Blair. The man seemed to be everywhere.

"Ah, I see you have a good eye, Sheila," Mike said, noting her absorption in the two men down the corridor. "Our star prosecuting attorney cuts quite a figure, ay?"

"Jed's not with the prosecutor's office, Mike. He's in private practice and—"

Mike's chuckle interrupted her. "Not Jed Blair. Tony Adams."

Sheila's head swiveled to Mike. "Tony Adams? Where?"

He waved a quick hand toward the two men. "Right there. The tall man in the brown suit talking with Jed. You never met him?"

Oh, my God! Sheila thought, closing her eyes and nearly sagging against the wall as the realization hit her. Tony Adams in the flesh. How could she have been so dense? And she'd talked to him and treated him like the handyman. This was going to be a hard one to live down.

Shock turned quickly to anger. The nerve of the man! He'd known full well what she was thinking, and he'd stood there and watched her make a fool of herself. Not a word, not a clue—he'd just let her bury herself deeper with each dumb statement. Why was he cutting his own grass anyway, walking about looking for all the world like a gardener? Why couldn't he hire someone to do it like a normal affluent attorney? Driving a Mercedes, then hauling trash. Honestly!

"Yes, ma'am," Mike was continuing, "Tony Adams is a man to watch. Been working for the state prosecutor for some time now. Maybe he's got his sights on politics, like old Maxwell T., his daddy."

Good! Perhaps he'd take those disarming gray eyes to Washington and get out of her hair. Still fuming inwardly, but with undeniable curiosity, Sheila put a tight smile on her face. "What's he like?" she asked the chatty policeman.

"Tony's good people. He knows everyone, the whole staff from the stenos and cops all the way up to the councilmen and the mayor. But you got to watch out for him." Mike removed his cap and smoothed his thinning gray hair. "He's the kind of man when he walks into the courtroom, he sort of takes charge, you know what I mean? Everybody sits up and takes notice. A bit of a maverick—don't mind taking the opposite side if he thinks he's right—

but everyone respects him, the other lawyers, the judges. Even the juries.''

''Sounds like a wunderkind. Is he a chip off the old block?''

Mike shook his head. ''Nah. He's nothing like the senator. Tony's tough, but he's honest. His father's got a reputation for being ruthless and for stretching the truth to suit himself.''

Sheila watched Jed throw back his head and laugh at something Tony said. ''How do father and son get along, Mike?''

''Well, the old man hasn't been around for four or five years, but rumor has it Tony's not thrilled that he's back. It took him quite a while to straighten out the practice after the senator left. He got Jed Blair in, and together they have a good, honest firm. Then two years ago Tony joined the prosecutor's staff. Now Maxwell T.'s back to muddy up the waters. Might be some fireworks there.''

What a great time to move into the building, Sheila thought. Oh, well, it wouldn't be dull. As she watched, Tony turned, undoubtedly sensing her eyes on his back. He was about thirty feet away, yet she could feel the intensity of his silvery gaze as he returned her look. He didn't smile, just studied her slowly and thoroughly. Yes, she could see what Mike meant. The man definitely had stage presence. She'd sensed something yesterday, but had made the cardinal mistake of assuming that because he was working in the yard he was a handyman. It wasn't Tony's fault, it was hers. An attorney who makes hasty assumptions. What must he think of her? That she was a rank amateur, probably. And right now she felt like one.

Mike adjusted his cap squarely on his head. ''Think that fellow's going places, Sheila. Got a brand new case, I hear. Might get him some good publicity. Something about a kidnapping.''

"Yes, I suppose he—what did you say, Mike? What case about a kidnapping?"

"Let's see, I heard preliminary was coming up soon. The Tremaine case. A rich young girl got kidnapped by an old boyfriend. Her daddy's got megabucks. Maybe you read about it a month or so ago. It was in all the papers."

"And Tony Adams is prosecuting that case?"

"From what I hear, he is."

Oh, no! Not only her landlord but her opponent as well. Sheila sighed heavily. Her instincts had been right. He certainly wasn't an ordinary handyman. If only she'd listened more closely to her instincts. With a last look at Tony Adams, she turned her back to him, said her goodbyes to Mike and headed for the elevators. Not yet noon, and she'd had quite a day.

She knows, Tony thought, watching Sheila walk away with short, angry strides. Angry with herself or him? He remembered how her voice had been hesitant and her eyes had flickered with awareness as they'd talked in her office late Saturday. There was hidden fire. He was sure of it. He'd soon find out, he promised himself, turning back to Jed and glancing at his watch. Time to go back into the courtroom.

Sheila took off her reading glasses and checked the time—nearly five. She'd been poring over various books in the law library across the hall from her office for the better part of two hours, and she still hadn't found what she was looking for. She remembered from her studies at the University of Michigan a case involving an intrastate kidnapping that had set a precedent. She needed to find it, but it looked very much as if she'd have to dig through some of her old notes at home to jog her memory further before she could search more intelligently.

Wearily she rubbed the back of her neck in an effort to ease the tight muscles, cramped after hours of bending over books. A cup of coffee would hit the spot, she decided, replacing the books she'd spread out over one of the sturdy walnut tables. Stopping to toss her notes onto her desk, she made her way down the stairs. Rosemary was just covering her typewriter as she passed the reception room.

"Are you leaving, or can I bring you a cup of coffee?" Sheila asked, pausing at the doorway. They'd shared a hurried lunch around noon, and she found herself liking Rosemary. Her warmth and manner invited easy confidences. Instinctively, Sheila sensed a person she could trust.

"Thanks, hon, but my oldest son and his wife are picking me up, and we're going out to dinner to celebrate." Slipping on her suit jacket, Rosemary came closer, her face wearing a wide smile. "They just found out they're going to be parents next year."

Sheila leaned against the doorjamb and smiled back. "Oh, how nice. Your first grandchild?"

"Yes, and I'm so excited. My other son just graduated from college, and he's not married yet."

"I have two brothers and a sister—all married—and nine nieces and nephews. It's like a zoo at my folks' house when we all get together."

"What a nice big family," Rosemary said, walking to the front door and peering out one of the side windows. "I only had the two boys. Your mother must be in seventh heaven with all those grandchildren to spoil."

Sheila nodded, smiling. "Oh, yes. She comes from a large Italian family. The more the merrier."

"I suppose your parents are always at you, wanting you to get married and give them more babies."

"Constantly."

Rosemary's blue eyes narrowed as she looked over the younger woman's blond hair and fair complexion. "You don't look Italian."

"My father's English. But he comes from a family of six. I don't believe the English are as cold as we sometimes think they are."

Shaking her short, peppery curls, Rosemary laughed. "Neither do I. Tony's English, and he's anything but cold. And his father's on his fourth marriage." The toot of a horn interrupted them. Rosemary pulled open the door. "There's my David now. Jed and Tony might be back yet, but I haven't seen hide nor hair of the senator all day. If no one's around, just lock up when you leave."

"I will. Have a nice time."

The coffeepot was empty. And that's the kind of day it's been, Sheila thought as she rinsed it out. Too late to make another pot with no one else around to help her drink it. A cup of tea would be just as good. Filling the kettle, she set it on the small stove and walked to the window to wait for the water to boil.

The weeping willow in the side yard was old, gnarled and drooping. It reminded her of one in the backyard of her parent's big house up north in Tawas, right on Lake Huron. Though the Detroit River was about a half mile east of the office, the tree seemed lonely for the water she knew willows always craved to be near; just as *she* was often lonely for her big noisy family, all of whom still lived near their childhood home—near her warm, loving mother and her soft-spoken, sensible father. She was the only maverick who'd ventured away to build a different life. She didn't regret the move, despite the occasional pangs of loneliness. Perhaps she'd find time soon to go back home for a visit. It would, as always, cheer her.

The whistling kettle drew her attention away from her rambling thoughts. Getting down the tea bags, she remembered something Rosemary'd said. Tony certainly wasn't cold, and his father was on wife number four. Pouring hot water into her cup, she had to agree that the little she'd seen of Tony Adams, cold was not a word that came to mind in connection with her thoughts about him. He was—damn!

Sheila set down the kettle, nearly tipping it, peering at her thumb where she'd grazed it along the hot metal. She should have taken the time to look for a hot pad. Popping her thumb into her mouth to cool it, she frowned in exasperation.

"Here, let me help," a deep voice behind her offered.

Turning, Sheila saw Tony coming toward her. Had she been so absorbed in her thoughts that she hadn't heard him approach, or did the man creep around on little cat feet? She removed her thumb and inspected it. "No need," she said quickly.

Ignoring her light protest, he took her hand in his, turning on the cold-water faucet with the other. "Turnabout's fair play," he said, watching her. "You fixed my finger, now it's my turn."

He'd removed his jacket. His white shirt looked as though he'd just taken it out of his closet, and his vest was buttoned over his broad chest and flat stomach. He smelled shower-fresh, with a hint of pine, very male. Sheila swallowed as he twined his arm through hers and thrust her thumb under the spray. "It's nothing, really."

"Sure it is. Wouldn't want you to sue the landlord."

His face was serious, but his voice had a teasing hint of humor in it. She fought an urge to shove his dark, curly head under the cold running water. "You could have told me Saturday," she said accusingly, wishing she could have hung on to her cool disdain. It was safer.

He turned away from the sink to look at her. She was close alongside him, leaning forward as he held her hand to the faucet. The scent of her, elusive yet already one he quickly identified as hers alone, drew him. She seemed to prefer simplicity, using only the barest trace of makeup, employing no discernible beautician's tricks. It only enhanced her natural loveliness. He wanted to bury his face in her hair, in her neck, in her.

"I thought I could learn more about you if you didn't know who I was," he told her.

Well, that was honest at least—manipulative, but honest. "And did you?"

He'd thought her eyes a deep brown, but on closer examination, he saw flecks of gold and lighter amber in their depths. Her lashes were thick, incredibly long and dark against her fair skin. His pulse quickened as he struggled not to reveal how her nearness was affecting him. A good attorney knows that an expressionless face and a motionless body are often his best weapons. He was sure he'd need an arsenal of weapons in dealing with Sheila North. "Yes, I think so."

Sheila felt herself trembling. He actually had her trembling. And his eyes. She could spend hours just looking into those mysterious silver eyes. How easy it would be to fall under the spell of this man. But she'd heard too many rumors about too many women who'd been in his life and had passed on through. They were for pleasant interludes only, to be discarded when finished. She'd never been good at that particular game. Time for a little distance here.

"You're freezing my thumb and soaking the cuff of my sleeve," she pointed out to him.

"Sorry." He turned off the tap and picked up a towel. Gently he patted her hand dry, dabbing at a few drops that had reached her cuff. Holding her hand between both of his, he studied the injury. "Looks like you'll live. I may still want you to sign a release-of-liability form."

Sheila decided to play it light, too. They needed to break the obvious tension between them. "Fat chance, fella," she said, taking back her hand. "I'm seeing an attorney in the morning. Know any good ones?"

He took a cup from the cupboard and threw in a tea bag. "There're a few around." He poured in boiling water, then turned to face her while it steeped. "Not many."

She took a tentative sip of her tea, but found it still too hot to drink. "So I hear. I also hear you're one of the better ones."

He gave her that slow smile, the one that changed his face, the one worth waiting for. "Rumors abound. You're not so bad yourself."

Taking a step back from him, she set down her cup. Standing too close to him wasn't wise. His nearness was beginning to awaken feelings she hadn't had to deal with for a long while. It wasn't that they weren't pleasant. They were—too pleasant. It wasn't even that she didn't want to explore these sudden feelings. She did, in time. But this attraction was happening a shade too quickly. Someone had to apply the brakes, to keep their conversation strictly business. Fleetingly she wondered how seldom that happened to Tony Adams.

"You don't know if I'm a good attorney or a bad one—yet," she told him.

"Yes I do."

"How?"

"Spies, Sheila. I have spies everywhere. Are you going to defend Jimmy Lee Morgan?"

She turned her back to the counter and leaned against it, crossing one foot over the other, her hands braced on either side of her against the ledge. There seemed to be a secret just behind his eyes, almost within reach. Or was it a professional evasiveness that had drifted into his personal life? she wondered. "Yes," she said, deciding that very minute. "Are you prosecuting that case?"

"Would that be a problem for you?"

"No. Why should it be?"

He shrugged, watching her. "Just thought I'd ask."

Her eyes got serious. "He's innocent, you know."

"Is he? Another of your snap judgments, Sheila? One of your quick assumptions? A baby-faced boy whose mother loves him couldn't harm a fly, is that right? Everyone on death row's innocent, too? Didn't some crusty old law professor a few years back point out to you that whenever you assume—"

"—'You make an ass out of you and me'," she quoted, nodding. "Yes, one did, as a matter of fact. He also suggested tossing out unexpected statements to open up your opponent."

He raised his left eyebrow and cocked his head. "Testing the waters, Sheila? You don't have to parry and thrust with me. Ask me anything you want to know. I'll answer all your questions."

Somehow she doubted that. "A cooperative prosecutor. How very nice. I noticed how open and willing to share information you were on Saturday." She watched his hand go to his shirt pocket, then drop away after barely patting the pack inside. The automatic reflex of the smoker, she guessed. Yet he didn't light up, though he seemed to want a cigarette. Puzzling—did she make him feel as though he *needed* one? Good, she'd take any advantage.

Tony took a step closer, placing his hands lightly on her arms. The silk of her lilac blouse felt good, but what he really wanted was to touch the satin of her skin. "I see you like shades of purple."

"Yes..." She broke off in midsentence, lost again in the fascination of his silver eyes. Funny how she'd never before today noticed how heart-stopping it could be just to stare deeply into someone's eyes. "Yes, I do like purple."

His hands moved on her ever so slightly. "Are you planning on beating the big bad prosecutor with a smashing win your first time up at bat in the courtroom and making a name for yourself?" he asked, deciding she was more the slow-simmer type, not the flash-and-fire.

His one hand traced the edge of her collar as the other slid around and made slow circles on her back. She felt a ragged breath feather across her own lips. "I play to win, if that's what you mean."

He was very close now, his thighs touching hers, his hand finding the nape of her neck, moving into the thickness of her hair. Sheila felt her blood heat, her knees grow shaky. Why wasn't she putting the brakes on now? she wondered, even as she continued to watch his face move nearer.

"So do I. *When* I play. But I'm out of this one. I quit the prosecutor's office today."

Her eyes widened in surprise. "You're returning to private practice?" At his nod her curiosity overcame her hesitancy. "Why?"

He shrugged noncommittally. "Many reasons." His hand moved forward along her jaw, then up, his thumb tracing the fullness of her bottom lip. "You have a beautiful mouth," he whispered.

Distracting—she wanted to ask more questions, but his touch was too distracting. She was sure he could hear the thudding of her heart, and still he just rubbed her back and caressed her lips.

"Beautiful," he said again.

Beautiful? It wasn't how she thought of herself. Actually, she gave little thought to her looks. She just accepted them.

"What time can you be ready?" he asked.

She frowned and her eyes filled with confusion. "Ready? For what?"

"Dinner," he answered, stepping back with a look of sweet reluctance. "I'd like to take you to dinner."

"Dinner?" she asked again, puzzled. "On a Monday evening?"

That quizzical eyebrow shot up again, and his lips twitched in a smile. "Don't you eat on Mondays?"

"Well, yes but—"

Picking up his cup, he moved toward the doorway. "Good. I've got a little work to clear up first. Pick you up at seven." He stepped out into the hall.

"But—"

He curved his head and shoulders around the corner. "Yes?"

"You don't know where I live."

He gave a patient smile. "Sure I do. Remember those spies I have everywhere? See you at seven."

Sheila drained her tepid tea and sighed. Outmaneuvered again. He made it seem as if he had all the answers and she scarcely knew the questions.

So he'd quit working for the state—another interesting development, and a sudden one at that. For many reasons, he'd told her. Was his father's return one of them? Sheila wondered. With quick movements, she rinsed her cup and reached for the towel.

Why had she agreed to go out with him? she asked herself. Tony Adams was devious, an expert courtroom manipulator and, rumor had it, highly successful with women. He'd built her up just now, then left her wanting. A clever maneuver, using her own attraction to him against her. But two strikes do not necessarily put you out of the ball game, she reminded herself. She was not going to let him get his way again. If he had big plans for her, he might just be in for a surprise. Dinner it would be, and dinner was *all* it would be.

Sheila put the dishes away and stopped a moment to consider. She'd have to be on her toes with this man personally even if they weren't opponents in court, a fact for which she was grateful. Tony Adams was one of those rare men to whom you gave a wide berth if you were at all smart. Sheila turned off the kitchen light and smiled. She'd always been considered, in most circles, to be quite smart.

Chapter Three

Tony turned onto Sequoia and headed the quiet Mercedes down the wide, tree-lined avenue. The small section on Detroit's east-side known as Indian Village was a gentle reminder of a wealthy era long past its prime. He passed large, stately houses, many three stories high, with billiard rooms and ballrooms, struggling to survive in modern times. Several had been renovated into separate apartments. Others were owned by single families who closed off upper floors as too costly to maintain. On the back of many lots sat huge three- and four-car garages, above which often were carriage-house apartments. It was in one of these that Sheila lived.

Turning into the drive and parking at the back next to her purple Volkswagen, Tony turned off the engine and sat for a moment gathering his thoughts. He wasn't quite sure why he was here or what impulse had driven him to ask Sheila North to have dinner with him. By anyone's standards he wasn't an impulsive man, and yet lately he'd made several impulsive decisions. Perhaps quitting the prosecutor's office wasn't as impulsive as it appeared to be on the surface. He'd been restless and unhappy there for some time. And then, the decision had almost been made for him. But asking Sheila out tonight certainly could be considered impulsive.

Automatically his hand went to his shirt pocket and reached for his cigarettes. Damn, but he could use one. Since meeting Sheila, the craving he'd vowed to conquer had returned to him, stronger than ever. She had him curious, restless, impatient. Running a quick hand through his hair, he left the car and climbed the steep steps to her apartment at a near run.

She opened the door on the first knock. Sunshine filtered through huge nearby trees, dappling the hair that hung to her shoulders with light and shadow. The dress she wore was dusty rose, simple, silky. Even in heels she came just to his chin. She wore a hesitant smile and held in her arms the biggest, whitest cat he'd ever seen.

"Meet Emma," she said, standing aside to let him enter. "She's my watch cat."

Stepping inside, he reached to bury his hand in the animal's soft fur. "She's beautiful," he said. His eyes locked with Sheila's. He trailed the backs of his fingers across her hand and along her arm and saw her eyes darken. Her warm scent tugged at his senses. Emma stopped purring and shifted her yellow gaze up at him.

Closing the door with a bump of her hip, Sheila turned and set the cat down, very aware of the sudden escalation of her heartbeat. During the short drive from the office to her home and while she'd showered and changed, she'd asked herself several times if going out with Tony Adams was a wise decision. If she closed her eyes, she could picture them in his small kitchen this afternoon, could still feel his hand on her back, his thumb tracing the fullness of her lips. Just now, she saw in his eyes the quietly simmering sensuality she'd sensed the first time he'd run that slow silver gaze over her, head to toe. No, getting this close to the heat this soon probably wasn't wise. But it was damned irresistible.

"Would you like a drink before we go? I have wine or—"

"I see you like Van Gogh," he interrupted, standing in front of a framed print on the wall, a field of wildflowers in a riot of yellows and golds.

She came to stand beside him. "Yes. His landscapes are uplifting. Like hanging a piece of sunshine on your wall. It's hard to believe he was such a disturbed man when you study his early work."

Tony shifted his stance to look down at her. "Maybe we're all a little like that, the smiling facade hiding a troubled soul."

Her eyes studied his a long moment. "Have you always been so serious?"

He considered that. "Am I?" he asked, raising a questioning brow.

She nodded. "I think so. I wonder if it's good for you."

His smile was slow. "Analyzing me already, Dr. Freud?"

She smiled back. "Sorry. I tend to do that. About that drink?"

"Let's have it at the restaurant."

"I'll just be a minute," she said, nodding and walking toward the bedroom.

Tony glanced around the large room, decorated in white and blues with touches of lilac and deeper shades of purple. Low, comfortable furniture, a small antique desk, a bookcase crammed full in hodgepodge disarray. Next to a small corner fireplace a stereo played softly, something sad, country and western. At the opposite end, on the drop-leaf dining-room table, sat a huge bowl containing a large goldfish swimming in slow, lazy circles. Next to it, looking deceptively sleepy-eyed, Emma watched the fish's maneuvers.

Her jacket over her arm, Sheila walked toward him as he watched the cat studying the fishbowl. "Are you going to leave these two here alone? I think Emma's just spotted dinner."

Shoving her keys into her small bag, Sheila shook her head. "Emma wouldn't dream of eating Jonah. They're pals." She switched on a small table lamp, turned off the music and moved toward the door.

Joining her, Tony looked skeptical. "How'd you get Emma to agree to this strange relationship?"

Sheila opened the door. "I put her in charge, made her responsible for Jonah's safety. I told you she was a watch cat." Her lips twitched mischievously.

Following her outside, Tony found himself grinning. "You're crazy, you know that? You make me feel like I've just stepped through the looking glass."

Smiling warmly, she took his hand as they started down the stairs. This was better, this was comfortable. Laughter was safe. It was his serious look that she had trouble handling. "Good. You could use a little silliness in your life, I think."

"And I think you're just the person to supply it."

"You may be right." She stopped as he opened the car door for her. "Did you pick out this Mercedes yourself?"

"Yes. Why?"

Her eyes roamed over his conservative suit, white shirt and muted paisley tie, then returned to his face. "The red. It's a surprise." Still waters, she thought. She'd be willing to bet on it. She got into the car.

Hand on the door, he winked at her. "Perhaps you'll find a couple more surprises, Sheila. If you look hard enough."

She watched him walk around the front. She hadn't a doubt in the world he was right.

* * *

The Roma Café was in a seedy section of town, surrounded by warehouses and abandoned buildings, yet was crowded nightly. What it lacked in location it more than made up for in mouth-watering Italian food, an impressive wine list and waiters who remembered your name. Seated in the back room at a cozy corner table, Sheila took a sip of the rich red wine Tony had ordered and smiled at him in appreciation.

"Mmm, this is good." Her eyes skimmed the room, taking in the dark woods, the spotless tablecloths, the crystal shimmering in candlelight, the rotund waiters who spoke with thick accents. "My mother would like this place."

Tony set down his glass and leaned forward on his crossed arms. The flickering light danced off her golden hair and warmed her dark eyes. She looked as appealing in the subdued atmosphere as she had in bright sunshine. He wanted to know more about her, to discover why she intrigued him. "Tell me about your mother."

Sheila shrugged, then let a soft smile break through. "Not much to tell. She was born into a large Italian family in Tawas in upstate Michigan, where she still lives. She married the boy next door, my father, her childhood sweetheart. When I think of my mother, the word nurturing comes to mind. She's very special, with jet-black hair and eyes the exact color of mine."

"Then she has beautiful eyes," he said, his gaze serious. "And you love her very much."

It wasn't a question. "Yes."

"And except for the eyes, you look like your father."

"A good guess. Yes, the only one out of four."

"Which undoubtedly makes you his favorite."

She shook her head. "My father has a gift for making each of us feel like his favorite."

"A good trait." Tony reached for his glass, took another sip. "And handy to have if he's an attorney. Is he?"

"No, he builds houses—wonderful houses. One of my brothers is an attorney."

"Did he inspire you to take up law?"

"Not really. Law has always fascinated me. Did your father inspire you to become an attorney?" She took a sip of wine, watching him over the rim. Not a flicker revealed what he was thinking—good courtroom control. But they weren't in a courtroom. His questions didn't bother her. She wondered if hers might somehow be breaking down his reserve.

He shook his head. "No, I think Jed did. We went to college together and then on to law school. We always talked about sharing a practice."

"And now you are, along with your father." She watched him drop his eyes, studying the crimson liquid in his glass. An imperceptible frown scurried across his forehead and then was gone. Or had she imagined it? His hand slid inside his shirt pocket but emerged empty. She'd seen the gesture several times before, yet he never lit up. Curious... she had to find out.

"Tell me, do you smoke or are you carrying those for a friend?"

He smiled sheepishly. "Old habits die hard. I used to smoke for years, but I quit three months ago. It was getting out of hand, the need controlling me, you know. So I stopped voluntarily, cold turkey. Damned difficult."

"I don't understand. Why do you still carry a pack with you always? Why tempt yourself?"

He shrugged, sitting back more comfortably. "I like to know they're there, in case I *have* to have a cigarette. This way, I could have one if I wanted to, but I *choose* not to. *I'm* in control."

Through the soft candlelight, she studied his bronze features. "Is control so important to you?"

"Over myself? Absolutely. If you don't have control over yourself, you lose control over your entire life."

Abruptly he changed the subject. "Why did you leave Babcock, Aimes and Whitney? They're a highly respected firm."

"Yes, I know. But they weren't right for me."

"In what way?"

The waiter arrived, interrupting their conversation as he deftly placed in front of them steaming plates of veal with lemon, baby asparagus and a fragrant side dish of spaghetti. After pouring more wine, he set down a basket of hot rolls and quietly withdrew. The fork-tender meat brought a smile to Sheila's face.

"Fabulous."

"Just like Mama makes?" Tony asked, his tone teasing.

"Almost as good."

"I admire your loyalty." Buttering a roll, he went back to their former conversation. "So why wasn't your position downtown right for you?"

Swallowing a mouthful of spaghetti, Sheila looked up, thoughtful. "Let me put it this way. Once, when I was a teenager, I was on a girls' soccer team. The first night I had a scratched knee and a scraped elbow. The second game I sprained my wrist. The third I nearly broke someone's nose. I had to admit I was holding everyone back. I learned that there's a time to quit, for yourself and the good of the team. It was the same at Babcock, Aimes and Whitney. I tried to be a team player, to do my best on the cases I worked on, but my heart wasn't in it—just like with soccer."

Fork suspended, he'd listened intently to her explanation. "That's a cute story, but this isn't a soccer game. It's life."

Resuming eating, she shook her head. "Same thing. If it doesn't work for you, and it could be harmful to others, best to get out while the getting's good."

"Quite a philosophy."

Her eyes searched his. "But you don't believe it."

He toyed with his food, thinking. "I'm not sure."

It was time to turn the tables. "Tell me about your family, Tony," she requested, her voice soft, only gently probing.

He took a fortifying drink of wine, deciding to satisfy her curiosity to a limited degree. "My mother is a wonderfully charming woman. She's beautiful in an offbeat sort of way, and quite talented. She currently operates a boutique in Soho, New York's somewhat bohemian neighborhood. After the divorce she went through two more husbands, each one handsome, debonair and penniless but the kind of man who looks great in a tuxedo, sends her a dozen red roses on her birthday and undoubtedly drinks champagne from her slipper—champagne *she* buys. She's an incurable romantic who keeps a man around until he turns into a husband with dirty socks, a five o'clock shadow and morning breath. Then she sends him on his way."

Taking his time chewing a bite of veal, Tony was unaware Sheila had stopped eating, her expression softening as she listened to him. Moving his plate aside, he continued.

"My father, on the other hand, is on wife number four. I didn't even meet one of them, she was in and out of his life so quickly. He's searching for a woman who can put up with his need to be center stage, his penchant for affairs and his frequent drinking bouts. The fact that most likely no such woman exists doesn't deter him in the least from continuing the search. Each one in turn thinks *she's* the one who will reform the charming scalawag. None have, of course, or ever will, because the good senator likes doing what he does and has no intention of changing for anyone."

With a last sip of wine, he raised his gaze to Sheila's and found her looking at him. He saw understanding in the warm depths of her eyes, not pity and not the answering humor his irrelevant litany had been trying to elicit. Compassion—it was the one thing that weakened him every time.

Her heart went out to him. She wondered if he knew how little-boy-disappointed he sounded under the glib recital. She doubted it. The urge to run around the table and take him into her arms was overpowering. Instead, she reached to place her hand on his, giving in to her need to touch him.

Tony dropped his gaze to the hand quietly resting on his. He'd thought it delicate, almost frail when he'd first held it. Now he saw the strength there, the empathy. He picked it up and studied her small finger with its chewed edge. The eyes he raised to hers once more held a hint of humor. "Maybe I should take up nail-biting. Not as addictive as smoking."

"I'm not so sure. We all have our crutches."

Signaling the waiter over, Tony reluctantly let go of her hand. "Would you like some coffee?" At her nod, he ordered two. "They have terrific raisin pie. I noticed you're fond of them."

Smiling, she shook her head. "I'm stuffed, really. I only resort to raisins when I've missed a meal or two. Lots of vitamins and few calories."

The waiter divided the last of the wine between them and left to fetch their coffee. Feeling encouraged by the slant of their conversation, Sheila decided to go a step further.

"Does your father's return have anything to do with your leaving the prosecutor's office?"

Holding his wine glass between his hands, he considered her question. A very perceptive lady was Miss Sheila North. He decided there was no point in evasion. "Yes, but there are other reasons, too. Maybe I'm not such a good team player, either. I like to make my own decisions, my own choices, not have to answer to the distric attorney. Or anyone else. And I discovered I wasn't cut out for the political arena."

"It's good you found out before you got caught up in it. Is your father disappointed in your decision?"

He gave a deceptively nonchalant shrug. "He hasn't shown up yet this week, so he doesn't know."

And won't it be interesting when he finds out? Sheila thought as she watched the waiter place coffee in front of them. Mike, her policeman friend, had hinted that the senator was less than scrupulous. Was that another reason Tony'd returned to his practice, to protect what he and Jed had built up during the older man's four-year absence? She hoped Tony's father would show up soon so she could meet him and judge for herself.

Glancing around the room, Sheila saw that nearly all the tables had emptied. Checking her watch, she noted with surprise the lateness of the hour. It'd been a far more interesting evening than she'd originally anticipated. She finished her coffee while Tony paid the bill, and they stepped out into the warmth of a star-studded, moon-drenched summer night.

Waving away the attendant, Tony took her arm and guided her toward the adjacent parking lot. "I'm not fond of others driving my car," he explained.

That need for control again, Sheila thought, standing quietly as he unlocked the door. Always there, underscoring everything he did. Having grown up in a shifting household, perhaps it was his way of coping, having something solid to hang on to. A far-from-simple man was Tony Adams, she decided.

He swung the door open and stepped back, but misjudged his distance and turned full into her, nearly knocking her off balance. His hands shot out, grabbing her elbows to steady her as she teetered from the bump. Then suddenly they were close, her upturned face inviting, her dark eyes shadowy in the dim glow of distant streetlights. Her scent reached out to him, entrapping him. Sliding his arms firmly around her, he lowered his head to capture her lips.

Her mouth seemed hesitant, though he guessed she wasn't. Her movements seemed inexperienced, yet he felt she wasn't. She responded to him slowly, cautiously, sweetly, and Tony knew a pull of desire he'd never before felt.

Sheila'd been expecting his kiss, had known the evening would end with it. But back at her doorstep, not here in a lighted parking lot with traffic cruising slowly by. She hadn't expected to collide with the hard wall of his chest, nor the sudden awareness that had flooded his gray eyes. She hadn't thought his mouth would be so soft, so arousing, the contact heating her blood. She hadn't known she wouldn't be able to control her arms, which wound around him, pulling closer and closer still. She hadn't anticipated the soft sigh of pleasure that came from deep inside her as she opened her mouth more fully to his.

Lifting his head, he shifted slightly, but his hold on her didn't slacken as he watched her eyes open, cloudy with the beginnings of passion. His hand touched the silkiness of her hair, so pale in the moonlight. Her mouth, damp from his kiss, trembled slightly, drawing him. On a soft moan, he dipped to taste her again, unable to resist a return visit.

She felt her breath catch in her throat as his tongue danced into her mouth, his obvious hunger exciting her. The sensuous, smoky taste of him mingled with his clean masculine scent had her senses swirling as her hands clutched the back of his jacket. This kiss was an exploration, a slow caress of lips, yet it had her heart thudding and her blood racing.

Equally stunned, they slowly drew apart. His arms remained loosely wrapped around her as if he didn't want to move too far away. Sheila's voice was none too steady when she spoke. "It seems I've discovered another one of those surprises you mentioned earlier, counselor."

Sliding his hand down her back, he hooked them together at her waist and leaned away from her, his gray eyes serious. "That surprised me as much as you."

Reaching up, she ran a hand down his cheek and around his jaw. "You're a puzzling man, Tony Adams. And I've always been intrigued by puzzles."

"I'll be interested to see how you plan to solve me," he said, dropping his arms and stepping back to hold the door open for her. "And just how long it will take you."

It was late Friday afternoon before Tony had a free moment to catch his breath or give serious thought to the effect Sheila North had on his emotions. Sitting behind his desk, he leaned back and rubbed the tense muscles at the back of his neck.

The week had flown by with meetings at the prosecutor's office as he completed his pending files and turned his caseload over to other attorneys more eager than he to make a name for themselves. There was always a ready supply dancing around the district attorney, dreaming up dramatic courtroom tactics in order to catch the right eye, hoping for that one big case that would launch them. Enough—after two years, he'd had enough.

He was relieved to return to private practice. Besides, with the senator back, he'd had little choice.

Jed had been carrying too large a load for the past few months. After several late-night meetings, they'd finally agreed on how to divide their present pending cases. The one Jed was most anxious to turn over was the Thornton case, so Tony'd spent the better part of the day immersing himself in the file, familiarizing himself with all the aspects of the Thorntons. A complicated mess if he'd ever seen one. Yet he found himself looking forward to the challenge.

Getting up, he moved to the large window and gazed out at the waning afternoon sun sprinkling the side yard with warmth. He stretched his tall frame, easing the kinks, running a hand through his untidy hair. He felt vaguely discontented and couldn't put his finger on why. Then it came to him—Sheila.

He'd known her such a short time, yet her image was always there, in his mind's eye, just below the surface. He'd deliberately avoided spending much time with her after depositing her on her doorstep Monday night. He'd passed her in the courthouse halls Tuesday, poured a cup of coffee for her downstairs late one afternoon and even spent a few minutes upstairs in the library with her yesterday. Not much contact, and still she dominated his thoughts, creeping in at odd moments throughout his days.

Where had these new feelings come from? he wondered. He'd always been so guarded, so careful, unwilling to get emotionally involved. Yet after one week around Sheila, she'd managed to pull a myriad of feelings from him ... *without* his permission. And after one simple dinner date and two stunning kisses she had him reliving the taste and scent and feel of her too easily and too often. More than that, she had him daydreaming like a teenager.

Slowly he removed two tickets from his pocket and stared at them. A popular country singer was appearing just north of the city at Pine Knob, a big outdoor amphitheater. Unable to attend tonight's concert, Jed had offered him the tickets. Tony had almost refused, but then he'd remembered that Sheila's stereo had been playing country music when he'd picked her up. She was probably a big fan. On impulse he'd taken the tickets and now stood studying them. Would she turn down a last-minute invitation? Maybe, but maybe not. Pocketing the tickets, he headed for the stairs.

Seated at her desk, head bent, absorbed in taking notes from a law journal, she hadn't heard him approach. She wore a white linen suit, a silky black blouse open at the throat and a pair of wire-rimmed reading glasses, lightly tinted. Oddly, instead of detracting from her classical beauty, the oversized old-fashioned specs gave her face a whimsical charm. He felt a smile take over his face as he cleared his throat and walked in.

"How's it going, counselor?" he asked as she looked up at him with a surprised but welcoming smile.

Leaning back in her chair, she removed her glasses. "Slowly."

"The kidnapping case?" She nodded wearily. He leaned against the edge of her desk, folding his arms across his chest. "Want to talk about it?"

She gave a small shrug. "Not much to talk about yet. I've spent most of the week checking Jimmy Lee's story. His school records, the pharmacist he works for, his mother. Not a lot to go on so far."

"You still think he's innocent?"

"Yes. I'm not saying what he did was very wise. I'm only saying he did it for understandable reasons. And, I believe, with Kim's permission. If I could just get to her."

"You'll find a way. You're bright, resourceful, quick."

From under lowered lashes, Sheila let her eyes feast on him. Navy slacks, pale yellow shirt, paisley suspenders today, the colors picked up in his tie. She wondered what those broad shoulders would look like bare, how that tan skin would feel under her touch, what he'd taste like. She felt her face flush lightly at the direction of her thoughts. Avoiding his eyes, she closed the book and shuffled the papers together into an untidy pile. "Thank you," she mumbled.

Seeing her sudden discomfort, Tony fought a smile. Was she remembering their kiss, the way her mouth had opened under his only days ago? Deliberately he got up and slowly walked behind her. "Have you talked with Kim's father at all?"

"No, but I've read his statement. Mr. Tremaine seems very sure of himself."

He lifted his hands to her shoulders, lightly massaging them. "Men like him usually are. They're comfortable with power and know how to use it. He might be the key to your case, but be careful. He's probably a cobra." He kept his touch light, though his fingers wanted to stray to her hair, to the soft vulnerability of her neck and around to the inviting roundness of her breasts.

Sheila felt the effects of his hands move through her, making her skin tingle and breathing go shallow, and forced herself to keep her mind on their conversation. "Not to change the subject, but I heard your father and his secretary move in earlier. Is he settled?"

"Yes, he's in," Tony said. He'd labeled Tremaine a cobra. Maybe Sheila hadn't changed the subject. Cobras came in many colors. "He wants to meet you."

Sensing the sudden tension in him, Sheila put her hand on his and swiveled to gaze up at him. "Are you going to warn me about him, too?"

"Are you susceptible to suave, impeccable English-bred charm?" he asked, taking her hand fully in his.

"I'm not immune to it," she answered. "My father's English."

"So am I."

"I know." Eyes steady on his, she let him make of that what he would. She'd thought about Tony a lot since Monday night—too much. She'd kept busy all week and hadn't realized until he'd walked in how very glad she was to see him again. There was no denying her attraction to him, and his for her. Why, she wondered, did he seem to waver between wanting to be with her and fighting his desire?

"Are you busy tonight? I have tickets for the concert at Pine Knob."

Her eyes widened in anticipation. "Are you asking me to go with you?" She watched his lips twitch into a smile, bringing out the dimple in one corner. She struggled with an urge to stand up and kiss it.

"Yes. Will you?"

She stood up, her hand still in his, a smile lighting her face. "I adore country music. How'd you know?"

"A lucky guess."

"Under cover or on the lawn?"

"On the lawn, I'm afraid."

"Don't be. I like it there much better. Reminds me of my decadent youth."

He released her hand and stepped back, shoving his own hands into his pockets, the need to touch more of her making them warm and damp. "Did you have a decadent youth?"

She laughed as she stuffed papers into her briefcase. "No, not really. Did you?"

"Yes, as a matter of fact he did," said a deep voice from the doorway. They both looked up.

Well, the great man himself at last, Sheila thought. Senator Maxwell T. Adams was an inch or so over six feet, nearly as tall as his son, with a full head of wavy white hair and a barrel chest. His eyes were a cold, silvery blue, confident and measuring. As a woman, she felt the heat of his bold appraisal, his appreciative approval. As a female attorney, from what she'd heard of him, she doubted if she'd ever earn his approval.

"Dad, I'd like you to meet Sheila North," Tony said, his voice level and expressionless. "Sheila, this is my father, Maxwell Adams."

Striding forward and extending a hand, he gave her a big smile. A duplicate of Tony's dimple nestled in the left corner of his mouth. "I've heard a great deal about you, Miss North." His hand was large, smooth, strong. "It's a pleasure to have you with us."

For a wild moment she feared he would kiss her hand, but instead he put his other one atop hers, enveloping it in a cocoon of warmth. "Thank you, Senator," Sheila answered. "I'm happy to meet you."

"Jed speaks very highly of you."

Her hand felt stifled in his firm grip. Gently she removed it. "We go back a ways. He's a talented attorney."

The physical similarity between the two men was evident, Sheila thought. Though the senator was slightly shorter and thicker, they shared the same heavy, curly hair, the ruddy complexion, the stylish, almost formal choice of well-cut clothes, the easy manner. The difference was mostly in the eyes. Tony's were a warm gray where his father's were an icy blue-gray. And in the mouth—the senator had thin lips, with a bit of a self-satisfied smile. Tony's mouth was full, sensuous and soft. The softest thing about him.

The senator adjusted an already perfect tie and checked his immaculate white cuffs, his shrewd gaze assessing her. "Is your family related to the Danford Norths of Grosse Pointe Farms? He's a neurosurgeon, a fine man. His wife plays tennis."

And that about sums them up, Sheila thought, but she kept her expression bland. "No, I'm afraid not. My family's from Tawas, up north."

"Oh, really?" The senator tried again. "I have a friend up that way. Sheldon North, a land developer. A relative, by any chance?"

"I doubt it. My father's a bricklayer." Which hardly explained her father's work, but she deliberately phrased it in such a way as to end this silliness. By the look on the senator's face, it had worked. From the corner of her eye, she saw Tony suppress a smile.

"Yes, well," he muttered, frowning. "Nice meeting you, Sheila. Tony, I've got to run. I'll be at my club if you need me."

They stood listening to his footsteps disappear down the stairway. Letting out a deep breath, Sheila sat down and looked up at Tony. His hand patted his shirt pocket longingly before he sank into the chair opposite her.

"I see you don't intimidate easily," he said, watching her.

Sheila cocked her head thoughtfully. "Did you think I would?"

"I wasn't sure. The senator cuts quite a figure."

"Is that what even his family calls him, the senator?"

Tony gave her a self-deprecating grin and stood. "I get around that nicely. I don't call him much. Pick you up at seven." He walked to the door, then swung around. "Dress casual."

"How casual?"

"Very. Jeans."

"You mean you're going to take off your vest?" she asked, unable to resist.

"I might. I have a blanket for us to sit on."

Sheila found herself smiling at the image of the two of them huddled together on a blanket under the stars listening to slow romantic ballads. Suddenly she stood, anxious to get going, for the evening to begin. "Are you feeding me, too?"

His head poked back around the corner. "I'll pick up this big bag of raisins and a bottle of burgundy. Will that be all right?"

Her smile broadened. "Perfect." She heard his laugh echo down the stairs. Feeling lighthearted, she snapped her briefcase closed. So what if she still had piles of work to do. And so what if the senator thought she had few redeeming social connections. She was going out tonight with a man who excited, intrigued and warmed her. What more could she ask for?

Chapter Four

"Here you go. One hot dog with everything." Tony handed Sheila her dinner, then sat down cross-legged on the blanket next to her, juggling his own. "Well, everything *except* raisins."

"Mmm," she murmured, already involved in a big, juicy bite. "Not even raisins could improve this. Delicious." Tucking her Adidas under her jeans-clad bottom, she sat opposite him, enjoying their picnic during intermission. A handful of other couples lounged on similar blankets along the sloping hill, a few older ones sat in lawn chairs and a group of teenage girls giggled in a cluster near the front. Others strolled the winding walks that led to concession stands located on the wide pavilion. The dusk of early evening brushed orange and gray streaks across the darkening sky. Sheila sighed contentedly.

Easing off the container top with one hand, Tony offered her a large paper cup. "Sorry about the burgundy.

They don't allow alcoholic beverages past the gates. You'll have to settle for root beer."

"No problem. I love root beer." She took a deep swallow, then studied the cup, squinting. "Oh, 1986. That was a good year for root beer."

Tony licked a dab of mustard from his finger and smiled at her. Fun, Sheila North was fun to be with...easygoing, adaptable, a lady who rolled with the punches. But the thing that shone through the mists was her intelligence—unmistakable, undeniable, and unexpected when you found it in a beautiful package along with a sense of humor and those wonderful brown eyes. This was a vastly appealing combination.

Even wearing an oversized pink sweatshirt, the sleeves shoved up high on her arms, she was sexy. Her hair was caught up in a ponytail and tied with a piece of pink yarn, making her look young and carefree. It occurred to him that it had been years since he'd become aroused simply by looking at a woman.

Finishing, Tony wadded up his napkin and tossed it in the paper sack. He scrunched forward, leaning his elbows on his knees, close in front of her. He watched her finish the last bite, then raise her eyes to his. For a long moment he just stared, as if trying to see deep inside her.

"What makes you so easy to be with?" he asked, sounding honestly puzzled.

She shrugged, smiling. "Am I?"

"Yes, I don't often feel this relaxed. With you, I do. I'm not quite sure why."

She thought she could guess why, and wondered if he could handle it. Her eyes twinkled at him. "Maybe you're too busy working to let yourself relax."

He gave her an exaggerated frown. "You think I'm a workaholic?"

She reached up to leisurely stroke his face to soften her words. "From what I've heard, sometimes." Slowly, she let her fingers trail down his neck and along the hard ridges of his chest. Then, abruptly, she lay back on the blanket. "From what I see, you're a little on the intense side. You must have had a very proper upbringing. Lightening up a little wouldn't hurt. Be good to yourself, I always say." She swung her gaze to his face. "For instance, aside from your work, where it's undoubtedly necessary, do you spend time around people difficult to be with?"

"More time than I prefer," he answered, flopping backward on the blanket beside her, cushioning his head on his crossed hands.

"There's a place to make a change. Why do you—a streak of masochism?"

He frowned, considering. "Business commitments, personal obligations, social manners. There's no escaping some people, I guess."

"Like your father?" she asked, turning on her side, propping her head with one hand.

"Hell, I don't spend time with my father. Never have."

She thought as much. Tony seemed in a receptive mood so she continued. "Does your mother come to town often?"

He shook his head. "No, she likes her little loft in Soho. I visit her occasionally. And my sister, Sandy, flies to the Big Apple often."

Scooting nearer, she leaned toward him, bracing one elbow on his broad chest, her hand fiddling with his pocketed cigarettes. "I didn't know you had a sister. Does she live on the east side?"

"She's got an apartment in the Jeffersonian that she shares with the current love of her life, Tim O'Connor."

The musky scent of his skin reached her through the thin cotton of his shirt. She tried to keep its effect from distracting her. "Ah, do I detect a note of disapproval of their arrangement?"

Almost absently, his hand moved to her back, making slow, lazy circles as he talked. "Not in their arrangement. But now, she's talking marriage."

"And you don't feel she should marry him?"

"No, I don't. Sandy's been engaged twice, broke both of them off. She's got a great job in an architectural firm. She's attractive, bright, together. What does she need marriage for? I think she should stick to relationships. Easier to get out of when you change your mind."

So that's how it is, Sheila thought, an interesting viewpoint. "You don't think Tim's right for her, or is it marriage in general you're opposed to?"

His hand drifted to her ponytail, his fingers threading through the silky strands...so soft. "Tim's a nice guy, but there could be a dozen men in her life that might be right for her. As to marriage, it's a highly overrated institution invented by bored florists, church organists and people who engrave silverware. Some marriages are over before the honeymoon. I've seen too many fail."

His parents, seven marriages between them. Yes, he'd seen his share of failures. She wondered if he'd ever had a chance to see a really good marriage up close. "And some have succeeded beautifully, like my folks."

"A miracle. You can't rely on miracles happening."

"And you can't base your life on fear. The people who worry about the what-ifs miss out on the miracles." His face drew her hand like a magnet. She reached up to touch, enjoying the light growth of beard, admiring the strong jaw. "Don't tell me you don't believe in miracles, either?"

His eyes darkened, and his hand strayed to the back of her neck. "Right now I do. I want to kiss you."

Her throat tightened. Quicksand—she was stepping into quicksand here, and willingly. "Then why don't you?"

The lightest pressure on the back of her neck brought her mouth close to his. His other hand encircled her, urging her upward, her breasts flattening against his chest. His eyes were on her lips as if he were memorizing their shape and texture. Heart pounding, she felt her mouth open in anticipation, her breath fan out between them. Gently the tip of his tongue touched her upper lip, then slid around to the bottom, completing the circle. Deep inside her Sheila felt an answering contraction as desire slammed into her, sure and strong.

His mouth settled over hers, lightly, perfectly, possessively. A deep-throated moan came from him as he pulled her closer, his tongue invading now, gradually bolder. Her fingers trapped between them tangled in the open throat of his shirt, in the crisp hair of his chest. His hard hands spread into her hair and along her back, sending shivers helplessly up and down her.

Needs raced wildly through Tony, an avalanche of feeling, demanding more. He twisted and turned her, rolling her over onto her back, needing to be more in control. It was impossible that this kiss was even more shattering than he'd remembered the first ones being. It was incredible that she could have him writhing and moaning so swiftly, so thoroughly, with just a taste of her mouth and the touch of her small hands. It was unbelievable that she made the hillside and the distant people, the noise and chatter, even the soft summer breeze disappear. And only Sheila remained. Only Sheila and his racing desire for her.

Feeling herself drowning, Sheila curved her hands over his shoulders, clutching him like a lifeline in a suddenly deep, suddenly dangerous sea of longing. Lifting his head, Tony took his mouth on a rapid journey over her face, kissing her closed eyelids, tracing her ear with his tongue, moving to nuzzle her neck. Blindly she reached and found his roaming mouth and claimed it again.

It was long moments before he pulled back, his eyes when they opened nearly as dazed as her own were. Slowly she raised a hand to smooth back the wild tangle of his hair, her breath coming out in jerky little puffs. Caressing his cheek, she smiled somewhat unsteadily up at him.

"Definitely not the modus operandi of a stuffed shirt," she said, her voice shaky. "You have the most incredibly inventive mouth. It...it does things to me."

He reached to take her hand from his cheek, pressed his warm lips into her palm, then moved it to the blanket, trapping it there. His eyes were serious, studying her, making her wonder what he was thinking.

"Do I bother you by touching you?" she asked, curious why he'd removed her hand from his face. When he didn't answer right away, she went on. "I'm a born toucher. My whole family's like that. I take it yours isn't?"

Tony thought about that and couldn't remember the last time his father had touched him, except to shake hands in greeting. He remembered his mother's quick, embarrassed hugs. And his sister Sandy was cool, often aloof. No, his family members weren't touchers, and neither was he—until Sheila.

She watched his emotions play across his face, unguarded for a change, so much going on behind those silvery eyes.

"Yes, your touching bothers me," Tony said finally. Shifting, his hands found their way under her, easing beneath her sweatshirt, feeling the warm skin there. He caught her swift intake of breath as her eyes widened. "But not in the way you mean. Does *my* touch bother you?"

"Yes, very much so. And I like it."

He brought his face very close, their breath mingling. "I want to make love with you."

I want that, too! She drew back a bit. "Oh, I think not. We hardly know one another."

"You don't have to know someone months to share a night of mutual pleasure."

She pressed into the blanket, into the hard ground beneath, moving back further so she could better see his eyes. "Is that what you're looking for?"

"That's part of it, yes. Aren't you?"

Swinging her gaze to the star-studded sky, she wondered if he could read her disappointment. "No."

He sighed. "We've probably discovered the greatest difference between men and women."

"Not necessarily. What we've discovered is an insurmountable impasse...at least for the time being."

Tony leaned back on one elbow, giving her a little breathing space. Why had he started this conversation? From the beginning, he'd known where it would lead. She was not a woman who'd compromise easily. "What is it you *do* want?" he asked quietly.

In the distance, ahead of them, the musicians had returned and were tuning up. Breaking away from him, Sheila sat up, brushing out her ponytail. "What makes you think I want anything more than an evening out under the stars, a hot dog and country music?"

Damn! She wasn't going to let him off easily. "You're looking for commitment." It sounded like an accusation even to his ears.

She swung her gaze to him, her eyes dark and direct. "You're looking for intimacy. Intimacy without commitment is the ultimate self-deluding lie. I've outgrown those games. Haven't you?"

Both barrels. The lady shot from the hip. He pulled himself up and leaned into her. "Look at me and tell me you don't want me."

She held his gaze for perhaps twenty seconds, then dropped her eyes, shaking her head. "I wouldn't exactly say that."

"Question my motives every which way. The pure truth is that *I want you,* and you feel the same."

A hint of amusement returned to her eyes. "I'm not sure where purity comes into this."

That questioning left brow of his shot up. "Are you that endangered species known as a virgin?"

She laughed. "No. Disappointed?"

"At twenty seven? I'd be surprised if you were."

Adjusting her sweatshirt, Sheila lay back again, crossing her feet at the ankles and folding her hands over her stomach. "Nonvirginal doesn't mean there've been hordes, you know," she said, wondering why she felt compelled to explain herself to him.

Tony joined her, leaning over to cup her chin and force her to look at him. "I never thought that," he said, his voice gentle.

Inexplicably she felt a hot rush of tears gathering. She blinked them away and looked at him again. "For me, it has to mean something. It *has* to."

The smile left his eyes, replaced by something she wouldn't have suspected—tenderness. She felt her heart opening wider.

His thumb traced the fullness of her lips. "I didn't know they still made women like you."

"Maybe you've been looking in the wrong places."

"Maybe," Tony said thoughtfully. He wanted her, he decided as he gazed into her darkening eyes. And he meant to have her. He just had to figure out his strategy. He was too much a master courtroom maneuverer not to have some of that filter into his personal life. Time...it would just take a little more time. He'd be patient and give her time. She'd be worth the wait.

The band began its rousing theme, and the impatient audience clapped along to welcome back the show's star. Tony and Sheila heard none of it as he lowered his head and captured her lips once more.

* * *

Sheila loved the early-morning hours, most especially on Saturdays. The sun had barely peeked through the blinds, and she was up and moving through her small apartment, dusting and vacuuming. After a quick shower, she completed her marketing and still it was not yet nine when she climbed into her car, carrying breakfast for two in a bag. Fresh orange juice, sharp cheese, tangy marmalade and the fragrance of warm croissants drifted to her as she turned onto Jefferson and headed for Riverfront West Apartments and Tony Adams.

It'd been an impulse to take breakfast over to share with him, and though she loved to act on her impulses from time to time, Sheila wondered as she drove just how he'd handle her appearing uninvited on his doorstep early on a Saturday morning. Since their visit to Pine Knob, she'd spent a busy week working on Jimmy Lee's defense in preparation for next week's preliminary hearing. And she'd had a couple of referrals—one was for the drafting of a will for an older couple and the other involved attending a real-estate closing for a friend's first house purchase. Dull, routine stuff, but it all helped pay the rent.

She hadn't seen much of Tony, but she knew he'd been immersing himself in the Thornton case and getting used to being back in his own practice. When they were both in, they'd fallen into the habit of sharing a cup of late-afternoon coffee together and talking. Sometimes about their cases, sometimes just idle chatter. She'd begun to look forward to these sessions more than she'd planned. Tony'd begun to matter to her, more than she'd have predicted. And while it warmed her, it also worried her.

She'd spent some time getting to know Rosemary, whose mother-hen ways often reminded her of her own parent. She'd stopped to talk with Jed a couple of times, and even the senator had shared a leisurely hour of conversation with her one afternoon in the library. But it was Tony who dominated her thoughts, Tony she wanted to be with, Tony who made her heart beat erratically. Unfamiliar with the role of pursuer, she nevertheless had decided this morning to take it on. Risks, though frightening, were exciting.

Stopping for a light, Sheila shook back her windblown hair and gazed around the light traffic, the cloudless blue sky, enjoying the beautiful summer morning. Even the high humidity, part and parcel of Michigan weather, didn't bother her today. Convertible top down, warm breeze caressing her face, she felt happy and glad to be alive. Starting up again, she prayed Tony was a morning person.

Morning wasn't welcome at his apartment. Tony loved to sleep, long and deep and luxuriously. He allowed himself few extravagances—he simply had a serious conservative nature—but sheets made of cotton so soft it could be mistaken for satin, silk shirts and butter-soft Italian leather shoes were not luxury items to him but necessities. They were creature comforts that soothed his soul—as was sleeping late on a weekend morning. Which was why, when he heard the insistent ringing of the doorbell and saw that it was only a little after nine, he muttered under his breath as he groped his way down the hall to open the door.

She stood there wearing white shorts and a forest-green collarless cotton shirt, her hands behind her back, a shy grin playing around her full lips. She looked like a Girl Scout leader who'd gotten off on the wrong floor. Unconsciously he felt his heart warm and a smile form on his face. She did that to him, regularly and effortlessly. Sliding one arm up the door, he tried to keep a sober expression.

"Yes, miss?"

"I—I wonder if you could help me out, sir? I'm working my way through college and I . . ."

"I'm sorry, but I have all the magazine subscriptions I need and—"

Bringing her arms forward, she waved a white paper bag under his nose. "How about warm, buttery croissants, straight out of the oven?"

He raised one eyebrow. "I suppose you think the way to a man's heart is through his stomach?"

"I'm counting on it," she answered.

Returning her smile at last, he reached for her arm, pulled her inside and into his embrace. Responding by letting her arms encircle him, Sheila breathed a sigh of relief. If he hadn't acted pleased to see her in just this way, she'd have turned tail and run in another two seconds.

Hands at her back, Tony hugged her close, nuzzling his face into her neck. "Mmm, you smell even better than breakfast." He kissed the soft spot under her ear and was rewarded by her quick shiver. "And taste better, too."

The night's growth of beard added to the rugged, sensual feel of him. Gently but firmly she moved away from him. "Ahh, but you haven't tasted Henri's croissants. They melt in your mouth."

Fully awake now, his body reacting to her nearness in a way that would soon be obvious and possibly embarrassing, he shifted and hoisted his pajama bottoms up more modestly. But he kept his hands on her arms, unwilling to let her move completely out of reach. "But I have tasted you, and I'd like to again."

His chest was as she'd imagined it so many times while tossing in her lonely bed—hard, muscular, and covered with golden brown hair. Sheila swallowed hard. "And so you may, perhaps later." Turning, she wiggled free and glanced about. "Point me to the kitchen, and I'll make coffee while you...get dressed."

He put an exaggerated leer on his face. "You sure you want me to?"

She retreated two more steps. "Uh, yes." Craning her neck she spotted the kitchen doorway. "I'll be in there. Don't worry, I'll find what I need." And she moved off.

Hiding a smile, Tony rubbed his chin and watched her walk away—nice tush, nice legs, nice woman. Chuckling, ιddenly not displeased at all to be awake early, Tony went to his bedroom.

Searching through the cupboards, Sheila smiled to her-self. She might have guessed that conservative Tony Adams slept in pajamas. Only the bottoms, but pajamas nonetheless. She wondered if he'd be shocked to learn she didn't even own a nightgown.

In short order Sheila had the coffee perking, the wooden kitchen table set and her goodies spread out. She moved back to the foyer and, hearing the shower running, took a moment to look over Tony's apartment. Like the man it-self, it was filled with surprises.

Sheila felt that you could judge who and what a person was somewhat by his home and the things he chose to sur-round himself with. But, oddly enough, that didn't apply to Tony's place, for it was as if a decorator had lifted it from the pages of *House Beautiful*.

Elegant couches, perfectly matching draperies, carpet-ing you could sink into, expensive glass-and-chrome ta-bles. A few knick-knacks that reeked of fashionable import stores, a crystal ashtray you'd be afraid to desecrate with ash, coffee-table books artfully arranged . . . lovely, im-peccable taste. Yet it left her with the impression of a beautifully appointed suite in a luxurious hotel. No warmth, no personality, no human touches.

Puzzled, Sheila returned to the functional but imper-sonal kitchen, done in pale wood and stainless steel, and poured herself a cup of coffee. Sitting at the table, she wondered at this new side of Tony she'd just discovered. She thought of her own cozy, disorderly, definitely lived-in apartment and shuddered to herself. What must he think of her taste if this was his?

She'd grown up that way—surrounded by good pieces not meant only to be admired but to be used lovingly, in

comfortable clutter. Even books, in her first home and her
present one, were not just for show but were read, one and
all. Tony'd seemed to appreciate the way she'd decorated
her office, yet by comparison his was the more expensive,
more formal, less inviting. She'd thought him a bit stilted
at first, had even told him he was a shade intense.

But she'd learned he had another side, warm and loving
and tender. Usually, in his dress and manner, his office and
home, he chose to hide that side of his personality almost
as if it were a flaw. His father was more like the public
Tony, giving off a to-the-manor-born aura that was reflected in his faultless taste and attire. Did Tony basically
admire his father and try to emulate him, or was it an unconscious thing? Was his bohemian mother's influence
trying to break through? Did he fight against it? And if so,
why? Sipping the hot brew, Sheila wondered at the many
layers that made up this mystifying man.

"I don't shave on Saturdays," he said, coming into the
kitchen wearing pressed denims and a striped knit shirt.

"That's all right. Neither do I," she said, striving for a
light mood. She got up, removed the reheated croissants
from the microwave and poured him a cup of coffee as he
sat down. Resuming her seat, she looked at him. Sunshine drifted in through the small window, landing
squarely on his russet head. She wished she didn't find him
so unreasonably attractive. "I think beards are sexy," she
couldn't help telling him, her voice a little husky.

He stretched to lingeringly caress her cheek. "I think
soft is sexy," he said, his eyes on hers.

Clearing her throat, Sheila tore her gaze away and unwrapped the cheese. "Maybe we'd better eat."

"Whatever you say," Tony said agreeably as he reached
for the butter. "I didn't have a chance to talk with you
yesterday. When's your preliminary hearing?"

Sheila took a swallow of coffee. Work was a much safer
topic. "It's set for Tuesday, but I'm excited about Mon-

day. I'm meeting with Sara Hendrix, Kim Tremaine's college roommate. I all but had to move mountains to get some private time with her.''

"A hostile witness?''

"Definitely. Her mother's going to be with her. I'm not quite sure why they're so reluctant, her parents so protective, if she has nothing to hide.'' She took a bite of cheese thoughtfully.

"I suppose it could be because she's only eighteen.''

"Don't they know you could have subpoenaed her?''

"That's probably why they agreed to meet with me. I wanted her to come willingly, not defensively. I'm not sure why, but I don't feel comfortable with her report, even after several readings. There's something missing...''

Tony swallowed and nodded at her. "You're probably right. Trust your instincts. It usually works.''

She'd always been one to do just that, though Tony couldn't possibly know that. Like coming to him in the morning. "And how are you doing with the Thorntons?''

He frowned. "I'm not sure. Neva Thornton is thirty-two, rather shy and very beautiful.''

"She's the third wife, the one his children think may have helped Mr. Thornton to his reward?''

"Right. She's either one hell of an actress and a gold-digging liar or a tenderhearted woman who genuinely loved her husband and made his last years very happy.''

"Thirty-two. And he died at seventy-two?''

"Yes. Forty years age difference. Makes you wonder.''

"And how long were they married?''

"Fifteen years.''

"Why, she was only seventeen when he married her!''

"Yes. She's so soft-spoken—from the south originally—and she's got this sincere manner.''

Holding her coffee cup between her hands, she smiled at him. "You believe her, I can hear it in your voice. Maybe she really loved him.''

"Maybe."

"There's no accounting for love, you know. It happens to the best people and against all odds."

He folded his arms and leaned forward, his eyes silvery and serious. "I have a tendency to believe you."

"Be careful, counselor, your soft spot is showing."

Breaking the mood, he popped the last morsel of croissant into his mouth. "And speaking of soft spots, these are terrific. Henri's you say? French?"

She laughed, a warm, delicious sound that dampened his palms and tightened his jeans. "So he'd have you think. But I drew up the lease on his building. Henry Goldblum. From New York."

Tony shook his head in mock sadness. "You can't trust anyone these days."

Glancing at her watch, Sheila got up to pour more coffee. "You have time for one more cup."

"Really? Then what happens?"

Briefly she touched his chest and upper arms, squeezing gently before sitting down again. "I see you've got good pectorals. We're going canoeing on Belle Isle."

"You're kidding? I haven't done that in...maybe ten years."

"High time you did then, I'd say." She drained her cup and stood. "Wouldn't want you to get flabby." Fat chance, Sheila thought, gazing at his flat stomach. She hadn't been sure how he'd react to her planning his whole day, but again he'd surprised her by looking almost eager to do something a little crazy. "And, if you don't tip over our canoe, I'll even buy you an ice-cream cone."

Gathering the plates, he took them to the sink and turned to give her a questioning look. "Two dips, one of them chocolate?"

"You bet."

Smiling at her, he grabbed her hand. "You're on. Let's go, counselor."

* * *

"Remind me to suggest more sedentary activities to you the next time we go out," groaned Tony, rubbing his sore shoulder muscles. "Don't you like spectator sports, like watching baseball games?"

Sheila laughed as she pulled him along up the grassy embankment toward the walk that led away from the canoe rentals and the shimmering water of the Detroit River. They'd driven over the connecting bridge from the city, the only way to reach the island park. The popular summer spot offered a woodsy atmosphere to many of the apartment dwellers who lived nearby. It provided several miles of winding, twisting roads, inviting leisurely drives, plus a boat club and restaurant, tennis courts, picnic areas and even a children's zoo.

"Sure I like baseball. But what could be more sedentary than sitting in a little boat and gliding it through the water? I warned you that you were out of shape."

"Easy for you to say. You sat in your end dragging your fingers through the water while I did all the rowing. I'll have you know I play tennis and handball at the club regularly."

"Mmm, if you say so. Next time, I'll row. And speaking of rowing, look over there."

Tony followed the path of her pointing finger. The canoe they'd vacated was rapidly moving downstream, rowed by a thin, wiry boy of no more than ten while a young friend sat across from him. The boat sailed past them with ease, the boy hardly straining.

Grinning, Tony turned back to her. "Yes, but his cargo's smaller."

"Oh!" Sheila yelped, then punched her fist into his upper arm. "Are you suggesting I'm fat?"

She was anything but, Tony thought. He cocked his head back and let his eyes survey her from top to bottom. He'd enjoyed his hour out on the water with her and was only teasing. He'd found he loved to ruffle her feathers now and then, to get a rise out of her, to watch her busy mind think up a rebuttal for him.

Tony had recently come to the conclusion that he'd spent far too many hours these past years working and far too few playing. Sheila, with her boundless enthusiasm for fun, drew him out, made him *want* to go, had him eager to try new things. Most of the women he'd dated up to now would have laughed somewhat hysterically if he'd suggested an afternoon canoeing on Belle Isle and wandering in the park. But then he probably would not have thought to suggest it.

Sliding his arm around her shoulders and drawing her near him, he smiled teasingly at her. "Not fat. Rounded in just the right places."

"Mmm, I guess I'll have to settle for that. And about to get rounder," she said, spotting the ice-cream stand up ahead. "Ready for a cone?"

"Right. Two dips."

Holding hands, they stood in line at the busy concession stand, watching the chattering children in front of them squirming impatiently.

Minutes later, they strolled away licking their cones as Tony reminisced. "I used to visit this island a lot as a teenager growing up on the east-side."

"Oh, you mean for the tennis courts?"

He chuckled, his tongue swirling the cold confection into his mouth. "Not exactly. There's a quiet spot for parking along the far side. I'd bring a date in the evening to watch the submarine races."

Sheila shot him a quick glance, busy with her own rapidly melting cone. "Submarines? I can't believe that river water's deep enough for anything resembling a submarine."

"It's not. But a few of us inventive adolescent boys would park here with girls and tell them that if they looked straight ahead long and hard, they'd see submarines racing."

"And while they watched for submarines you had your way with them?" she asked in mock horror.

"Well, we sure tried." He shook his head, smiling. "All that seems a hundred years ago."

"You really did have a decadent youth, as your father told me."

Tony crunched the last of his cone and stopped, wiping his hands. "Nah, I was basically your shy, awkward, studious type."

The sun highlighted his wind-tossed hair as he stood looking down at her, his gray eyes smiling, his face appearing more relaxed than she'd seen it since she'd known him. "Sure you were," she said, finishing her ice cream. "And pigs can fly."

He laughed and slung his arm across her shoulders companionably. "What's next on our agenda, coach?"

"Tony! I can't believe it's you!" came a voice from the bicycle path behind them. As they turned, a slim auburn-haired woman stopped her bike alongside them and was quickly joined by a tall man who had two tennis rackets sticking out of his wire basket. "Are you slumming?" she asked with a mischievous grin.

His arm still around Sheila, Tony smiled at her and his companion. "Sandy, Tim. Good to see you. Sheila North, meet my sister, Sandy Adams, and the big guy's Tim O'Connor. Sheila has a law office in my building."

Smiling, they shook hands all around.

"I didn't know you came here to Belle Isle?" Sandy probed, looking at her brother.

The resemblance was there, Sheila thought as she studied Tony's sister, in the dark curly hair and the slow smile. But, as with the senator, the eyes were different, more blue than gray, with squint lines that seemed to say she laughed easily and often. Tim was big, redheaded, round-faced and freckled. He had the map of Ireland stamped on his ruddy features.

"We come here all the time," Sandy explained, her gaze on Sheila as she spoke. "It's you I can't believe bumping into here, Tony. Sheila, are you responsible for dragging my brother from his stodgy apartment and his fuddy-duddy club out into the sunshine?" The woman's affection for Tony was obvious, her manner open and direct.

"I guess I am," Sheila answered, relaxing, very aware that Tony's arm was still firmly around her. He seemed not the least inclined to remove it. She wasn't quite sure why, but the gesture pleased her.

"Well, good for you. It's about time you broadened your horizons, big brother."

"How about a game of tennis, you two?" Tim suggested before Tony had a chance to reply. "We've got extra rackets in the car."

Tony rolled his shoulders, a pained look on his face. "Thanks, Tim, but not today. Sheila's had me rowing for hours."

"Hours! More like one."

Sandy laughed. "You're finding out that most of the time Tony's idea of exercise is turning the pages of a book. Are you new to the area, Sheila?"

"No, I've lived in Indian Village over three years."

Shrewd blue-gray eyes measured the two of them. "But you two have only recently met?"

"Hey, I thought I was the interrogator in the family?" he said, softly but with unmistakable firmness of tone.

Tim caught it immediately. "Come on, Sandy. Our court will be taken if we don't get a move on."

A sudden sound made them turn to look. Sheila saw it coming but was helpless to stop it. A young boy running across a portion of open field, looking over his shoulder at the kite he was trying to launch, ran pell mell into Tony, nearly jostling him into the two bicycles. Sheila shifted aside several steps as Tony steadied himself.

"Whoops!" Tony said, reaching to grab the boy, who'd almost lost his footing. "You okay?"

He looked to be seven, eight tops, with a gap-toothed grin. "Yeah. Sorry, mister."

"Having a little trouble getting that thing up in the air, are you?" Tony asked, reeling in the bright red kite and checking it for tears.

"There's not enough wind today," Tim told him, leaning forward on his handlebars.

Tony glanced up at the sky, then wet his finger and held it aloft to check the wind's direction. "Sure there is." He squinted down at the boy. "Want some help?"

His round face lit up. "Sure. My brother said he'd help but he went off to talk to some girls." His tone clearly indicated what he thought of anyone who'd rather talk to girls than fly kites.

"Do you mind?" Tony asked Sheila with raised brows.

"No, go ahead."

"See you two later," Tony said with a wave to Sandy and Tim. Then he was jogging across the field alongside the boy, who was looking up into his face and listening intently to whatever it was he was explaining.

Sandy stared a moment, dumbfounded. "Well, will you look at that...am I crazy or was that my brother who just ran off to fly a kite?"

All three of them watched as Tony and the youngster ran, feeding out the kite line just so, trying to get the summer breezes to catch it and carry it higher. The first attempt failed. With his quiet determination, Tony changed their direction and went back the other way. He wasn't going to let it lick him, Sheila thought. He wanted to control the wind, too. Amazing.

"We're throwing a party the end of next week, Sheila," Sandy said, bringing her attention back to the two people

standing straddling their bikes. "I haven't mentioned it to
Tony yet, but perhaps you'd both like to come."

Tim's big hand touched Sandy's briefly. "An engagement party, at long last. I've only been asking her for a
year."

"Oh, congratulations," Sheila said warmly. It was obvious these two had something special between them. And
yet Tony'd told her he didn't approve of their marry-
ing...interesting.

Sandy smiled warmly at Tim, then brought her eyes to
Sheila's. "The second generation of Adamses aren't nearly
as impulsive as the first. I take it you've met my father, the
senator?"

There was affectionate humor in her voice, which
pleased Sheila. Sandy, it seemed, had come to grips with
her father's idiosyncrasies. Tony would do well to do like-
wise. "Yes. He's...he's..."

Again, the light, bright laugh. "Yes, he's definitely difficult to describe. Will you come to our party?"

Deciding she liked Sandy Adams, Sheila smiled. "I'll
mention it to Tony."

"Good. A week from Friday, eight o'clock at our
place." Adjusting her pedals, she climbed on her bike, as
did Tim. "We'll look forward to seeing you again."

"Bye, Sheila," Tim said, already moving.

"Bye." She stood watching them ride off companionably, experiencing an unexpected pang of envy. Sandy and
Tim were a little like her parents, so sure of their feelings
for each other, so in agreement with their thoughts that
Sandy even spoke in the plural on their behalf. Would she
ever share in that close a relationship? Was that what she
wanted?

She'd been raised to view independence as a must, not a
possibility. But it was an independence of spirit, coupled
with a generous nature that allowed a sharing of self with
her loved ones—more than allowed, it was required. She'd

known she wouldn't settle down until she could find just that mix in a mate.

Unconsciously she chewed on the nail of her little finger as her eyes moved to the dark-haired man in the field standing next to a little boy who held a ball of string, on his face a big grin. They both had their heads turned upward to where the kite dangled and twisted on a breeze that hadn't been there minutes before. He'd done it.

Sheila smiled. Yes, she decided that very moment, she did want that strong, close relationship. And Tony Adams was the man with whom she wanted to share it.

Chapter Five

Several tiers of cement steps led up to the triple set of revolving doors of the state courthouse, wide concrete railings flanking each side. At high noon on Tuesday, Sheila sat down on the wide ledge with a heavy sigh, waiting for Tony to join her.

She'd already had a busy morning at Jimmy Lee's preliminary hearing. It'd gone surprisingly well, despite the somewhat formidable presence of J. D. Tremaine, seated in the back row, taking in the proceedings with a seeming nonchalance that hadn't fooled Sheila for a moment. Beneath that hooded gaze lurked a steely-eyed strength she was certain Kim's father would not hesitate to exercise. He must have pulled a few strings just to get inside the courtroom, for usually only the principals were in attendance at the closed-door hearings. Tony'd been right. The man was a cobra, Sheila decided with distaste.

Afterward, having checked the docket, she'd discovered that Tony was trying a case that morning, and unable to resist seeing him in action, she'd slipped into the back of his courtroom. Running a casual hand through her hair, Sheila tipped her face up to the warming rays of the sun. Impressive—Mr. Tony Adams was most impressive.

He'd been defending one of his newest cases, a young accountant at a small firm who was accused of misappropriation of funds. Tony's rhetoric was persuasive without being ponderous, his questions concise and fearless, his style one of quiet assurance rather than flamboyance. The man was a study in contradictions, Sheila concluded—all fire and thunder and hot eyes in her arms, a cool professional in the courtroom and yet gentle as a spring rain and pliable as a marshmallow if he wanted to be. There was no question about it, Tony Adams fascinated her.

He'd caught her eye at the break and asked her to linger and have lunch with him if she had the time. He didn't have to ask twice. As she waited, she thought back to last Saturday and the delightful day they'd spent together. When he set his mind to it and forgot to be starchy and proper, Tony could be fun.

After he'd gotten the boy's kite flying well, he'd smiled at the lad's exuberant thanks and had come back to her. They'd walked along the pathways holding hands, talking, simply enjoying their time together. Finally, pleasantly worn out, they'd found a bench and had sat watching the wild ducks at the shoreline, bobbing and quacking. It was still daylight when he'd turned into his apartment's parking lot and pulled alongside her car. She'd wanted to go back up and let him make dinner for them as he'd suggested. But she'd turned him down, explaining she'd promised her aunt Irene that she'd visit that evening.

If she'd gone inside, she knew how their day would probably have ended. Despite her growing feelings for Tony, she wasn't ready for that quite yet. And she hadn't been prepared for the way he'd scooped her into his strong arms and kissed her long and hard. "You can't kiss me here in broad daylight," she'd told him, trembling as always from the effect of his mouth on hers. "Who said?" he'd asked, and had kissed her again. What had happened to the conservative Tony Adams? she wondered, smiling at the memory.

Walking briskly, Tony came rushing through the whooshing doors and spotted Sheila sitting on the ledge, her face turned to the sun, smiling softly to herself. He slowed, then stopped, watching her, his stomach muscles tightening. She was beautiful. Was she thinking of him as she smiled so sweetly? he wondered. He'd thought about her the past few days more times than he'd felt comfortable with, the memory of her warm response to his kisses filling him and making him ache for her. This had to end. He had to get her to bed and end this conjecturing soon.

She was wrecking his concentration, diverting the mind he'd always held in rigid control, sapping his strength. He felt oddly complete when he was with her. The part that worried him was that it might follow that without her he'd be incomplete. Tony squared his shoulders. No woman had ever been indispensable to him. Sheila would be no exception. He'd have her, then he'd be over this need to know her, this absorbing fascination with her that he'd let put a stranglehold on his emotions. He needed to get back on track.

Sensing his presence, she turned to look at him. The sun filtered through the golden strands of her hair as he watched her eyes warm to the sight of him. Soon, he thought, answering her smile as he walked to her. Soon she'd be his.

"Hello," he said, coming up close and trailing the backs of his fingers along her cheek. "I hope I didn't put you behind schedule asking you to wait."

He was becoming a toucher, Sheila thought, flooding with warmth. And she loved the way his touch made her feel. With the unconscious feline grace of a purring kitten, she turned her face into his hand. "No, you didn't," she said.

Tony felt his heart thud in response to her sensual gesture. "Where do you want to have lunch?"

Rising, she let her gaze roam over the sidewalk area below them. A pushcart with a perky red-and-white canopy stood several yards from the steps, doing a thriving lunchtime business. She smiled and pointed. "Over there," she told him, taking his hand and starting them down the stairs. "Willie's lunch stand."

"Anyone ever tell you that you're a cheap date?" he asked.

"That's what *you* think. These are New York dogs, with sauerkraut and mustard and melted cheese. Very special, and not so cheap."

He ordered one for each of them as Sheila chatted with Willie as if they were long-lost friends. She seemed to charm everyone with her friendliness, her open warmth. Tony envied that about her.

"Something inconsistent here," Tony commented, handing her a diet cola. "All these calories washed down with a diet drink. Why bother?"

They walked leisurely down toward the waterfront amid other lunchtime strollers seeking fresh air, sunshine and a break from their office routine.

"Perfectly logical to me," Sheila answered, taking a sip. "Why add more calories unnecessarily? So, how'd your morning go? Anyone ever tell you that you're dynamite in the courtroom, counselor? I may make it a habit to drop by and watch you. I could learn a lot from you."

He tried not to let her praise warm him. He almost made it. Shrugging matter-of-factly, his expressive eyes moved to hers. "Too early to tell how the Brewster case is going. Did you learn anything yesterday from Sara Hendrix?"

Sheila swallowed a messy bite of hot dog and kraut and frowned. "Her mother sat at her elbow the whole while, nervous as a cat, frowning at me, answering for Sara half the time, bordering on threatening me for bullying her daughter.''

''Were you, tough lady?'' he asked through a busy mouthful.

''In the immortal words of Abbott and Costello, she ain't seen nothin' yet. Wait'll I get the girl on the stand. I'm convinced that Sara's not telling us everything. But I couldn't get her to open up yesterday. What I wouldn't give for fifteen minutes *alone* with her.''

They reached the river's edge and sat down on a bench facing the water. ''You say that Kim didn't know Sara before she went away to college?'' Tony asked.

''No, she didn't. Why?''

''This is probably a long shot, but maybe not, knowing what men like J. D. Tremaine are capable of. Have you checked into Sara Hendrix's finances, whether some kindly benefactor might not be sliding her a little extra money to keep an eye on his daughter and report to him?''

Sheila stopped in midbite. ''My God! Why didn't I think of that? I'll bet that's it. And that's why they won't let me see Sara alone and why her mother's so nervous.'' She turned to face him, her eyes warm with appreciation. ''You're really good, you know? I wonder how long I have to be at this before all the angles will occur to me so readily.''

He shrugged. ''I could be wrong, you know.''

''But it's a lead to check into, one I didn't have this morning.'' Spontaneously she hugged him. ''Thank you, Tony.''

''Just how appreciative are you?'' he asked, crumpling up his used napkin.

''Moderately,'' she answered cautiously. ''What'd you have in mind?''

"Dessert. I'm a growing boy, and this hot-dog diet you've got me on lately will have my stomach growling all through this afternoon's courtroom session."

Laughing through her relief, she finished her drink. "Well, let's find you something gooey and filling before you keel over from malnutrition." Taking his arm, she led him toward a little confectioner's shop she knew of around the next corner.

As they walked, they paused to listen a moment to a group of teenagers playing an impromptu concert—drums, guitar and banjo. Summer fever had evidently hit some of the passersby, for several were dancing in an uneven half circle in front of the musicians while others stood about, tapping in rhythm to the happy tune.

"Come on," Tony said after a moment, tugging on her hand.

"Wait," Sheila said, coming up close in front of him. "I've never danced with you."

"I don't think this is the time or the place," he answered, frowning in surprise at her offbeat suggestion.

Slowly she opened his jacket and ran the fingers of one hand under the vest of his suit, up and down, her touch lingering.

"What are you doing?" Tony asked.

"Checking out your stuffed shirt," she answered, her impish gaze meeting his. She saw a slow, reluctant change as his eyes darkened. After a long moment the frown went away and a smile appeared. "You're intent on stripping me of all my dignity, aren't you?"

Laughing up at him, she moved into his arms and guided him into the dancing crowd. "Come on, counselor, be human. It only hurts for a little while."

And so they danced, a jerky, weaving jitterbug of sorts that left them both sweaty and smiling. Then the boys switched rhythms and drifted into a low, mellow tune. Easily a dozen couples swayed to the bluesy sound while just as many watched from the grassy embankment. It was summertime, and the livin' was easy.

Tony's first thought was that he hoped none of his colleagues, and most especially none of the judges, would stroll by and see him making a fool of himself. His second thought was that Sheila felt very good, very right close up against him, in his arms, her scent clogging his throat, her hair so soft against his chin. He never got to a third thought, for the second wrapped itself around him, and he held on, realizing he was falling fast. Lord, how was he going to keep from going over the edge with this woman who had him canoeing in parks, dancing in the streets and stepping out of character regularly? And learning to love it.

"You're working too hard again, Tony," Rosemary said the following Monday as she watched him lean back in his desk chair and pinch the bridge of his nose tiredly. The late afternoon sun slanted in through half-drawn blinds, casting shadows on his handsome face. "I thought a return to private practice would lessen your load, not increase it."

He raised his head and viewed his secretary affectionately. He'd first met Rosemary Norris years ago when she was a court stenographer and he was fresh out of law school and working for his father. She'd come to him, needing help. It seemed her husband liked to drink almost as much as he liked to use his wife for a punching bag afterward. There'd been two young boys, a small house and an old station wagon. Tony'd made sure, after the messy divorce, that Rosemary got to keep them all. She'd never forgotten. When he'd felt comfortable in the firm he'd asked her to join him. She hadn't hesitated a moment. Rosemary was like family.

"So did I, Rosie, but it's not surprising we're behind. Jed was carrying a hell of a load in my absence. It's only fair we reverse roles for a while."

She stood up to her full five-foot height, snapped her shorthand pad closed and gave him a tender smile. "Be careful you don't get caught up in it, Tony. Like your father did. A man loses himself in his work, doesn't take the time to develop and nurture a relationship, and pretty soon he doesn't remember how." She glanced meaningfully toward the ceiling in the direction of Sheila's overhead office. "How do you like the new addition to our building? I say she's a much-needed ray of sunshine around here."

Tony straightened, grinning at her. No one else talked to him the way Rosemary did. He wouldn't have allowed it. But he knew she loved him like a third son. "Subtlety was never your strong suit, Rosie."

"Sometimes you need straight talk." She moved across the room. "I'll type these letters for you right away." Opening the door, she stepped back in surprise. "Oh, hello, Sandy."

Sandy Adams smiled at her brother's secretary. "You caught me in mid-knock. You're looking good, Rosemary. I was wondering where everyone was around here." She moved closer to Tony's desk as Rosemary left, closing the door behind her.

"How are you, Sandy?" Tony asked, wondering what brought her to his office. Sandy was not the drop-in type. She sat down in the chair opposite his desk, piercing him with her blue-gray gaze. Though she was four years his junior, he often had the disconcerting feeling that his sister was the older of the two.

"Fine. I was just passing by and thought I'd stop for a minute and tell you again what a great time Tim and I had with you and Sheila at the ball game yesterday. Those Tigers are something, aren't they?"

Skeptical of this preliminary small talk, Tony gazed at her thoughtfully. "Yes, they are." The ball game had been Sandy's idea. Though he'd been doubtful when he'd phoned Sheila, she'd been delighted. The day had turned out to be filled with carefree laughter, lazy summer chatter and fun. And more damn hot dogs, this time with beer.

Crossing her long, slim legs, Sandy lit a cigarette. "Sunday afternoons at the ballpark. Brings back old times, doesn't it, like when you and I used to go just to get away from the bickering at home? Your Shiela is a darling. A really nice, warm human being, isn't she? Are you busy tonight?"

Not unusual for Sandy to rattle on nonstop, Tony thought, but she wanted something. He was sure of it. Inhaling her smoke, he patted the pack of cigarettes in his breast pocket and smiled at her. "In answer to your questions, yes to number one, yes to number two and probably to number three."

"Okay. I take it dear old Dad's gone for the day?"

Idly Tony fingered his gold pen. "Is he? I don't keep track."

"Are you two getting along?"

Nonchalantly Tony shrugged. "We always get along."

Sandy inhaled deeply. "But you still don't like him?"

Tony sighed. This was an old discussion between him and Sandy. One he wasn't eager to pursue further. "Is that what this visit's all about?"

"You're a shade touchy today. I just asked."

"All right, I respect him as my father. At times, I actually admire him. I suppose I even love him. But like him? Not really. Now I'm going to have to ask you to excuse me. I have a lot of work to do and—"

Sandy went on as if he hadn't tried to brush her off. "You don't like him because you see too many traits in yourself that you also see in him. And some of them aren't to your liking."

"What? That's ridiculous!"

Calmly she blew smoke toward the ceiling. "Not at all. You're both handsome, charming, charismatic. You're respected, admired and successful in your chosen field.

Workaholics, you might say. And you both have a bit of a reputation as a ladies' man who loves 'em and leaves 'em, never moving beyond surface relationships.''

He didn't need this today, Tony thought, closing his eyes as he leaned his head back. There was a fluttering in his chest, a lump in his throat and his hands shook slightly as he fought the knowledge. He wasn't like his father, never had been. Then why was it that two people—two who he knew loved him—had indicated just that within the last half hour? They couldn't be right, could they?

"You have to admit," Sandy went on, "he's come a long way, our father. He's clever, cunning, even ruthless and very astute in his dealings. A lot of people owe him favors, and he collects. If his public image's a bit cold, well, people forgive him that small flaw."

Tony brought his head forward and opened his eyes, pinning her with his cool silver gaze. "Are you saying *I'm* cold?"

"I didn't say that."

She'd hesitated a moment too long. "Why are you bringing all this up today?"

"Because I see a chance for you here and I don't want to watch you blow it. The first step was getting out of the prosecutor's office, away from the lure of politics, separating yourself from *his* image, establishing your own. And now this."

"Now what?"

"Sheila. She cares for you. And she's the first woman I've seen you with that is truly right for you."

Tony threw down his pen and exhaled a deep gust of air. "You are truly an incurable romantic, Sandy. Just because you and Tim—"

"No! Not just because of me and Tim. Because it's obvious as the nose on your face, you big, dumb clod."

He shook his head in disbelief. "You're wrong this time. She's fun and she's bright, and we like one another. But she wouldn't even...that is, we haven't—"

"Made love? You don't have to. Besides, there's a hell of a lot more to it than that, and you know it. I watched you both yesterday very carefully. It's in the way she looks at you, listens to you, smiles at you. And, for that matter, you're hooked, too, big brother. Yes, you, too."

"Look, Sandy," he said, trying for a businesslike tone, "I don't have time for this. I—"

She stood, flinging her purse strap over her shoulder. "Okay, I'll go. I've said my piece. No, you're not like him, Tony. *Not yet*." She maneuvered neatly around the chair. "Are you and Sheila coming to our engagement party Friday?"

"Probably," he answered vaguely.

She nodded, then turned toward the door. Hand on the knob, she turned to him. "See you Friday. Bye."

And she was gone, leaving him with a lot to think over.

Sheila frowned at the empty box of raisins on the library table, then glanced at her watch. Six o'clock already, and she'd skipped lunch. She was overly warm despite the air-conditioning, suddenly hungry and frustrated at not finding anything in a huge stack of law books to help her help Nina Costello. Damn!

Perhaps the best thing to do would be to go home, change into cooler clothes, eat dinner and go over her notes. Tomorrow she'd be refreshed and ready to tackle things with a better attitude. Decision made, she closed a heavy book and moved to pick up the second volume just as it slid off the corner of the table, falling onto the Oriental rug with a dull thud.

"Damn!" she muttered, bending to pick it up.

"Having a little trouble in here?" Tony asked from the library doorway.

Straightening, she looked up into his smiling face. "Just a small case of fatigue and frustration."

Loosening his tie and unbuttoning the top button, he sat down in one of the leather chairs and leaned back. "I know how you feel. It's been one of those days for me, too."

Sheila sat down again, noticing the tired lines around his eyes. "Would talking over your problems help?" she offered.

Considering you're one of them, I doubt it. "Well, let's see. For starters, they're exhuming Mr. Thornton tomorrow and his widow is very upset, his three children are getting nastier and now we've got an ex-wife who wants in on the action. And I've discovered that the accountant I'm defending seems to have a past history of gambling, though he swears he took no money from his firm." He raised his eyebrows at her. "Want me to go on?"

Leaning forward, she picked up her pen, sliding her fingers along its length thoughtfully. "Perhaps the exhumation is a good thing. If Thornton's widow is innocent, they won't find anything. If she's not, it's best you discover it now. And maybe your accountant is a graduate of Gamblers Anonymous and just happens to be a man in the wrong place."

He smiled. "You have a way of narrowing things down, Sheily."

Her head swiveled to him, her eyes widening. "What did you call me?"

"Sheily. I went to school with a girl whose name was Sheila, and we called her Sheily. You don't like it?"

"My father calls me that."

"It's the name I give to you in my thoughts."

Suddenly she felt her blood heating, her palms dampening. Always with him it was this way. Moments after he entered a room, he had her purring. "You think about me?" she asked softly.

Tony leaned closer, touching the end of her nose lightly with a fingertip as his silver gaze roamed her face, finally returning to meet her eyes. "Yes. A lot more than I'd planned." After a long moment, he leaned back again. "And what has you so frustrated?"

You. You have me very frustrated. She'd deliberately avoided him the past week, needing some time to put things in perspective. So by the time he'd called her yesterday morning asking her to the ball game with Sandy and Tim, she'd jumped at the chance. She knew she was getting in deeper each minute she spent with him. If she were smart, she'd run from him. Yet it was probably already too late. How had she made the colossal mistake of learning to care for a man who thought marriage was a joke?

Buying a little time, Sheila slid her legal pad in front of her and skimmed her notes. "I have a new case, a referral from my aunt Irene when I visited her the other evening. She has a housekeeper she's used for years, Nina Costello. It seems that Mrs. Costello bought a house five years ago on land contract. She doesn't speak very good English, but she's never missed a payment. However, when she signed the papers, she didn't understand that there was a balloon note due at the end of the five-year period which ended last month. The gist of it is that the deedholder, one Joseph Ward, wants the twenty-eight-thousand dollars that's due him now or he'll take back his house."

She could almost see his busy mind working as he absorbed what she'd told him, discarding one thought and considering another. He was a man who loved puzzles, the challenge of coming up with solutions.

"Did she have an attorney at the closing?" Tony asked. He saw Sheila shake her head. "A real-estate broker?"

"Yes, I've checked. He died two years ago, and the small firm dissolved."

"Did you check out the witnesses on the closing papers?"

"Yes. One was the realtor's secretary, and she's moved out of state. The other was Mrs. Costello's daughter, who remembers nothing about a balloon-clause explanation at the time." Sheila crossed her legs and leaned toward Tony, warming to the discussion now. "You know, I vaguely remember a case that set a precedent some years back. Something about the seller being unable to hold the purchaser to terms that hadn't been fully disclosed at the time. I recall that shortly after that, in order to be valid, the purchase agreement and the land contract had to state that all parties were aware that, after a certain period, a balloon note for a specified amount would be due and payable," Sheila finished.

The lady was sharp. Tony moved to the bookcase, his fingers already searching for certain volumes. "I remember something about that, too. I think it was in the late seventies or the early eighties. Let's see here."

Sheila joined him, and together they pored over one volume, which led them to another and still another. Their assorted separate problems, their hunger and fatigue, forgotten, they scanned and read and copied information for the better part of an hour until Tony finally found the case.

"It was in all the newspapers at the time," he explained, his voice carrying an edge of excitement as he recalled the details. "In the early eighties, mortgage interest rates were really high, so land contracts, with a ceiling set at eleven percent, were in great demand. The plaintiff was an older black man who'd used his life savings of five thousand dollars as down payment on this little house, which he bought from the defendant on a two-year contract with a twenty-thousand-dollar balloon note. When they discovered that the seller had more than a dozen of these going, all to poor uneducated people or foreign-speaking individuals who wouldn't easily understand the terms even if he had explained them, that did it. The reporters had a field day. Realtors, attorneys and sellers were cautioned to apply the truth-in-lending disclosures to all land contract sales." He turned to her, grinning. "So there you are, lady. Does that help?"

They'd been standing, leaning over the book spread open on the library table. Slowly straightening, still smiling with pleasure, Sheila turned to him.

"I don't know how to thank you. This is twice you've helped me. Did I tell you that I petitioned the court and got permission, through the new prosecutor, to examine Sara Hendrix's bank records?"

Standing close in front of her, he slowly slid his hands along the length of her arms, his eyes warming as he watched her face. "And what did you learn, pray tell?"

"You were right. Unfortunately for her, Sara's mother wasn't too smart. She'd opened a bank account for Sara's school expenses last fall with a couple of hundred dollars. Then, starting the first of October, four hundred dollars were deposited to Sara's account each and every month through last May. The checks were from J. D. Tremaine."

Tony nodded. "He was paying Sara a hundred dollars a week to spy on his daughter." Moving a hand up and into the thickness of her hair, he lazily caressed the back of her neck with the other.

"Yes, like an insurance policy. Only you'd think a man like Tremaine would cover his tracks, pay her in cash."

"He probably never thought it would come this far, go to court and all."

"True," Sheila said, her voice catching as his magic hands had her straining to concentrate.

"That, in itself, is no crime, I'm sure you're aware. Morally it's a rotten thing to do, but—"

"I know, but I have an idea. What if . . ." Her voice had become ragged, her breathing irregular.

Tony's hands moved forward to frame her face as he lowered his head. "Could we possibly discuss this case later, counselor?"

Sheila was all for that. Her heavy eyes drifted closed while the familiar weakness crept over her. His mouth barely touched hers at first, his lips teasing, his tongue tasting leisurely. Heat, red-hot heat, shot through her, colors exploded inside her head, and the need to get closer became almost unbearable. On a soft moan, Sheila pressed into him, her arms going around and curling about his shoulders, her mouth opening under his.

She tasted his passion and gloried in it, meeting it with her own. She felt the hard muscles of his back under her searching hands and longed to explore further. She heard the thunder of her own heartbeat as she shamelessly allowed his hands to press his hard frame into her softness. Without leaving her lips, he changed the angle of his kiss, taking her deeper. Sheila let a stream of pure pleasure pour through her.

Needs pounded at Tony, making him a little crazy. He wasn't one to lose control easily, but he was close now. Desire was no longer an old friend who came to him slowly, easily satisfied until the next time. Desire slammed into him when he held Sheila, making him tremble with the force of it, making him desperate to have her.

Sucking in air, he moved his face into the hollow of her throat, tasting the silk of her skin, nipping at her ear as small sounds came from deep within her, urging him on. His hands moved between them, along the row of buttons at the front of her blouse. His mouth on her face distracted her while his fingers opened the buttons, then pulled the material free of her skirt.

Suddenly she seemed to come back to herself. "Tony, I—"

He leaned back from her, his hands going around to unfasten her bra. "I want to see you."

Her hands flew to his, stilling them. "Someone could come up. I—"

"Everyone's gone. The door's closed, and I locked up downstairs before I came looking for you." Determined fingers fumbled the clasp open, and slowly he moved aside the wisp of lace.

Helpless—she felt helpless to stop him. Her flesh grew fuller, wanting his touch. She bit down on her lip to keep from crying out as she saw his eyes devour her, his hands slowly cup her. When his thumbs circled, then gently rubbed the swollen peaks, she did cry out as her knees nearly buckled under her.

He held her near-sagging weight with one arm around her while his other hand caressed, teased, explored. She was pale and soft and incredibly beautiful. He wanted to feel her nakedness against his chest. He wanted to put his mouth to her. He wanted more than he ever remembered wanting before.

Easing her away from the table, he tried urging her to the softness of the thick rug. But she shook off the mists and stopped his hands again.

"No. Tony, please."

"Why? I know you want to as much as I do."

Taking a deep breath, Sheila stepped back from him. Want him? God, yes, she wanted him. But there was a reason. A very good reason. "I have to leave. Please understand."

His own breathing ragged, Tony ran a shaky hand through his hair. This frustration was becoming habit-forming. He looked at her as she straightened her clothes, wanting to rip them off her, to throw her to the floor, to feel her under him. "Sheila, I *don't* understand."

"Then I'm sorry." She moved to the table, gathering up her things. At the door she turned to face him, tears glistening in her eyes. "I'm not a tease, Tony, please believe me. You'll have to trust me this time. I have my reasons."

He didn't look angry. He looked disappointed and confused. It was almost her undoing. Quickly, before she could change her mind, she turned and groped her way down the stairs, blinking rapidly, not even stopping in her office to pick up her suit jacket. If she didn't get away from him fast, she knew she'd give herself away. She'd reveal to him what she'd only recently discovered herself, the one thing she knew Tony Adams would run from. She was in love with him.

Chapter Six

Contracts and wills, deeds at house closings, child-support delinquencies—Sheila turned away from the papers strewn over her cluttered desk and stared out her office window at the summer rain showering the leaves of the big maple tree. Her mood was as gloomy as the weather forecast. The work she'd been doing the last few days to keep busy required little more than notarizing papers. Most of it could have been handled by a first-year law student. She longed for something more challenging, something she could sink her teeth into. When they were passing out patience, she must've been standing in another line, she thought with a sigh.

The Jimmy Lee Morgan case was not going well. She'd pinned Kim's father down about the checks to his daughter's roommate, and he'd readily admitted to them. There was no law against helping a deserving young lady, his daughter's friend, with her college expenses, was there? he'd asked, a look of cunning innocence on his face. He'd had his story ready, obviously alerted by the prosecuting attorney. If she'd dared suggest bribery, he'd have probably slapped a libel suit on her for defamation of character.

Sheila chewed on her nail and pondered the possibilities. Everyone she'd talked with who knew Jimmy Lee—the school counselor, his teachers, his mother's friends, the people he worked with and for—all spoke of him as a good person, a hard worker and crazy about Kim. No, a boy like that wouldn't force the girl he loved to run away with him, she felt certain. Kim had to have gone willingly. Then why did she change her story? Did Daddy Tremaine have something on her to force her to lie? What she needed, she thought with exasperation, was fifteen minutes with Kim Tremaine without her father present.

Enough gloom and doom, Sheila decided, swinging around to face her desk. At least she'd be able to help Mrs. Costello. She was meeting with opposing counsel next week. Perhaps they'd be able to work something out without going to trial. Thanks to Tony, who'd found the ammunition she needed, she was ready for bear on that one.

Tony... They'd walked wide circles around each other since the incident in the library. But, at odd moments, she'd get a feeling and look up from her desk to find him pausing on his way past her doorway, his eyes hungry and yearning. He'd nod and she'd wave, and he'd be on his way. But the impact of his need remained. She understood and shared it. As for herself, there were few moments when he wasn't on her mind.

Suddenly inspired, she grabbed her purse and made for the door. Raindrops or not, she'd go out and get something by way of thanks for Tony. Maybe the gesture would clear the heavy air between them. If it didn't please him, t would make her feel better, anyway. Humming to herself, she skipped down the stairs.

* * *

Tony drove north on Jefferson Avenue on his way to his office from the courthouse, his movements automatic, his eyes on the traffic though part of his mind was on other things. On the radio, in a silky tone, a country-and-western singer sang of endless love. Tony wished he believed in it. He wasn't even sure he believed in love at all. But Sheila did.

When he'd chosen a career in law, he hadn't done so, as some had thought, to follow in his father's footsteps. He'd wanted the challenge of the work, to be financially independent, to be free to run his practice his way, and for the satisfaction of being able to help others. And he'd let no personal complications interfere with his goals. Success was a greedy taskmaster, one that entrapped you with its reluctant rewards. Getting to the top of his profession and staying there had occupied most of his waking hours for years. Until Sheila.

Perhaps he'd allowed himself to get a little stuffy, a shade too conservative, often putting enjoyable activities on the back burner in favor of work. Maybe, as his sister had suggested, he'd had only surface relationships with the women in his life, such as Gail Whitney, an attractive architect from Sandy's office, whom he'd frequently dated. But he had good reason. There seemed little point in delving deeper, getting to know someone really well, then having them move on or tiring of them yourself. His mother had adored his father, but he'd moved on. And it had changed her, shattered her, and was in part responsible for her other stabs at marriage and her many relationships. Still hoping to find what she'd lost. He hadn't ever wanted to be a part of that scene. Until Sheila.

He cruised the big Mercedes to a halt at a stoplight and adjusted the air-conditioning vent, aiming it at his face. The windshield wipers slip-slapped across the front window, rearranging the light rainfall. Here he sat, hurrying to the office, wanting to see her, hoping she'd be there. He shouldn't be wanting her with thoughts of permanency in mind. Hadn't he decided some time ago that permanency was an illusive dream and forever a myth? Until Sheila.

Unconsciously he grimaced. He shouldn't be wanting her at all. She wasn't smooth sophistication, poised and polished, with a willing body. She was country charm, warm brown-eyed laughter and fragile feelings. She was Christmas Eve and long walks in the woods and fresh-baked cookies in front of a crackling fire. She was trouble, and he damn well knew it. The light changed, and he zipped forward.

Once again he enjoyed his days after the rat race of the prosecutor's office. Enjoyed the intricacies of his cases, the challenge of preparation, the combat of the courtroom. A sigh escaped from him unbidden. But it was the aimlessness of his nights lately that bothered him. He knew women who could fill them, women with eager mouths and clever hands who'd give him physical pleasure that would have him gasping. But when it was over, the lingering memories weren't warm, and he could hardly wait to leave them and head home.

He turned onto Seminola, the winding road that ended at his office. Recently he'd found himself wanting, reaching, needing something more real, more solid, more permanent. There was that word again. But was there really such a thing? Or would he achieve it—only to have it disappear as it had for his mother, his father and so many others? Could Sheila change all that?

She seemed to see inside his mind, to somehow know what would please him, to draw him out. Perversely, the more she was able to get to him, the more he tried to keep her from seeing too much. He recognized it for the defense mechanism it was and wondered why he was doing it. Because she was getting too close, that's why. She wanted him, of that he was certain. She wanted more than a love affair. She wanted more than he could give.

Tony pulled the Mercedes next to her Volkswagen and turned off the engine. Not even glancing at her car, he made for the stairs. He would ignore her. He *could* ignore her, he was certain, if he put his mind to it.

His father wasn't in, and he was relieved. He was in no mood for one of his hearty, probing father-son chats. The less the senator involved himself in the practice, the better. Let him play the returning elder statesman a while longer. It was definitely safer.

Rosie looked up as he walked in and smiled her usual welcome. Moving to his desk, she followed with his messages, mentioning a few specifically.

Setting down his briefcase, he returned to the mail neatly lined up for him and stopped. In the center of the desk pad was a delicate crystal bud vase containing a perfect red rose. He moved closer. No card. He turned to Rosemary.

"To what do I owe this?" he asked, puzzled.

"It's not from me."

"Oh? Then who sent it?"

Rosie's eyes slid to the ceiling and back to his, a knowing smile forming on her face. "Your tenant."

"Really? What for?"

With a smug smile, Rosemary placed his messages on the desk. "She didn't say, just asked if she could put it on your desk. I imagine you must have done something she wants to thank you for." Swallowing a chuckle, she scooted her compact little body out the door.

Sitting down, he stared at the rose. Damn! The woman had a way of getting under his skin, way under.

The rain wasn't going to let up, Sheila decided, standing looking out her office window. Puddles had formed in the flower beds, and the graveled parking lot looked like a wading pool. The sky was gray and darkening rapidly. A good night to go home and curl up with a good book, she thought. But the sound of footsteps on the stairs had her turning toward the door.

He paused in the doorway, looking uncertain. She waited, standing behind her desk. Slowly he came into the room, his gray eyes very soft, like the gentle summer rain clouds.

"You brought me a flower," he said.

"Yes."

"I've never...that is, no one's ever..."

The warmth of her smile broke through. "Then it's high time someone did. I'm sure you've made many women happy with a gift of flowers. I wanted to surprise you. It appears I have."

He came nearer, around to her side, close enough to touch her, but he didn't. She felt her breathing go shallow.

"Yes. But why?"

"To thank you for all the help you've been to me on several of my cases. And to make you happy. Have I?"

He gave her his slow smile, the one she loved, the one that crinkled the corners of his eyes. "You always make me happy, Sheily."

With a small laugh, she shook her head. "Not always, as I recall."

He rubbed the back of his neck, dropping his eyes. "Yes, I've been meaning to apologize to you for that episode. I didn't mean to come on so strong. I've never forced myself on a woman yet."

She melted at his choice of words, melted into a small, helpless puddle like the ones in the flower beds. Raising her hand, she caressed his cheek. A late-afternoon beard shadowed his face. She found it incredibly sexy. "You weren't forcing yourself on me, Tony. I want you every bit as much as...as you seem to want me. But I've told you, for me it has to mean something. I can't just...just...." Dropping her hand, she looked away. "Well, it's a little complicated."

"It *would* mean something, Sheily. I care about you."

That stopped her. She raised her eyes to his, studying their silver depths for long minutes. "Do you?"

"Yes, dammit!"

Folding her arms across her chest, she leaned against the desk and sighed. "I see it pleases you a great deal."

"Do you want the truth?" he asked, his hands on his hips, his stance defiant. Was he challenging her or himself? she wondered.

"Yes, please."

"All right." Running a hand through his already untidy hair, he began to pace the small room. "I've never been in love. Thirty-four years old. Never." He stopped, turned to face her. "Have you?"

"No." She thought she saw a flicker of relief in his eyes before he resumed his pacing.

"I've never wanted to be. I've watched so many people *think* they are, *feel* they are, *know* they are. Then, in weeks or months, a year or two, it's gone. I don't want to make promises I can't keep. So I've never made any." He moved to her, close, very close, his breath warm on her cheeks. "Then you came along, only a short month ago. And you ruined it for me."

"Ruined what?"

"My alone time, my privacy, that I've always protected and enjoyed. Now, without you, I'm lonely."

"Oh, Tony," she whispered, her arms sliding around him, her face turning into his broad chest. The man definitely knew the right things to say.

He held her, just held her, and it felt so good. But he had to tell her all of it. "It's obvious that I care about you, but it doesn't change the way I feel. I don't want to lead you on, to let you think this may go somewhere one day. Sure I want to take you to bed, but that's not by any means all of it. I like being with you, talking with you. I like seeing you smile, hearing you laugh. Yet the fact remains, I'm not interested in marriage. I'd make a lousy husband. But don't want to lose you either. Can't we just . . . just be together?"

Slowly she leaned back to look up at him. "Let's take it one day at a time, Tony. Let's get to know one another and see where it leads us. I promise not to make any demands of you if you'll just go slowly with me. I've never cared for anyone before in quite this way, either. And it's all happened a little fast for me, too. It takes some getting used to."

He gave her a mock scowl. "You make me sound like some new medicine you have to take for a while before your system gets used to the effect."

"Not a bad description," she teased.

"Hey!"

"Only kidding." She hugged him to her, feeling better than she'd felt in days. One day at a time, she thought.

"Sandy and Tim's party is tonight. Do you want to go?"

"Yes. I like them both." Nuzzling his neck, she breathed deeply of his special scent, committing it to memory. How good it felt to be back in his arms. She raised her face to his, needing more.

He saw it in her eyes, the desire she couldn't quite hide. It excited him. Bending, he pressed warm lips to hers, his arms tightening about her.

Sheila closed her eyes, letting the now-familiar sensations take her on the roller-coaster ride she recognized from each time before when he'd kissed her. She was lost in him, so quickly lost in him.

Tony could smell the rain in her hair, fresh and summery in flavor, clean and sweet. His tongue swirled with hers, tasting her need, her passion. But he clamped down on his hunger. She wanted to take things slowly. Reluctantly he moved back from her and rested his head for a moment against her forehead. As he waited for his breathing to normalize and the throbbing heat to subside, he wondered how long he could hold out.

The Jeffersonian was a high-rise apartment building on the east side of town, situated almost on the back of the Detroit River facing the Canadian border on the other side. By the time Sheila and Tony arrived at his sister's tenth-floor apartment, the party was in full swing.

Sandy herself opened the door, looking lovely and poised in a bright red dress that seemed to emphasize her gay mood. "Hello, you two," she said, hugging them both warmly. "I'm so glad you came." Her pending wedding had evidently filled her with a bubbly enthusiasm. She positively glowed.

"I told you we'd probably make it," Tony said, recovering from her unexpected display of affection.

"She has to worry about something besides the caterer not showing up on time, doesn't she?" Tim asked, giving them each a hearty handshake. "Sheila, you look beautiful."

"Thank you," Sheila said, hiding a smile, for he'd sounded so surprised. Of course, he'd only seen her in casual clothes, and tonight she'd worn an emerald-green jersey with soft lines, the color a vivid contrast with her pale skin and fair hair. The overall effect was stunning, or so Tony'd told her when he'd picked her up.

"Well, come on in and mingle. Tony, you know most of the people here. Oh, there's Hal Fisher. Tim, let's go over and see him. Catch you later." With a wave, they were off.

Tony's hand at her waist guided them inside, and Sheila was glad he was with her in the sea of unfamiliar faces. Some glanced up at the new arrivals with a smile, several greeted Tony in passing and a few gave them long, measuring looks. Briefly he introduced her to a couple of people, but his arm never strayed from holding her at his side

She'd never been particularly shy, yet Sheila felt oddly pleased at his nearness.

"What did you say Sandy does for a living?" she asked as they worked their way through the crowd. "This place is gorgeous." Her gaze took in the huge sunken living room, decorated in muted colors with exquisite furniture and a magnificent view from the open French doors leading to the terrace. Understated elegance, she thought. A lot like Tony's place, only on a grander scale and with an added warmth that was somehow missing in his apartment.

Grabbing two glasses of champagne from a passing waiter's tray, Tony handed her one. "She's an architect, and Tim's a partner in the firm. They do all right."

She took a sip of champagne, turning to face him. He wore brown slacks, a yellow silk shirt open at the throat and a tweed sport coat, casual but classic. Sheila had been relieved he hadn't shown up in his usual three-piece dark suit. "Have you revised your opinion of their proposed union?"

He took a bubbly sip before he answered. "No, I haven't but if they want to become a statistic, it's up to them."

She frowned. "What a doomsayer you are. They haven't even walked down the aisle, and you have them divorcing."

"Law of averages, lady." Turning toward a small commotion at the door, he took a deep breath. "Brace yourself. The senator's just arrived."

He had indeed, with full flourish, resplendent in white slacks and a navy sport coat, looking tan and fit, his thick white hair combed just so. Sheila watched him work the crowd with ease and charm, admiring the politician in him that drew people like magnets while his shrewd blue eyes missed nothing. She felt a slight chill as he spotted them by the terrace doors and made his way to their side.

Clapping Tony on the shoulder, he shook hands with him. "Tony, I've been back several weeks, and we haven't even had lunch together," he chastised, hinting at avoidance.

"Next week maybe, Dad," Tony said, smoothly if somewhat evasively. "I've been pretty busy catching up."

Turning next to Sheila, the senator took her hand. "My dear, you're a vision tonight, a woman any man would be proud to have on his arm. How is it that you've singled out my son for that particular honor?"

The man was fishing, curious about her relationship with Tony. That alone would make her deliberately vague. That and the fact that she didn't trust the good senator and felt her feelings for his son were none of his damn business.

Smiling sweetly, she eased her hand from his. "I've a weakness for Englishmen with cool manners and warm eyes, Senator."

She felt more than heard Tony's muffled chuckle of approval, but the senator's laugh was a shade too hearty. "Well said, young lady. I'm hearing some mighty fine compliments around town about your work."

"Is that right?"

Stopping to order a Scotch on the rocks from a hovering waiter, he resumed his conversation. "Yes, from several sources. I ran into an old friend at lunch today. He tells me you're defending that young lad on the kidnapping charge." He shook his leonine head. "Shoddy business."

Tony's arm around Sheila tightened. "What friend was that?" he asked before she could respond.

"J. D. Tremaine," the senator said with a salt-of-the-earth smile. "Been a member of the party for years." His eyes narrowed as he looked at Sheila, daring her to question his friend's credentials.

"I see," she said, glancing at Tony and noticing his carefully expressionless face. "Yes, I'm defending Jimmy Lee Morgan."

Making a little ceremony of it, the senator straightened his pocket handkerchief with long, lean fingers. "Well, of course, everyone's entitled to a defense under the law, no matter how weak their case."

"That's pretty judgmental, Dad," Tony commented, his voice dangerously low. "I don't imagine you've had the time to read up on both sides of the case."

Accepting his drink, the older man took a hefty swallow before raising his eyes to his son's. "No, no, I haven't. But I know Jim Tremaine." Swinging his gaze back to Sheila, he smiled benevolently. His tone became companionable, almost fatherly. "As I used to tell Tony years ago, Sheila, someone has to represent the underdogs of the world. But a lawyer who wants to go places would do well to steer clear of them. I might offer you the same advice."

Suddenly she was reminded of Tony's description of J. D. Tremaine—a cobra. And here was another one. Feeling Tony's fingers flex at her side, she returned the senator's cool smile. "Thank you, Senator. However, I think there are plenty of law firms around to represent the top dogs of the world, especially now that you're back. Those of us new and inexperienced have a tendency to stick to what we believe in."

His eyes registered mild annoyance as he quickly revised his opinion of her. "Yes, well, you're young. You'll learn." Sipping his drink, he spotted someone over the rim. "If you'll excuse me," he said with a curt nod of his head, "I see another old friend. Have fun."

"He seems to have a lot of old friends," Sheila commented as he walked away. "All in high places, I imagine."

"Not as many as he'd have you believe," Tony said, turning her to face him. "You okay?"

"Certainly," she told him with a bright smile. "It takes a whole lot more than your father's cool disdain to get me down. I'm half-English, too, you know. Besides, I rather like sparring with him. He's challenging."

Tony let go of the annoyance that had seeped into him since his father had arrived. Sheila had the right idea. The senator should be taken with a grain of salt and a sense of humor. If only he could do that. He looked down at Sheila and smiled. "Yes, he's definitely challenging. And..."

"Oh!" Sheila said, jumping back as someone jostled a heavyset man who then bumped into her, spilling her drink on the side of her dress.

"I'm *so* sorry," the man said, leaning over and dabbing at the spot near her hem with his soaked paper napkin.

Sheila stopped his hand and gave him a smile. "It's all right." She checked the remaining contents of his glass. "White wine comes out easily enough. I'll just go take care of this."

"The powder room's down the hall, first door on the left," Tony told her.

"If it doesn't come out," the red-faced man went on, "I'll get it cleaned for you."

Glancing over her shoulder as she moved away, she gave him another smile. "Honestly, it'll be fine. I'll be right back, Tony."

Reassuring the embarrassed man that all was well, Tony strolled out onto the deserted balcony for a breath of fresh air. Sipping his champagne, he looked down at the peaceful river, the winding drive along the Canadian shoreline where the lights of cars could be seen passing by. The city noises didn't reach this far up, and the party clatter was beyond the doors. He inhaled deeply, enjoying the moment of quiet solitude.

Smiling to himself, he felt he had to hand it to Sheila. She'd handled the senator with finishing-school good manners, yet had zoomed in with a couple of perfect squelches. Her adaptability amazed him. She'd rushed off to spot-clean her dress with a dismissive smile that had changed the atmosphere from strained to pleasant. Most of the women he knew would have become tight-lipped and furious. Sheila reserved her anger for bigger things, he was certain.

"Well, big brother, how goes the battle?" Sandy asked, coming toward him.

He turned to smile at her, uncertain if it was the champagne or Sheila who'd put him in a decidedly mellow mood. "It goes well, Sandy." He gestured toward the crowded room. "I didn't know you knew so many people."

Sandy leaned on the railing next to him and shrugged. "Sure. The whole world loves lovers, didn't you know that?"

"Then you're going through with it?"

"The marriage? Yes, I am." She tossed back her thick auburn hair and looked up at him with eyes wide and sincere and so like his own. "I'm going to take a chance, Tony. I know I love Tim, but I'm still scared to death, despite my brave talk."

"I don't blame you there."

"But I've decided love is worth it. It doesn't come along very often, and even if you have it only for a year or two, it's the *best* thing we have going for us. *The very best*. I'll make a good wife for Tim. I'm sure as hell going to work at it."

Silently Tony absorbed what she'd said, wondering if she was trying to convince him or herself.

But Sandy couldn't let it rest. "You still don't agree?"

"If you think it's what you need, then it probably is," he answered quietly.

"Need? Tony, you make the word sound like one of those four-letter ones you find scrawled on public lavatory walls. Why do you think it's such a weakness to *need* someone? Only fools think they have to show the world they can go it alone."

Stubbornly she stood her ground, warming to the one-sided argument. "It's no sin to admit you care for someone, that you need them. It doesn't make you a weaker person. It just might make you a stronger one."

"Maybe."

"Maybe?" she asked, puckering her brow at him. "Well, at least we've moved from 'not on your life' to 'maybe.' I guess that's progress." She touched his chin affectionately. "You always were a hard sell. I don't mean to lecture you. I just want you to be happy."

His smile was warm as his arm came around her. "I want that for you, too."

"Can I get in on this hugging?" Sheila asked, walking out to join them, smiling at the close scene she'd glimpsed.

Quickly Tony's other arm reached out and brought her into the circle. "Anytime, lady." He pulled them both to him, then swung his eyes to the stars overhead. "Mmm, this is living. A starlit night, a warm summer breeze and two beautiful women. What more is there?"

"There's chaos if I don't get back inside and rescue Tim," Sandy said, extricating herself. "We have a pact. Every ten minutes we check on each other to see if one of us is stuck talking with a bore. I see he's cornered by that very large lady with the bright orange hair. I think he may need rescuing. See you later."

Even if her recent nagging hadn't been getting a bit annoying, Tony'd have been glad to see Sandy go back in. He was always glad for a few minutes alone with Sheila. As she stood looking out into the night he moved close behind her and encircled her with his arms, burying his face in her fragrant hair.

"Mmm, you smell so good. Did the spot come out?"

"Thank you, and yes, it did. It's lovely out here."

"It is now."

She snuggled closer. "Mmm, that's nice. What all's across the river? I've never been there."

He raised his eyes to the shoreline. "Windsor, Ontario. A nice little city. And up past that is—"

"Past that be dragons," she interrupted.

"Dragons?"

Smiling, she turned within the circle of his arms so she could see his face. "Yes, dragons. You've never heard the story?" He shook his head. "Well, then, let me tell you. Once upon a time, very long ago, the wise old men of this particular village set out to make road maps of their town, painfully walking each pathway. And then they mapped out the next town and one more beyond that. Wearily they returned home, their work done. In the months to follow, when someone pointed to the far boundary line and asked 'But what is beyond that?' the elders, too tired to explore further, simply answered, 'Past that be dragons,' and the fearful villagers didn't dare venture outside the perimeters set up."

"That's the end of the story?" he asked, enjoying her flight of fancy.

"No, of course not. One day a young man fell in love with a young maiden in the first village, and she with him. But her family didn't approve of him because he was an adventurer, a man who wanted to leave, to seek his fortune elsewhere, to make his own way. And he wanted the woman he loved to go with him. But she was fearful of going too far, for surely he would lead her to the edge and 'past that be dragons.' However, the young man said to her, 'We love one another and we belong together. You must believe in me, and if you do, wherever we go, if there be dragons, I will slay them for you.' And so she believed in him enough to follow him, and when they ran across dragons he did slay them for her."

"And they lived happily ever after?"

"Certainly."

"Did you make that up right this minute on the spot?"

Her eyes danced with mischief as she ran light fingers inside his jacket and along the hard ridges of his chest. "How could you think such a thing?"

"Is that what you want, Sheila, someone to slay your dragons for you?"

"Is that what you want, Tony, someone to believe in you?"

He hadn't seen the trap coming. He'd have probably fallen into it anyhow, he decided. In her dark gaze he saw a depth of feeling he didn't want to put a name to. Later, maybe, but not right now. "Yes," he answered softly.

"You got it," she whispered as she reached up and pulled his head down, capturing his lips with hers.

Chapter Seven

Tell me the truth, Miss North," Jimmy Lee said, his dark eyes filled with concern, "it doesn't look good for me, does it?"

Seated across from him in the barren conference room, Sheila tried to look encouraging without giving the boy false hope. "We could use a break. Does that answer your question?"

Grimly he nodded and took a deep drag from one of the cigarettes she'd brought him. She met with him several times a week, bringing him up to date on her meager findings, trying to keep his spirits up, hoping he'd remember something else that would give her a new lead. For she'd come to like Jimmy Lee Morgan, and from the first she'd never stopped believing in his innocence. Proving it was another matter.

She hated to go to trial basing her case on not much more than character witnesses testifying on Jimmy Lee's behalf while trying to cast aspersions on the Tremaines's motives and character. A sort of his-word-against-Kim's-word approach. If she attacked Kim on the stand, the boy would undoubtedly react badly. And yet what choice did she have? One of them was lying, pure and simple, and she chose to believe her client. Would J. D. Tremaine, if in fact he had coerced his daughter into supporting his story, allow her to be put on the stand, knowing how that might affect a young girl? Hard to climb into the mind of a cobra.

The new prosecutor assigned to the case, Alan Sherman, was overweight, overworked and, most of the brief time she'd spent with him, overwrought. While he'd been cooperative in assisting her, he hadn't been too friendly, giving her the feeling she was adding to the confusion of his life by defending such an obviously guilty defendant. She held out little hope for help from that department.

She and Jimmy Lee had just spent half an hour rehashing everything, and Sheila felt their case was about as strong as the wispy tendrils of smoke drifting toward the ceiling. Jimmy Lee had been quieter than usual, smoking incessantly, his movements jerky and nervous. Was it all just getting to him, or was there something else bothering him? Sheila wondered.

"You seem a little distracted today," she began, studying his young features. "Have you perhaps thought of something that we could use?"

Eyes downcast, he fingered his thin mustache for a moment, then crushed out his cigarette and looked at her. "Have you talked to Kim alone?"

"No, I haven't been able to. You saw what it was like at the preliminary hearing. Her father was on one side of her, their attorney on the other. Why?"

"I think something's bothering her."

Sheila kept her voice level through a rising sense of excitement. "What makes you think so?"

"My brother came to see me. Kim called him last week crying. Said she had to talk to me."

"We can arrange that."

He gave a snort of derision. "Oh, sure! I tried. I called her house, and they wouldn't let her come to the phone."

"*I* can try. Let me—"

"No! Last night she phoned me here. But they wouldn't call me right to the phone. They took her name and number and had me call her back on my free time. When I did—" he shrugged helplessly "—same thing happened. Only this time her father got on and told me to leave Kim alone and never call her again."

"If I talk to their attorney..."

"Uh, Miss North, what would happen to Kim if—if they find out she lied?"

Sheila crossed her legs and sat back. "Before she goes on the witness stand, not much. Falsely accusing a person of a serious crime—as she's done with you—is punishable, but you'd have to press charges against her. If, however, she lies on the stand, the court doesn't forgive perjury."

He sat staring at his burning cigarette as if he could find the answers he needed in the lengthening ash.

"We know she *is* lying, Jimmy Lee," Sheila reminded him.

"Only because *he* forced her," Jimmy Lee snarled. There was no question who "he" was.

"Nevertheless, lying. And if she won't come forward before trial date, then you'll have to trust me to get the truth from her on the witness stand."

"No! I don't want her hurt."

Anger moved into her, coupled with weeks of frustration. Her eyes bored into his. "Do you know that you're facing twenty years to life because of *her* lies, and you don't want her hurt?"

His Adam's apple bobbed up and down in his thin neck as he swallowed nervously, but his eyes remained steady on hers. "Better me than her."

"Is that right?" Sheila stood and, flinging his file inside, slammed her briefcase shut and snapped the lock. At the door she turned to look back at him, her eyes still blazing. "You'd better think that over long and hard, because I'm not wasting my time representing a fool who's protecting a girl whose lies are going to ruin his life."

Her knock brought the guard quickly. Without a backward glance, she walked out on him and marched down the corridor, more furious than she could remember being in a long while. Love, in Jimmy Lee Morgan's case, was not only deaf, dumb and blind, it was downright stupid.

An hour later, seated at her desk staring out at the leaves of the big maple tree swaying in the light breeze, she wondered if she'd been too harsh, leaving Jimmy Lee like that. No, dammit, she hadn't! It's true he was in a terrible fix with the girl he loved holding the key to his freedom, but it was time for him to grow up and face facts. He'd either have to let Sheila use all the pathetically little ammunition she had to free him—and if that included hurting Kim, so be it—or he'd have to resign himself to the possibility that, innocent or guilty, he might be locked away for a very long time.

No easy solutions here, she thought, taking off her glasses. But she was tired of reading and rereading the Morgan file in the scant hope that she'd overlooked something. Putting it all neatly into her briefcase, she decided that tomorrow she'd take the bull by the horns. Whether Jimmy Lee liked it or not, she'd show up on the Tremaine doorstep and see what she could learn in a face-to-face encounter with old J. D. and his daughter. She wasn't naive enough to think she'd bully a seasoned cobra like Kim's father into a full confession. But maybe she could pick up something useful from the way they'd act, some nuance, some gesture, *something*.

Snapping her case closed, she headed for the stairs. A cup of coffee would taste good. If in fact Kim had been trying to reach Jimmy Lee, something undoubtedly was on her mind, Sheila knew. If she could just talk to the girl, even if it had to be in front of her father, perhaps she could use her feelings for Jimmy Lee to prod her. If she hinted Kim's testimony could well put her ex-lover behind bars for life, would it intimidate her enough to stand up to her father and rise to Jimmy Lee's defense? Sheila didn't know, but she meant to find out tomorrow.

Peeking in, she found the reception area empty. Both Jed's and Tony's office doors were closed. It was silent across the hall in the senator's quarters as well. Rosemary must be downstairs in the kitchen with the senator's secretary. As she was about to join them, Rosemary's ringing phone stopped her. Listening, she heard no footsteps approaching. She decided to answer the phone and take a message.

"Adams, Blair and Adams," Sheila said.

"Hi, Rosie," a young male voice said, "this is Billy Jackson. Is Mr. Adams around? I got some great news for him."

"No, I'm sorry, he's not," Sheila said, reaching across Rosemary's desk for a pad and pen, not bothering to correct his assumption. "I can take a message for him, if you like."

"Yeah, I like," he singsonged happily. "Just tell him his talk with my friend, Reuben Tate, did the trick. Reuben's going to join the tuition program."

"All right," Sheila said, writing. "Anything else?"

"Hey, Rosie, you should have seen Mr. Adams Sunday night down at the center. We got no chairs yet, you know, but it didn't bother him none. He's down there on the floor with us guys, the music's bongin' in the background, and he's sitting there explaining his program to Reuben. And that dude bought it, just like I did. Moved out of his old man's rattrap, and he's livin' with me now. And we're going to hit the books together come September, Reuben and me. I tell you, Rosie, your boss is one hell of a guy."

Straightening, Sheila tried to make sense of the conversation. Perhaps if she explained she wasn't Rosemary. "Billy, this isn't—"

"Yeah, I know, this isn't the best time to call. You probably got a hundred things going. Just tell Mr. Adams for me, will you? Tell him Billy and Reuben are gonna make him proud. Catch you later."

"Do you want to leave a number where he can reach you?" Sheila asked, then realized the phone was dead. Replacing the receiver, she stared at the message pad reflectively. Who were Billy and Reuben? she wondered, her curiosity piqued. Why did these young men need an attorney to talk with them and where was this center without out chairs? Interesting.

But none of her business, really. She left the message clearly in sight on Rosemary's desk and walked out into the hallway just as Tony came in through the back way. He looked warm, winded and a bit harassed, yet his smile as he came to her was broad.

"I was hoping you'd be here," he said. "Have you got anything going this afternoon that you can't put off?"

Sheila cocked her head, considering. "No, not really. Why?"

Placing his briefcase just inside the reception-room doorway, he shrugged out of his suit-coat. "Because you and I are going to play hooky for the afternoon."

"We are?" she asked, smiling and folding her arms as she watched him whip off his tie and vest and put everything on top of his briefcase. "Are you shedding *all* your clothes for this event?"

His arms scooped her close, and he nuzzled her cheek with his. "You just keep those lecherous brown eyes off my gorgeous body. Besides, aren't you the one who's always telling me I dress a shade too stodgy?"

Enjoying his embrace, she nodded. "Yes, and I'm glad you're taking my advice and loosening up." She drew back to look into his dancing gray eyes. She couldn't remember seeing him looking more carefree. What was happening to the serious Mr. Adams? "And where are we going to play hooky?"

"Greektown," he announced. "We're going to wander down there and fill up on souvlaki and grape leaves and baklava and drink ouzo until it's running out of our ears. I've decided we've both been working hard, and since we couldn't be together last Sunday, we deserve an afternoon off."

"I can't believe you. Is this the staid and proper Lawyer Adams suggesting we set aside all work, and play on a weekday?"

"You bet," he said, grinning down at her. "I've reformed. To hell with business. My new hedonistic approach. Do you like it?"

She rose on her toes and kissed his chin. "I *love* it."

"Good," he said, releasing her and glancing back into the reception room. "Where's Rosemary?"

"Downstairs, I think."

"I'll just run down and ask her to tell all callers we're out for the day and they'll have to postpone their problems. Go climb into the Mercedes. I'll be back in a flash."

What a pleasure it was, Sheila thought, hurrying back to her office, to see Tony beginning to enjoy life more. She hoped he wouldn't regret her drawing him out a bit. They'd both probably have to burn the midnight oil later to catch up again, but it'd be worth it. She hadn't visited the old Greektown section of the city in ages, though she'd loved the area when she had.

Grabbing her purse, she decided to leave her jacket. The white linen slacks and black-and-white striped blouse she wore would do, but she slipped out of her pumps and into flat shoes, for she knew they'd be doing a lot of walking. Humming to herself, she closed the door behind her.

"There's one more stuffed grape leaf left," Tony said. "We can't leave it."

Leaning back in her chair, Sheila shook her head. "I can't handle another bite just now. You eat it."

"Well, if you insist." He scooped it onto his plate as the dark-haired waitress poured them each a cup of very black, very thick coffee.

As she departed, Sheila leaned forward to gaze into her cup. "Looks a little like the last time I had the oil changed in my car."

Tony took a cautious sip, then arched his brows. "Hot, strong and black. Delicious, but you might have one problem with it," he said, finishing the last morsel on his plate.

"What's that?"

"It might be strong enough to put hair on your chest."

She laughed. "Just what I need. But after those two glasses of ouzo, I could use something to unfuzz my brain."

Elbows on the table, his shirtsleeves rolled up, Tony leaned toward her, his eyes lingering on the soft swell of her breasts. "I think I'd like your chest any which way, and I like your fuzzy brain, too."

Glancing quickly around at the other diners at the Pegasus Taverna from their secluded table by the window, Sheila felt the heat move into her face. She wasn't sure whether it was from the effects of the ouzo or from Tony's words. "Could we please *not* discuss my chest in public?" she whispered.

"All right, I'm an agreeable guy. Let's go somewhere private and discuss it. Of course, that would probably entail a thorough examination and..."

Crossing her arms defensively over the subject in question, Sheila gave him a tolerant smile. "Drink your coffee, counselor."

He grinned at her, enjoying her discomfort enormously. "Yes, ma'am."

Brushing aside the fringed curtains, Sheila gazed out onto the narrow sidewalks of Monroe and St. Antoine Streets, the heart of Greektown. Browsers strolled, enjoying the summer sunshine, the tiny fragrant shops peddling their mysterious imported wares and the vibrant music piped up and down the avenue. In the Hellas Cafe the old men gathered to reminisce about their youthful escapades.

She and Tony had spent several hours wandering through the many stores up Trapper's Alley—bookshops, boutiques, a fudge emporium—and out past the flower stands on each corner. After much looking, Tony'd bought her a delicate lilac scarf with fine embroidery in each corner. And, over his protests, she'd insisted on buying him a white fisherman's cap which she'd immediately set atop his thick head of hair. Uncertain at first, he'd finally adjusted it at a jaunty angle and left it on, even through their late lunch. Turning to gaze at him now as he sat back, looking sated and pleased with himself, she smiled wondering what the senator would say if he could see his son now.

She caught Tony's eye, and he smiled at her, warming her, melting her. Love—the word floated to the surface from her subconscious. Yes, love. She loved this handsome, intelligent, wonderful man. And he didn't believe in love nor the power of it. He didn't think love could move into your life and change it and change you forevermore. But he would. She would show him the way. She simply had to, for she'd never felt anything so powerful before, so right. And she knew he felt more than he would admit. But admit it he would one day. As she returned his smile, she felt certain of it.

"That's a mysterious smile, lady," he said. "Like there's a message in it for me, but I'm not quite sure what it is."

A message! She'd forgotten all about his message. She wasn't sure whether it was important or not, but perhaps she'd better tell him about the call. "That reminds me, a young man named Billy Jackson phoned just before we left. He was anxious to tell you about Reuben Tate."

He frowned, leaning forward. "How'd you come to talk with Billy?"

"I'd gone into the reception room to ask Rosemary if she'd like to join me for a cup of coffee, and the phone rang. She wasn't around, so I answered."

"And what did he want to tell me about Reuben?"

"Something about Reuben had left his father's place, had moved in with Billy and was ready to join in the tuition program." That evidently pleased him, for he nodded and smiled. Sheila was relieved. For a moment there, she felt as though she'd inadvertently intruded on something personal.

"Mmm. Is that all?"

"Well, he chattered on a bit, thinking I was Rosemary, though I tried to interrupt and clarify that. He said something about you sitting on the floor of the center last Sunday, explaining your program to the guys, and that you were one hell of a guy yourself."

He smiled a little sheepishly. "Billy's a good kid and a great recruiter."

She leaned forward, hoping he'd go on but hating to pry. When he didn't, she decided to risk it. "I don't suppose you'd like to tell me about Billy."

Toying with his spoon, he shrugged. "Not much to tell. He's a kid from the wrong side of the tracks. I ran into him a couple of years ago when he was sixteen, defending him on a stolen-car charge. Got him off as a first offender. Besides, he didn't steal the car, but he was with the kid who did. Billy's poor, black and pretty much alone.''

She was beginning to see the picture. "And you decided to help him."

"I gave him a little boost, yes. We all need one now and then."

"What kind of a little boost?"

He hesitated a long moment. "I told him if he'd stay in school and graduate, I'd help put him through college. He just finished his first year at Wayne State." Looking up, he gave her a proud smile. "As an honors student, can you believe it?"

No, Sheila thought, her heart expanding. Tony Adams didn't believe in love. Of course he didn't. "Billy's an honors student because someone believes in him," she said, her voice soft. "And now you've convinced Reuben Tate to follow suit. How many others are there in your program, counselor?"

He finished his coffee before answering. "Just those two. Don't canonize me, Sheila. Jed and I set up this trust fund. We take turns meeting at this recreation center a couple of times a week. Maybe it'll help a few kids stay on the straight and narrow. No big deal."

No, Sheila thought. No big deal to Tony. But she saw it as quite a big deal. She reached over, her hand twining with his. "Billy's right. You're one hell of a guy."

He stood, a little embarrassed. "One hell of a sleepy guy. Come on, let's walk off that ouzo before I nod off in my coffee."

And so they did, up and down the winding streets, in and out of shops and boutiques until dusk found them in front of a large building with a flashing red sign that read Mykonos.

"Oh, belly dancing!" Sheila exclaimed, reading the sign out front. "I've never seen it. Can we go in?"

"Sure," Tony said, smiling indulgently at her enthusiasm. It'd been years since he'd been to Greektown, and never had he enjoyed it as much as this day with Sheila. Seen through her eyes, everything was new and exciting.

The main room was large, with many small tables crowded around a good-sized stage with a bandstand at the far end. Most of the tables were filled, but with a surreptitious exchange of a folded bill from Tony's hand to his, the smiling maître d' found them an empty one near the front. The band was warming up as the waiter brought them each an ouzo.

"You may have to carry me back to the car if I drink another one of these," Sheila told him, speaking close to his ear in order to be heard over the music.

"Glad to accommodate." He clinked his glass against hers. "Here's lookin' at you, kid."

Tony shifted his chair alongside hers and placed his arm across the back as the music became loud and rhythmic. Warmed by the drink and Tony's nearness, Sheila saw the lights dim and the first entertainers appear on stage to wild hand-clapping and foot-stomping from the crowd of onlookers, many of whom were evidently regulars at Mykonos. Eight folk dancers, the men in white shirts, tight shorts and knee socks and the women in peasant blouses and full skirts, marched out and moved into the regimented steps of a traditional Greek dance.

When they finished the first one, white-aproned waiters appeared and placed hefty stacks of small crockery plates along the edges of the stage. As the dancers went into their next number, following what was obviously a prescribed routine, several of the people from nearby tables came up and, one by one, smashed the plates hard on the stage floor. Tony smiled as Sheila gasped. Crockery flew every which way as the clever dancing feet avoided each new arrival while the crowd cheered and the ouzo flowed.

Laughing along with the rest of the audience, Tony and Sheila applauded and cheered until their hands hurt and their throats ached. So they drank more ouzo and smiled at one another, stealing a small kiss now and then, caught up in the gaiety. Sheila couldn't remember when she'd had more fun, or did it just seem like that because Tony was near?

As the dancers swaggered off the stage, two waiters with brooms swept aside the largest piles of broken plate pieces, the lights dimmed even lower and the band began a slow, slinky tune. Into the spotlight came a tall woman wearing a wispy veiled costume. Her long black hair was straight and shiny, flying out behind her as she whipped her head about, gazed seductively at the crowd through long lowered lashes and gave them a small smile from her pouty red lips. Eagerly they drummed on the tables, urging her on. Sheila leaned forward, watching intently.

The slithery music enveloped her as she moved into the heady gyrations of the belly dance, undulating in impossible contortions, her flesh rolling and tossing as if it had a mind of its own. Castanet-like sounds came from her fingers, and occasionally she stopped to remove another veil from the seemingly endless supply she had draped about her.

When she was down to the last few filmy coverings, she slinked off the stage and approached the nearest table. Weaving and bobbing the upper half of her body toward the man seated there, she thrust her ample bosom into his face until finally he took a folded bill and inserted it between her breasts while the woman with him cheered him on. With a haughty smile, the dancer gave him a bump and grind and moved on to the next table.

"What an easy way to make a living," Sheila said to Tony's ear. "Why didn't I think of this?"

He reached down and patted her flat stomach. "Stick to the law. I don't think you've got the belly for it."

Laughing, she pulled his hat down over his eyes and returned her attention to the dancer, who was working her way through the crowd. It took her nearly half an hour to circle the room and find her way back onto the stage, her bra bulging with dollar bills. The rousing finish was a rollicking fast belly dance, accompanied by drums and much plate-smashing by waiters and patrons alike as nearly everyone in the restaurant got into the act. Exhausted, the dancer ran offstage and the musicians ended on a high note to wild applause. Sheila couldn't help feeling sorry for the poor cleanup crew of the Mykonos if this was a twice-nightly event.

As they made their way to the door amid the boisterous crowd, Sheila felt very warm and more than a little woozy. "Oh," she said as a fat man pushed an elbow into her. Tony's arm steadied her.

"Are you all right?" he asked.

"I think so, but I'm not sure ouzo's my drink."

Tipping his head back to better see her flushed face, Tony smiled. "Why, counselor, I do believe you're a little tipsy."

"I am not," she protested feebly. "But I sure hope you remember where we parked the car."

"Come on, you little boozer," he said as they emerged into the warm night air. "This way. I think I'd better take you home."

"No," she said, trying to keep up with his long-legged stride. "I have to go back to the office. My car's there, and I need my briefcase first thing in the morning."

"All right, but I'm not sure I'm going to let you drive. We'll see when we get there."

Reaching the car, he unlocked the door and held it for her. "Don't be a chauvinist, Tony Adams."

"I thought you liked strong, masterful men," he said, going around and getting behind the wheel.

"I do. Sometimes." Without another word, she lay back her head and went to sleep.

Smiling, Tony turned on the engine.

The sudden stopping of the car as Tony turned the Mercedes into his apartment parking space woke Sheila. Blinking a moment to clear her vision, she turned her head to find him studying her with ill-concealed amusement. She brushed her hair back from her forehead and gave him a smile.

"Just what do you find so funny?"

"You. Funny and fascinating."

"Fascinating? Not me. I'm an open book, not at all mysterious, unfortunately." She yawned expansively. "I have to go up and get my briefcase." As she glanced out, she suddenly came to life. "We're not at the office. What are we doing at your apartment?"

"I thought you might need a little coffee."

"Are you going to make it?"

"Sure thing. Come on.

She yawned twice again during the elevator ride up to his floor. He hoped she would stay awake long enough for him to get the coffee into her. As he searched through his crowded key ring for the door key, Sheila grabbed them playfully.

"Race you to your door," she said as the elevator opened. Sprinting down the hallway with Tony close behind her, she still felt a little wobbly, but the night air had cleared her head somewhat. Bending to the lock, she tried to get the key to work. But he was beside her, trying gently to move her aside.

"Here, let me give that a try," he insisted.

But she wouldn't let him. Laughing, she bumped him out of the way with a quick hip movement. "I've almost got it."

"You are *one* stubborn lady. Why don't you—"

She dropped the keys and her purse and nearly dropped herself as well. Grabbing her arms to keep her from toppling, Tony pulled her upright. Slowly her head came up, her thick blond hair falling back from her uptilted face. The hall light reflected in the brown of her eyes, which were calm and clear and suddenly aware.

In slow motion, his hands moved to frame her face, his fingertips tracing its lovely features as a blind man might, memorizing its contours. Her eyes darkened with desire for him, letting him know, letting him see. She was his, all his.

Tony lowered his mouth to hers as his arms slid around and pulled her closer. She opened her lips under his, welcoming his tongue inside her, breathing in the exciting taste of him mixed with traces of the pungent ouzo. Her body moved against him, delivering a message her mind had denied but could no longer. She stood there pressed hard into him, no longer aware of the public hallway or the elevator's noisy departure or the overhead light shining on them. She knew only Tony, only this man, only him.

Reluctantly breaking from her, Tony picked up the keys and unlocked the door, swinging it open. With a hand at her back, he guided her inside, then locked the door behind them. Not bothering to turn on the lights, he bent to pick her up, cradling her in his arms. Standing in the dim light sprinkling in through the large picture window, he placed a kiss on each of her eyes, the gentle gesture making her feel fragile and cherished.

Through the vestibule and across the living room he carried her. Stopping in front of the fireplace, he placed his mouth on hers again, drawing her in. Shifting, he allowed her to slide down the length of his body, letting them both enjoy the sensual contact.

Desire. It clamored through her, pounding in her head, rushing through her veins. His fingers, undoing her buttons, weren't moving fast enough. Her own hands, removing his shirt, weren't quick enough. She wanted to be flesh-to-flesh with him. Finally he touched her swollen breasts, and a moan she couldn't control broke free. In striped shafts of moonlight, he inspected and learned and explored. She was reeling with the feel and taste and scent of him.

Need. He was burning with need, but he dared not rush it. His lips moved over her face while his hands rid her of the rest of her clothes, and then he struggled out of his own. The couch by the fireplace was large and soft and welcoming as he lowered her to it.

Beauty. He saw so much beauty in the silken softness of her body as she lay with him. And in the expression in her eyes as she watched him slide his hands over her. Moving his face into the hollow of her throat, he inhaled the wondrous fragrance of her, his tongue tasting the enticing flavor of her warm skin. She was everything beautiful and gentle and soft in the world. And she was offering her gifts to him.

Passion. It ripped through him, no longer able to be stilled. His mouth on hers was hard and hungry now, no longer patient, but greedy and seeking. His hand slid down and found her, swallowing her gasp as he touched deep inside her. Her movements were near frantic now, making him lose his pacing; his passion a roar in his ears as he moved over her while her hands on his back clutched at him. Then he was on her and in her, filling her body.

Pleasure. There was only pleasure now, wild and soaring and pushing them onward. Moving together, they climbed, letting the feelings build and build. Until there was nothing but blinding light behind closed eyelids and a rushing sound in their ears as their minds emptied to all but feeling. The world went away as they gave to each other.

Love. As she floated back, Sheila could think only love. She'd experienced closeness with a man before, but she'd never experienced love. Until tonight. Until Tony.

Chapter Eight

She was a snuggler. A toucher and a snuggler, Tony thought as he awakened to find Sheila sprawled half-across him, cuddled up close. Involuntarily his arms, which had been resting on her, tightened, and she stirred slightly in sleep, making a soft sound, then went still again.

He lay on his back, looking at the moonlit shadows dancing on the wall, cradling her carefully in his embrace. From long habit, he took out his feelings now and examined them. He found them warm and comforting. Gently he moved the pale hair from her cheeks, enjoying the flush of loving on her face, which he had put there. Sheila.

Tenderness. She exhibited such tenderness effortlessly, and still she had such strength. It drew him, more than anything she might have knowingly done.

She made him feel young and uninhibited. She'd kissed him in a canoe and in a public parking lot and in a crowded restaurant, kissed him openly and naturally and unashamedly. She made him Fourth-of-July happy, amusement-park joyful, last-day-of-school giddy. And she did it all by looking at him with those deep brown eyes, by touching those soft lips to his and winding her arms tightly about him. Oh, but more than that. So much more than that. She did it by looking into his mind and soul and heart. And by caring. Yes, mostly by caring. Sighing deeply, he wondered what he was going to do about Sheila and this incredible way she made him feel.

Unconsciously, as he lay thinking, he rubbed the satin skin of her back. Now she moved under his hand, her face rising from where she'd had it pillowed on his chest. Slowly she gave him a smile.

"Mmm, it seems I drifted off."

"Yes, you did," he said, pulling her up closer to his face and kissing her long and sweetly. "Did I wear you out?"

"In a nice way, but yes, you did. You and the ouzo."

With a quick movement he rolled her over onto her back on the textured couch and loomed over her, his silver gaze once more caressing her face. "Ah, but I see you have amazing recuperative powers. A short nap and you're ready for more." His hand moved lingeringly down her throat, then drew lazy circles along the soft swell of her breasts.

"Am I?"

"Don't you think you might be?"

"I can't think at all when you touch me like that," she said, feeling her flesh quiver and dance under his knowing hand.

He paused. "Do you want me to stop?"

Her eyes sparkled as she met his hot gaze. "Did I say that?"

He shifted to watch his fingers on her pale flesh. "What a wonderful barometer of a woman's arousal breasts are. Watch. When I breathe on one, like this—" leaning down, he blew warm air on her "—you shiver. When I cover it with my palm, see how it grows and swells to fit my hand? And when I put my mouth to you..."

Sheila hardly heard the rest as his lips closed over her and her restless body squirmed under his loving touch. Impossible to believe, he had her wanting him again so swiftly. Closing her eyes while he continued his ministrations, she felt passion explode behind her lids. Then his mouth moved up to capture hers as his strong arms pulled her into his long, hard frame.

Murmuring into her mouth, he broke the kiss and moved to whisper in her ear. "This is a hell of a time to bring this up, but was this safe?"

She paused, feeling suddenly uncomfortable. "Meaning?"

"Well, let's just say I'd make a lousy captive bridegroom."

Sheila felt a sudden chill settle over her, the mood for her totally broken now. She pulled back from him. "Is that why you think I came up here with you, to get pregnant and trap you?"

He pulled her roughly into his embrace again. "Of course not. But unwanted pregnancies do occur. I don't want that to happen to us."

Slowly but firmly she moved from him. "I certainly don't either." Leaning forward in the dim light, she searched for her clothes. Damn, how could he think that of her? She had to get away from him. Now!

He put a hand on her arm, stopping her. "What are you doing?" he asked, sounding genuinely puzzled.

"Leaving. I think it's time." She stood. "I presume the bathroom's down this hall." She started walking toward it.

"Wait!" Tony got up clumsily, uncertain what he'd said to dispel the mood and turn her off so when moments before she'd been as ready and willing as he. Surely a sensible conversation about birth control wouldn't upset her so. "Sheila," he said, going after her. "What's wrong?"

"Nothing!" She made it to the door before he caught her and swung her around. She stood clutching her bundle of clothes in front of her, her eyes blazing.

"I'm sorry. My timing was bad." She didn't move, didn't speak. "Dammit, I wasn't accusing you. I just didn't want..."

"Didn't want me to trap you. Yes, I know. Well, don't worry, I haven't, so now will you let go of my arm so I can get dressed?"

Icy cold and yet filled with sadness, her voice cut through him. He hadn't meant to hurt her. He'd gone about it all wrong. He'd have to explain.

"Sheila, my mother and father had to get married because she was pregnant. I was that child. He never let either of us ever forget it."

She searched his eyes and realized he was telling the truth. Instantly she softened. What a horror that must have been for a little boy growing up, feeling unwanted, in the way, the inadvertent reason two people who no longer even liked each other had to be together. It explained a great deal. Dropping her clothes, she moved into his arms. "Oh, Tony, I'm so sorry."

He held her close, just held her, pushing back the old pain. He didn't dwell on it, seldom thought of it anymore, really. But when he did it always surprised him how much the old memories could still hurt. Now that Sheila understood, it was somehow easier, the pain lessening more quickly. So good for him. She was so good for him.

"I'm the one who should apologize. I hurt you by blurting it out like that. I..."

Her mouth moved to his, spilling soft kisses on his lips, his chin, his cheeks. "Shhh, don't apologize. I overreacted. Just love me, please, right now. Love me, now."

She was a wild thing, her mouth doing crazy things to him, her hands moving all over him. There was no time to think, to move to a better place. So he lowered her to the carpeted hallway, covering her body with healing kisses to wash away the pain he'd caused her, hoping she truly understood. Never before had he felt such a need to make amends, never before had he been so swept up in a fiery desire that left him trembling and gasping. Never before had he let someone come so close to knowing him, *really* knowing him. Never before.

The world grew soft and hazy for Sheila as Tony entered her swiftly, then stopped, opening his eyes until she met his gaze. Clinging to the edge of the precipice, they held the moment, absorbing the wonder of being joined.

"I love you," she whispered, so filled with the feeling she could no longer contain it. Wordlessly Tony began to move, slowly at first.

He watched her face as her rising passion brought a soft blush to her features. Faster and faster now, as a fine damp sheen appeared on her body and she strained with him, moved with him, reached with him. Though his need was great, he wanted hers to be desperate, and he saw she was almost there, her hands pressing into his back, her breathing ragged. Another moment and he heard her soft moan as she closed her eyes and let the world slide away. His throat choking with the beauty he saw in her face, he let himself join her.

Sheila came back to herself slowly, savoring the aftershocks. Was it her love for this virile, exciting, complex man that made their coming together so powerful, so all-consuming? she wondered. The first time, in the living room, they'd had no patience, needing to discover one another swiftly, thoroughly. And now, this time, it'd been like a raging fire rushing through her, a mindless desperation. Had he even heard her whispered declaration of love? And would he say anything if he had?

Raising her head, she shook back her hair so she could see his face. Her mouth twitched nervously at the corners.

"Oh, lady," he said, his voice husky, "I love the way you love me." And he hugged her tightly, possessively.

She did love him. Oh, how she loved him. But obviously he hadn't heard her, so she choked back the other words she wanted to shout to him, fearful they would make him turn from her. "Is it proper for a lady to say 'thank you' to a compliment like that from a gentleman, I wonder?"

"One mustn't take credit for an innate talent such as you possess."

"I assure you, I've never before seen a hint of this particular heretofore-hidden talent of mine. Perhaps you bring out the baser side of my nature."

He grinned at her. "Good. Let's keep it between the two of us, shall we?"

If only he weren't joking, Sheila thought. She eased back from him. This was definitely not the way she usually did things, on the floor in a man's apartment. "I think it's time I head for home."

"Please don't go," Tony coaxed, his hand gentle on her face. "Stay the night. I promise to rise early and take you to your car so no one will be the wiser."

She was tempted. He looked so little-boy pleading. To spend the night in his arms...but no. "I can't. I want a shower, and I haven't any clean clothes."

"Take a shower. There's a blue terry-cloth robe on the back of the door. It might be a little roomy but—please, Sheila?"

He had her. Those damn silver eyes. "I would if you just had a bed. Making love on your couch and on the floor is very sexy, but..."

Laughing, he jumped to his feet and pulled her up. "I do have a bed, a great big comfortable one. Go take your shower, and I'll show it to you."

In the kitchen, Tony filled a glass with cold tea and ice and, tilting his head, drank thirstily. He filled another for Sheila, his thoughts in a jumble. Automatically his hand moved to where his breast pocket would be, wishing bitterly for a cigarette. Perhaps it'd been a mistake giving up smoking. He desperately needed something, for he felt that all his defenses were down. It'd been years since he'd felt so vulnerable.

He'd never felt about another woman exactly the way he felt about Sheila North. If her passion when they'd made love in the living room surprised him, then the open way she'd given herself to him just now stunned him. He'd revealed something intensely personal about himself to her and in that unguarded state he'd demanded nothing from her. Then she'd given him everything. And she had so much to give that it nearly overwhelmed him.

I love you, she'd whispered, or had he imagined it? he wondered as he sipped the rest of his drink. He'd told her he didn't trust feelings of love, didn't believe in commitment, didn't believe in the forever myth. And she'd marched right past all that and declared herself anyway. But how much credence could you give to feelings expressed at the height of passion?

If he didn't believe her words of love, he couldn't mistake her physical message of love. She was all flash and fire, clever hands and seeking mouth, hot blood and pounding heart. But she was more than that. She was tenderness and caring, she was sweet patience and a slow climb up the mountain. And when he came down, she was there, still holding him, her brown eyes shining.

He'd always liked women, liked the way their minds worked, their subtleties, their curiosity. Not just in his bed but in his life. But on a short-term basis, where he called the shots.

And now he wanted Sheila to stay the night, he wanted to hold her through the long hours, to sleep beside her, to awaken with her. And the feeling jolted him, for usually in the past, when the evening was finished for him, it was finished. He was the one who left, because he'd always made sure it was the woman's place they'd go to. Yes, he entertained in his apartment, used it for business and social meetings, but he never brought women to his bedroom. It was far too important a room to him. But now he wanted Sheila in it. There had to be an explanation here somewhere. Picking up her glass, he decided to just accept his feelings for now and worry about the implications later.

After twenty minutes she came out, wrapped in her warm dreams and his soft robe. She smelled of his talcum. Dreamily she breathed it in.

"I see you discovered my secret weapon," Tony said as he came down the hallway with a towel wrapped about his waist. Smiling, he handed her a frosty glass of iced tea.

"Yes, baby powder. And here I thought you used some sinfully expensive and exotic men's cologne." She took the tea and drank deeply. "I think ouzo dehydrates a person worse than sunshine."

He nuzzled his scratchy face along her cheek. "I think you smell sensational. Are you hungry?"

"Not for food," she answered, her eyes wide and teasing.

"Mmm, we'll see what we can do about that. I'm going to take a quick shower." He inclined his head toward the far door. "Why don't you wait for me in my bedroom?"

Nodding, she turned and walked slowly down the hallway, sipping her tea. At the doorway she stopped and leaned against the frame, studying his bedroom. So this was Tony's haven.

A huge four-poster bed of rough-hewn pine dominated one end of the room, flanked by matching twin nightstands. A well-used fieldstone fireplace was on the wall opposite, with a long corduroy couch angled cozily facing it. On a free-form table in front of it rested a black lacquered tray with several cut-glass decanters, a bucket of ice and two crystal glasses. On the wall above a highboy dresser was a framed coat of arms, the Adams family crest. A magnificent oak rolltop desk with a soft leather chair rounded out the totally masculine room done in warm browns, gold and splashes of yellow.

As Sheila moved into the room, her bare feet sank into the luxurious pile of the high-low tweed shag carpeting. This comfortable disarray was so unlike the perfection of the less private rooms. Books were scattered and piled on a low side table, on the floor and even on the end of the couch. Thick, heavy pillows were clustered randomly next to a stack of law journals, several open and lying face-down.

She walked closer to study the pictures on his desk. Jed and Tony in their college days. Sandy alone, then with a younger Tony, and Sandy standing with her arms around an older woman, tall, thin and dark, obviously their mother. Conspicuous by his absence was the senator. Tonight he'd given her a reason why.

Slatted wood blinds covered the two high windows, the lighting was muted and, from somewhere, low bluesy music drifted in. The room looked lived-in and loved. Such a contrast to the rest of his apartment. She wondered as she finished her tea if Tony realized how much this special room and the way he'd put it together revealed about him. Would she ever stop discovering new facets of this complex man?

His hair damp and curly, Tony came to her in bare feet, wearing a yellow terry-cloth robe.

"You have a whole wardrobe of robes in assorted colors, I see," Sheila told him, curling up on one end of the couch.

Setting aside a stack of books, he joined her and nodded. "Sometimes on weekends I don't bother getting dressed at all."

The thought sent shivers through her. From where he sat, his scent drifted to her. Soap and baby powder, a ludicrous combination on a grown man. It captivated her, as nearly everything about him did. She drew her knees up and hugged them, trying not to let her emotions show. "This room, it's wonderful. I might never leave."

She fit in beautifully. Suddenly it occurred to him that he might want her to stay more than one night, and the shock of that thought had him reeling. "Will it go to your head if I tell you no woman's ever been in this room before you?"

Eyes softening, she reached out to run her fingers down his arm, then to rest on his hand. "Yes, I think it will." She glanced toward the bed. "That bedframe looks handmade. I love that rough wood look."

"It is handmade—by me." He smiled at the surprise registering on her face. "When Jed and I were in college, we decided we needed some variety, so we took this woodworking course. I discovered I loved working with wood." He leaned back comfortably, running his hand through his damp hair, his long legs stretched out in front of him. "There's so much character in wood, so much feeling. It has a history, memories. So I kept at it. It was a welcome change from hitting the books."

Sheila remembered that Rosemary had said he'd refinished the office building alone, not wanting to entrust it to anyone else. It was a source of pride to him, as was this beautiful furniture.

He nodded toward the bed and chest. "I made a similar set, only smaller and more feminine, for my mother. She had it hauled all the way to New York, to her loft."

Another surprise—he had a wide romantic streak. "I don't blame her. It's beautiful." Her hand still on his, she squeezed it. "You're multitalented, counselor."

He leaned closer, his head resting on the couch back, his brows raising in an exaggerated Groucho Marx leer, drop ping ashes from a nonexistent cigar in the familiar gesture. "Want to see a demonstration of some of my other talents?"

"I think I've already seen a sample of that particular talent, and it's 'awesome,' as the California 'valley girls' would say."

He grinned, foolishly pleased. Leaning forward, he poured a small amount of amber liquor from one of the decanters into two glasses and handed her one. "Have a little brandy. It'll warm you."

Warm me? Did he think she needed warming when just being near him had her palms damp? She took it anyway. "Just when I've almost gotten over the ouzo." She sipped slowly. Yes, very warming. She settled more comfortably in the corner, leaning back to look at him over her glass. Just to look at him. It felt so good just looking at him. "Tell me about your mother, Tony."

He stared into the contents of his glass, reaching for an explanation that would best explain Deanna Adams Cartwright Forbes. "She's tall and on the thin side and Greenwich Village chic, I guess you could say. Her clothes choices are somewhat theatrical and a little haphazard. Sort of like an older version of a flower child. There's a simplicity about her, an innocence I don't believe she'll ever lose." He smiled, caught in memory's web. "Life seems to *happen* to her, as if without her permission, or even her knowledge. She's naively trustful, maddeningly vague and wonderfully kind."

He loves her, Sheila thought, but she knew better than to say it aloud. "She doesn't sound like the type of woman who'd have appealed to your father, even years ago."

His gray eyes narrowed thoughtfully, as cool as a cloudy day. "I think she was everything he was not—and she still is. At her essence, my mother is honest and sincere. Maybe he thought some of her good qualities would rub off on him. Or perhaps he wanted to conquer her, which is certainly in him. Along the way, he ruined her.''

He's never forgiven his father for hurting his mother. Or for the pain the senator caused him in his early years. Why then, Sheila wondered, was he in business with him? "You seem so different from your father. I'm surprised you ever got along sharing a practice.''

"We didn't share a practice,'' he said, his voice a little too loud in his need to emphasize. "He's always had his clients, and I've kept mine separate. I don't even handle referrals from him. When he went to Washington, a lot of his clientele drifted away, especially when I joined the prosecutor's staff and Jed didn't want to work with them. Neither of us is too fond of the members of the old-boys network of friendship my father thinks is his life's blood.''

Sheila took another warming sip of the brandy, then set it down, wondering how he'd handle her next question. "Did you join the prosecutor's office in an effort to disassociate yourself from your father and his following?''

She'd expected a flash of anger, perhaps annoyance. Instead he turned to face her, a slow smile forming. "Did you study psychology along with your law courses?''

She had her answer, and a warmer reaction to a probing question than she'd dared hope for. How far they've come, Sheila thought, returning his smile. "As a matter of fact, I did. Comes in handy in the courtroom.''

He slid one arm around her, drawing her close up against him, her head resting on his shoulder, her face tilted up to his. "And in the bedroom, from time to time, I imagine. You seem fascinated with trying to figure out what makes me tick.''

"I'm fascinated with *all* of you, counselor.'' She insinuated her hand inside the opening of his robe, her fingers tangling in the dark, curly hair on his chest.

"Not just my incredibly intriguing mind?" he whispered, his mouth close to her ear, his tongue moving inside.

A shiver shook her, harbinger of more to come. "Not at the moment," she was able to get out just before his mouth closed over hers.

The sweetness of the kiss caught her unprepared. Always with them, it seemed, unbridled passion lay lurking beneath the surface, waiting to shoot out of control at a look, a touch. But his lips moved gently over hers, lingering lazily, savoring the moment. Their breathing merged, their scents mingled, their tastes mixed until she couldn't tell where hers left off and his began.

He brushed light kisses over her face and neck, yet returned often to her waiting mouth. He could afford to take his time with her now, to bank his own needs already building, for she was here for the night, his to explore, his to kiss at leisure, his to love completely. All his. The thought made him giddy with wonder. Using only mouth and tongue, he worked slowly to arouse her, delighting in the soft sounds she made, pleased at the way her body began to move as her passion built.

With shaky hands he eased open her robe and slid it from her shoulders. Lowering his head, he touched the tip of her breast with his wet tongue, and she arched against him, his name a sigh that escaped from between her parted lips. Slipping the rest of the garment from her, he trailed kisses along the soft underside of her breasts, over her shoulder, nibbling at the tender skin inside her elbow, down the throbbing pulse at her wrist. Fighting his own growing need, he buried his face in the satin of her flat stomach as her hands moved into his hair, pressing him closer.

Her breathing raspy, she lowered her head and spoke softly. "I thought you promised me a bed the next time."

Shifting, Tony stood up on unsteady legs. "So I did." Effortlessly he picked her up, then, unable to resist, moved his mouth to capture the peak of one breast, drawing in deeply. He heard her groan as he felt her grow hot and hard under the gentle onslaught of his lips. Carrying her to the bed, he set her down, pulled back the covers and eased her onto the mattress. Whipping aside his own robe, he lay down beside her, one arm stretched above her head, one hairy leg angled over hers in lazy possession, enjoying the way her dark eyes watched him.

Far below, a siren droned in the distance, the air conditioner gave off a muted hum and the soft music continued, but Sheila heard none of it. For her, there was only Tony with his magic hands, his sensuous mouth and his loving ways.

Tony awoke to bright sunshine and the smell of bacon and coffee drifting to him. As he stretched lazily, he became aware that there was a smile on his face. He couldn't remember the last time he'd awakened smugly satisfied and smiling. Pulling on a pair of jeans, he rinsed his face and joined Sheila in the kitchen.

She was standing at the stove, her back to him, wearing one of his shirts, the sleeves rolled up, the tail riding low on her curvaceous thighs. Moving up behind her, he shifted her hair aside and kissed her sweet-smelling neck.

"A sex fiend who cooks. What man would ask for more?"

Turning the bacon over on the griddle, she peered up at him. "*I'm* the sex fiend?"

Swiveling her into his arms, he kissed her long and thoroughly. "I'd say we're well-matched," he said with a grin. He moved to pour himself a cup of coffee. "What time is it?"

"Nine-thirty, would you believe it? I can't remember the last time I've slept so late."

He took a long hot sip. "I can't remember the last time I've slept so well. You're better than a sleeping pill." He eyed her over the rim. Her breasts were pink and clearly defined under the thin shirt. Watching, remembering, he found it difficult to concentrate on their conversation. "I like your outfit. It looks much better on you than on me."

"Thank you." She sent him a frowning glance. "Do you really take sleeping pills?"

"Occasionally. Sometimes I'm too tired to fall asleep easily." He moved closer to her, sliding a suggestive hand down her back and lower. "But I think I've found a better remedy for fatigue."

"Oh, you have, have you?" Deftly she placed the bacon on paper towels to drain. "How do you like your eggs?" she asked, aware that his hand was busy at her back. She turned to face him, placing her hand over his, halting his progress. "You're very distracting. And we've got to get going. I talked with Rosemary, and I've had a very important call."

He set down his cup, placing his hands lightly on her arms. How'd she manage to look so damn appealing, her face shower-fresh, her eyes alive and alert, her skin practically humming? He didn't want to talk about calls. He wanted to carry her back to bed. With a great effort he made himself appear interested. "What important call?"

"Kim Tremaine—she wants to meet with me." Her voice fairly quivered with excitement. "This may be the break we need, Tony."

"That's great. What time are you meeting her?"

"One o'clock. How do you like your eggs?"

"Later." He nuzzled her cheek. "I'd like my eggs later."

She squirmed but didn't pull away. "Tony, I have a million things to do before I meet Kim."

"A million and *one* things," he said meaningfully. Reaching to shut off the stove, he turned them toward the hallway. He had appointments, too. But first things first.

One mustn't confuse one's priorities. Now that he'd tasted her, would he ever have enough of her? Tony wondered.

She couldn't stop her smile as she let him lead her, his fingers already fumbling with her buttons. "I warn you, the bacon will get cold."

"Did I ever tell you that I read this article—very scientific—about cold bacon being good for you?" He ushered her into the room. "Let me tell you all about it." With his foot he kicked the bedroom door closed behind them.

Chapter Nine

Tony sat down at the table in the quiet restaurant and watched Janie Brewster wend her way through the late-afternoon lunch crowd to the door. She held her head tall and proud, as she had in the several weeks he'd known her. No small accomplishment, since the prosecuting attorney had a nearly airtight case against her husband, Andy Brewster, Tony's client.

Signaling the waiter for a refill of coffee, Tony crossed his long legs and sighed. He'd begun to doubt the young accountant's innocence some time back. Too many coincidences, too many weak witnesses, too many unanswered questions. He'd be summarizing his case tomorrow, but in his heart Tony really felt Andy was guilty of embezzlement. But Andy's wife, Janie, didn't agree. She'd never once wavered in her belief in her husband. She was beautiful in her love and her loyalty on Andy's behalf. Sheila'd be like that, Tony decided, the thought making him smile.

The coffee arrived, and he took a swallow, then pulled out his legal pad and gold pen and leaned forward, making some notes for his summation. For a long while he sat thoughtfully, writing an occasional word or sentence. Then he set it aside and drank some of his tepid coffee.

Tony couldn't remember ever being steeped in a case, really caught up in it like this one, when he'd hit a wall, a wall that stopped him cold. He thought of the case, the people, their needs, and he was usually so lost in his work, so wound up in preparation, that no one and nothing in his personal life could interfere. And here today he had yet to put a coherent paragraph down on paper. His scrawls were all doodles, and the doodles all led to one word—Sheila.

Putting his pen back in his pocket, he looked toward the ceiling with weariness. Fortunately his briefcase was bulging with facts and figures, and he knew, come the morning in court, his extensive training and unfailing memory would not let him down. He'd give his all in his final plea on behalf of his client. It was the overall picture that bothered him.

Quite simply, Sheila North dominated his mind. Sheila, his brain screamed. Sheila, his heart purred. Sheila, his body yearned. Sheila.

He didn't understand it, not any of it. Why did she keep crowding his mind, creeping in at the most unexpected moments? He should have been able to push her into some isolated corner to be dragged out when business problems were solved and leisure hours were upon him, waiting to be filled. Instead she was there, diverting his moods, stealing his concentration, seeping into his pores.

No wonder he'd never let himself get seriously involved before. This was ludicrous, this was madness, this was total loss of control. The one thing he couldn't abide. And he felt helpless to do anything about it. How did people survive this craziness? he wondered, looking around the near-empty restaurant, a popular downtown luncheon spot.

Two tables away sat a couple he studied with growing interest. The man was in his early thirties, with a stocky build and a short haircut. He looked like a high-school football coach. With his right hand he shoveled food into his mouth, hardly noticing what was on his fork, while his other hand held the sports section of the newspaper. The woman with him was about the same age, with mousy brown hair and a discontented look about her small, pinched face. She poked at her food disinterestedly, her gaze skimming about the room without curiosity. She wasn't as much annoyed at the fact that the man ignored her as resigned to it. Probably a daily occurrence in their lives. Her gold wedding band was still shiny.

With the divorce rate in the United States over fifty percent, Tony wondered how much longer she'd be wearing that lovely symbol of their spoken vows. If Sheila were here, would she, too, recognize and admit that such a poor, sad couple represented not the unusual but the commonplace? Marriage, it seemed, brought an end to romance, to that deep abiding interest in each other and, worst of all, to love. He picked up his coffee and drained it.

Sheila had tried last night after they'd made love to not let the hope show in her eyes, but he'd known what she was thinking, what she was dreaming would happen, what she was undoubtedly already planning...wedding bells. He didn't blame her. Women—and Sheila was no exception—had a strong nesting instinct. The only thing stronger was man's resisting instincts, this man's, anyway.

The fact that he cared for her he would admit, though it had caught him unaware and unprepared and had taken over his life without his permission. But marriage was an altogether different ball game. Rising to go pay the check, he wondered how long it would be before Sheila started pressing him.

"You look different, somehow," Jed said as he sprawled in the chair on the other side of Tony's desk. "I'm trying to figure out what it is."

"Worry, that's what it is," Tony semi-growled at him. "The Brewster case goes into summation tomorrow, and I have a hunch Andy better like stripes."

Jed wouldn't be diverted so easily. "Nah, that's not it. I've seen you worried countless times before. You've got a *different* look about you, a cat-that-ate-the-canary look. That's closer. A Cheshire cat-satisfied look. A...a...wait a minute! I've got it. Where's Sheila? She hasn't been in all day."

Shuffling papers, Tony frowned. "How should I know where she is? You need her for something?"

Jed's grin was wicked and knowing, his black eyes dancing with the certainty of discovery. "Yeah, to confirm my suspicions. You've fallen for her, haven't you?"

Tony's hands stilled, and a sigh of resignation escaped from deep inside him. Sixteen years he'd known Jed Blair, from their college-freshmen days. You don't lie to a friend with that kind of history between you, not even if you've lied to yourself. "Okay, so you figured it out. Probably temporary at best."

Jed snorted, pleased with his powers of detection. "Who you kidding, pal? I knew when you'd fall, it'd be hard. That lady's quality." Suddenly his dark brows drew together as his forehead creased into a frown. "You're not playing her along, I hope."

It almost sounded like a threat. Used to Jed's deep loyalties, which he only extended to a privileged few, Tony didn't flinch. "Have you ever heard me admit to seriously caring for a woman before?" he asked quietly. He watched that sink in as Jed slowly shook his head. "Then that answers your question. I care for her, but that doesn't change much. I'm rotten husband material and you know it, so don't go renting a tux."

Jed stuck an empty pipe into his mouth and clamped down on it angrily. He, too, had given up smoking, but instead of carrying around a reassuring pack of cigarettes he took his frustrations out on a smelly old pipe. "Says who? Listen, Tony, do you think good husbands are born and bred? Show me the man who whistles through life saying, 'I can hardly wait to find a sweet little thing to marry and a vine-covered cottage to stash her in so we can have a couple of fat babies with runny noses needing braces and future college tuitions so I can work my ass off for them.' Come on, man. Grow up! We were all like you once. We go down, kickin' and screamin', but *we do go down*. And you want to know why?"

It didn't matter if he did, Tony thought, because once you wound Jed up on *any* topic he was strong on there was no stopping him. Leaning forward on crossed arms, he decided to enjoy the show. "Please, tell me why."

"Because we *need* 'em, Tony." Jed thought for a fleeting moment of his Tanya, without whom life would have *no* meaning for him, and his voice became eloquent. "We need that woman more than the air we breathe."

Tony remained unconvinced. It'd been a while since he and Jed had debated this topic, and he wasn't crazy about opening it up again, but it seemed he had little choice. "The woman, yes. The forever bit, the cottage and kids, no! She'll have to take that or leave it. Her choice."

Jed stuck the pipe back in his pocket and leaned forward, zeroing in on his friend. For years he'd wanted Tony, whom he loved like a brother, to find someone who'd make him complete. He'd known it wouldn't be easy, for he knew Tony's background. But when Sheila'd come on the scene and he'd witnessed the obvious chemistry between them, he'd hoped that Tony'd finally met his match in that beautiful, feisty little lady who seemed so right for his best friend.

"Have you told her?"

"That I love her? No, she doesn't need the words. She knows I care."

Exasperated, Jed shook his head. "Tony, all women need the words. And men, too."

"But I warned her some time ago that I don't dance to a forever tune. And don't give me any shining examples like you and Tanya or her mother and father—flukes. I'm not gambling my life on a fluke. I have obligations...to the law, to my career, to myself. I'm happy with the way things are, and I'm not committing myself to any one person, no matter how much I care, because I know—*I know*—it won't last."

Tony watched Jed lean back, absorbing that, thoughtful and contemplative, dangerous.

"Okay, friend," Jed said finally. "You have obligations. Many of them self-imposed, some even selfish, but nonetheless very real obligations. You have the law, a career, your goals. Just one question, my friend." Jed stood now, the dramatic lawyer presenting his final argument. "Who nurtures you? Who's there for you when you need a shoulder for support, or someone to share a laugh or a smile, or when you long for an ear at the end of a bad day, or when you hurt, *really* hurt? Who, Tony?"

The silence was deafening as they stared at each other, each in turmoil. Then a voice from the open doorway shattered the mood.

"Hey, guys, is this private or can anyone join in?" Sheila's bright voice interrupted.

Recovering first, Jed moved to greet her. "Sheila, you're looking particularly scrumptious today. Come on in."

Looking from Jed's welcoming face to Tony's frown, she walked slowly toward them, feeling the sudden need for caution. What had they been discussing that made the air thick with tension? she wondered.

"Yes, Sheila," Tony said, shaking off the effects of the previous conversation and putting on a smile, "come tell us how your visit with Kim Tremaine went."

Hands in the pockets of her yellow shirtwaist dress, Sheila sat down opposite Tony while Jed took the chair next to her. "I've just come from the D.A.'s office. I believe by this time tomorrow Jimmy Lee will be a free man."

"I'll be damned!" Jed said, whistling softly. Sheila had kept him updated on the case's progress, but he'd voiced serious doubts that Jimmy Lee would win over the Tremaines.

"Atta girl," Tony told her, his pride evident.

Crossing her legs, Sheila sat back and shook her head. "I'd love to take the credit, but I can't. We moved for a dismissal because the plaintiff has seen the light and is withdrawing the charges due to new evidence."

"Which is?" Jed asked.

"Jimmy Lee was telling the truth all along. Kim loves him and went willingly with him. They drove for hours, looking for a justice of the peace who'd marry them. The first one they found was out of town, according to his wife. The second told them they needed a blood test first. So they pulled off the side of the road to get some sleep, thinking they'd get the blood test first thing in the morning and go back."

"Only the state police found them first," Tony finished for her.

"Yes, because, as we'd suspected, her roommate, Sara Hendrix, had called her father and alerted him. So old J.D. used his impressive pull and had everyone except the marines looking for them."

Jed stuck his pipe in the corner of his mouth and played with it. "I still don't understand. Why did she go along with her father's accusations?"

Brushing her hair from her face, Sheila's eyes narrowed. "Mr. Tremaine told her that if she wouldn't back up his every word he'd pull strings and get Jimmy Lee put behind bars for life. But if she did as he said and agreed never to see the boy again, he'd make a deal with the prosecutor and get Jimmy Lee off on probation. Well, we all know Alan Sherman, the prosecutor assigned to the case, is far from perfect, but stupid he's not. Nor dishonest. There were no deals, made or hinted at. Mr. Tremaine was lying to his daughter, and if she'd have stuck to her story and perjured herself, Jimmy Lee most likely would have been convicted because our case was weak."

"Did that girl honestly believe her father had the prosecutor's office in his pocket?" Tony asked.

Nodding, Sheila answered him. "Yes, of course she did. You have to realize Kim's barely eighteen, the only child of a very wealthy and powerful man. And he'd been wielding power over her all her life. He had no trouble convincing her he'd do exactly that, see her boyfriend behind bars rather than married to his darling girl."

Tony couldn't resist a smile. The boy had gotten off because the charges had been dropped, and she was as pleased for him as if she'd fought tooth and nail for Jimmy Lee's freedom in a long courtroom trial. It was people who mattered to Sheila, with justice the end result. She'd never compromise her ideals, in law or in life. She was a woman you could trust and believe, one who'd keep even promises she made to herself. He wished he hadn't stopped believing in promises years ago. "All right, Sheila," he said finally. "Tell us. Why'd Kim change her mind?"

Sheila's smile was tinged with sadness. "It seems the night she and Jimmy Lee pulled over on the side of the road, they didn't go right to sleep. Last week Kim discovered that she's pregnant."

"Oh, no," Jed said.

"So that's why she'd been trying to reach Jimmy Lee through his brother and at the prison," Tony added.

"Yes, and frankly I think, in this case, it's the best thing that could have happened. It took a lot of guts for Kim to call me, to decide to go against her father's wishes. She realized that she wanted their baby, wanted to quit college and marry Jimmy Lee, and that gave her the courage to stand up to her father."

"And you've already informed Alan Sherman?" Tony wanted to know.

"I took Kim right over to his office, and she told him the whole story. Of course, Alan explained that there was no way her father had made a deal with him, verifying that her father was again trying to manipulate her. Alan called J. D. Tremaine and told him to meet him at his office, so I left Kim with him."

Sheila shook her head sadly. "Kim still has a tough row to hoe, but she'll have Jimmy Lee by her side. Of course, her father will probably always be a problem for them. Men like J. D. Tremaine, they just can't keep from meddling in their children's lives. He was willing to send a young, innocent boy to prison for God knows how long just to get him away from his daughter. He's a real cobra."

Suddenly Sheila was reminded that Tony had first labeled Tremaine a cobra and that the senator was of a similar nature. Quickly she glanced at him and was relieved when he gave her an understanding nod. He'd caught it, too, but was letting her know it was all right.

"So it looks like you'll have a dismissal, right, Sheila?" Jed asked. "That's the second case lately that's practically solved itself for you. That's no way to pay the bills, lady."

"Perhaps not, Jed, but I was really worried on this one. I had a gut feeling about Jimmy Lee's innocence and yet I had nothing but a few strong character witnesses to put on the stand against Tremaine's money, reputation and clout.''

"I'm glad it worked out, for Jimmy Lee and you," Tony told her.

"Me, too. And I called Sophie, Jimmy Lee's mother. She's ecstatic." She nodded, satisfied. "So it was worth it. Maybe I'll make money on the next one."

"Good attitude, babe," Jed said, getting to his feet and checking his watch. "Got to run. I promised Tanya I'd eat dinner home at least once a week." He grinned boyishly. "The woman can't stand to be without me. See you tomorrow, and congratulations on your client getting out." He swung his dark gaze to Tony as he made his way to the door. "And you think over what we talked about, okay?"

"I will," Tony said with a wave.

"Hey, you two, how about dinner at our house one day next week?" Jed asked, his hand on the knob.

"Sounds good," Tony said.

"Sure," Sheila agreed.

As Jed left, Tony rubbed a hand across his gritty eyes and raised them to look at Sheila. "How do you manage to look so damn good this late in the day, when I know you didn't have much sleep last night?"

He looked a little tired, she thought. A little tired and a little worried. She smiled tenderly at him. "And whose fault was that?"

That brought a slow grin to his face. "I hope you don't think I'm going to apologize for it."

"I certainly don't expect you to. Besides, I remember being a willing and active participant in those midnight diversions."

"Mmm, I remember that, too."

"You look a little beat, Tony. Is anything wrong?"

He sighed and tapped his pen on the open file on his desk. "Well, you're getting a dismissal and I'm probably going to get a conviction. We go into summations tomorrow, and I've got this niggling feeling that Andy Brewster hasn't told me all he knows.''

''Is there anything more you can do?''

Shaking his head, he got up and stretched. ''Not that I can think of. I sure hate to disappoint his wife. She's some lady, sticking by his side through thick and thin, never wavering in her faith in him.''

''Isn't that the way it's supposed to be, for better or worse?''

Tony didn't feel like having another discussion on the merits of marriage right now. He'd had about enough for one day. He moved to her, glancing at the closed door. ''Come here.'' He pulled her up into his arms, close up against him. ''I've been thinking about this all day.'' He kissed her long and lazily and thoroughly. ''Mmm, how is it possible? Away from you a mere six hours, and I missed you.''

Her breath mingling with his, she smiled. ''Me, too.'' She leaned in for another quick kiss. ''But I'll go home now and let you finish writing your summation. Besides, I have to get up early. I want to be there tomorrow morning when they release Jimmy Lee.'' She reached up to touch his face lingeringly. ''Don't stay too long. You could use some rest.''

''I won't.'' He kissed her again, then loosened his hold on her. ''You taste so good. It draws me back again and again, that special taste.''

''I hope you *always* feel like that,'' Sheila said, smiling at him as she scooted toward the door.

Slowly Tony walked around and sat down heavily at his desk. There was that word—always. She's already thinking always. Taking a deep breath, he picked up his pen and started rereading his notes.

Seated in the back row of the courtroom, Sheila listened as Tony summarized his client's case for the attentive jury members. He looked calm and self-assured in a navy pin-striped suit, and no one seeing him would ever have thought he had the slightest doubt about Andy Brewster's innocence. He was eloquent, convincing, believable. He was the kind of man you'd want defending you if you had to be brought to trial. He was the consummate professional.

Arriving a bit early for her meeting with Alan Sherman and Jimmy Lee in the prosecutor's office, she'd stopped in to hear Tony, for she admired his style and felt she could learn from observing him. Except for his resonant voice, it was quiet in the packed courtroom, with even the earnest-faced judge leaning forward to listen. Tony's very presence seemed to command that kind of attention.

She studied him as he moved about the courtroom, tall and handsome and confident, and remembered the wild sensuality behind the steely exterior. The judge, jurors and observers saw a soft-spoken, intelligent man of the law, never guessing the primitive streak that lay beneath his deliberate disguise. But she did, and her blood warmed as she watched him.

The memory of that first time he'd made love with her burned in her mind, lightly coloring her face. She hadn't known she was capable of such passion. She'd been loved before, but never so powerfully, so deeply, with such urgency, such a feeling of rightness, such a sense of completion. She wondered if Tony honestly felt the same way.

Glancing at her watch, she knew she had to leave for her appointment. Reluctantly she slipped out the door, her thoughts of Tony putting a bounce into her steps as she hurried down the hallway.

It was dusk before Tony left his office building, locking the door behind him. After the jury'd been charged and had gone into deliberations, he'd come back and immersed himself in paperwork, a sometimes cleansing ther apy for a troubled mind. And it had worked to a degree, he decided, climbing into his Mercedes. He and Rosemary had cleared up a lot of correspondence and made some headway updating some of his open files. The secretary had left a couple of hours ago, and he hadn't seen Jed or Sheila since morning.

But the senator had been in for a while, he thought, frowning as he started the car. In and madder than hell that Sheila'd embarrassed his friend Jim Tremaine. Tony shook his head in wonder as he maneuvered down the drive and into the street. Embarrassed was the word the senator had used. Never mind that Tremaine had falsely accused an innocent person, had encouraged his own daughter to commit perjury and had bribed another young girl to spy on his daughter. Guilty wasn't a word the senator applied to his friends. He was angry that Sheila had had the unmitigated gall to *embarrass* Tremaine, as if he'd only committed a small social error and should be readily forgiven, his reasons meriting his conduct. It was pitiful.

Tony was nearly to the turnoff when he spotted a familiar purple Volkswagen parked on the side road, its top down. On impulse he pulled up behind Sheila's car and glanced toward the sandlot baseball game going on in the field across the street. She wouldn't, would she? Getting out, he shaded his eyes from the setting sun as he studied the players. Sure enough, there she was, in the midst of a dozen young boys, the oldest no more than fourteen.

Shrugging out of his suit coat and yanking off his tie, he flung them both on the car seat, closed the door and walked toward the protective mesh fence. She was playing shortstop, crouched down, eyes alert, body tense, one small hand buried in a huge leather mitt. She wore sneakers, purple slacks and a lilac jersey blouse, sleeves shoved up high on her arms. He could see her jacket hanging on the end of the fence.

His mouth twitching into a grin, Tony moved closer into the shade of a gnarled old tree. What on earth was he doing, serious and sophisticated Tony Adams, standing around a vacant lot watching this childlike woman play ball with a bunch of kids? he asked himself. This was a forever woman. A softhearted, tender, house-in-the-suburbs, kiddies-in-a-fenced-in-yard woman.

He'd have probably been better off sticking to his flashy dates, the ones who knew dinner and dancing led to bed, breakfast...and goodbye. They knew the rules, and they didn't expect promises he wasn't willing to whisper.

But not Sheila North. She didn't follow anyone's rules but her own. He'd probably be better off leaving now, walking away, forgetting her. But he knew he wouldn't. She had him hooked, and if she didn't know it already, she would soon figure it out.

Tony returned his attention to the game as a freckle-faced, redheaded boy of about twelve came up to bat to the wild applause and cheers of his teammates. Tapping the end of the bat on home plate like a pro, his mouth working on a wad of chewing gum, he acknowledged their encouragement. A runner danced on second, teasing the baseman with the possibility he might make a dash for third base. The pitcher looked to Sheila and gave her a curt nod, then picked up the signal from the catcher and threw a fastball. The redhead swung at it, the heavy bat making a whooshing sound at the miss.

"Stri-i-ike one!" called out the umpire, one of the older boys. Leaning a hand on the tree and sticking his other deep inside his pocket, Tony watched closely, enjoying the scene.

The pitcher went through his windup ceremony again and the ump decided it was ball one. The boy on the mound followed up quickly with a deceptively slow throw that had the redhead swinging before he realized he'd been had. Grimacing now, he hunkered down and waited for the next pitch.

Pulling his hat low over his eyes, the pitcher wound up slowly, then let go with a curve ball that the redhead hit straight to Sheila. Eyes on the ball, she took several quick steps backward, caught it easily for the out, then ran at full steam and tagged the runner from second who'd dared to venture toward third but wasn't fast enough.

Pandemonium broke out as the fellows realized Sheila'd gotten two players out and won their game for them. From the outfield they came rushing in to clap her on the back while the pitcher spun her around in a frantic embrace and the catcher, tossing off his face mask, ran out to join in the melee. Tony felt like cheering along with the kids, but instead stood smiling broadly as Sheila endured the good-natured backslaps and hand-pumps from her young teammates.

In the middle of the fracas, she looked up and across and saw him standing there watching her. It was foolish, Tony thought, to feel so good when she grinned and waved at him...silly and foolish and fine.

The boys begged and coaxed, wanting another game, but Sheila declined with a happy laugh, grabbed her jacket and walked slowly toward him as the boys huddled together, rechoosing sides.

"Well, well," Tony began, "aren't you the reckless one!"

She squinted up at him. "Aren't you—just a little, maybe?" she asked.

"Hardly ever anymore," he answered regretfully, slipping an arm along her shoulders as she hugged his waist. Strolling, they moved toward the cars. "Looks like you were having fun out there. Are you a regular on that team?"

"Oh, I play with them once in a while," she said, wiping her brow with a tissue from her pocket. "When you grow up with two older brothers and a tomboy of a sister, you play a lot of ball. I kind of miss that, so these guys have adopted me. The little redhead who was last up to bat cuts the grass where I live, and he talked me into joining them. They needed a shortstop.''

He leaned down to place a kiss in her hair. "You're pretty short. I guess you qualify."

She gazed up at him. "I'm not short. You're just very tall." They reached her car and stopped. Sheila patted the crumpled pack of cigarettes in his shirt pocket. "I see you've still got your security blanket handy."

Reaching down, he picked up her left hand, brought it close up between them and singled out her little finger. The nail was still chewed down and ragged. "And you're still gnawing on this?"

She nodded, looking chagrined. "I wish I could give it up. At least you've done that." She smiled up into his eyes. "I guess I'm a mess."

She was hot, sweaty and perfectly wonderful. He pulled her to him, nuzzling her soft cheek, his nose in the fragrance of her hair. "A very lovely mess," he said, realizing again how very much she'd come to mean to him. "Jimmy Lee and Sophie out celebrating tonight with Kim?"

"Probably. They're pretty happy. And your Brewster jury's still out?"

"Yup. How would this messy little ball player like to share a cool shower and a bucket of chicken with this weary old attorney while we wait for them to call me?"

She cocked her head, considering. He moved his mouth to her ear and whispered something outrageously risqué. Leaning back, he saw her eyes widen in shock, then soften in response. She looked as if his bold suggestion was delightfully appealing.

Standing on tiptoe, she spoke softly into his neck. "Can we hold the chicken an hour or two?"

Chapter Ten

Well, Sheila," Rosemary said, "no one can say you waste your time on the easy ones. This new Davis case looks like a whole Pandora's box of problems."

"It does at that," Sheila answered, sitting down at her desk. They'd just come up from the downstairs conference room, where Sheila had asked Rosemary to take notes as she talked with Dottie and Ed Davis. During the last few weeks, as her workload had increased, she'd found the sharp, efficient secretary invaluable in aiding her. She also felt very good about the mutual respect and the genuine friendship forming between the two of them.

"If the case goes to trial," Rosemary went on, taking a seat opposite Sheila, "I don't know how the jury could help but be moved by a plaintiff who rolls into court in a wheelchair. He had my sympathy from the start."

"Mmm, I know," Sheila mused. "But there are a lot of unanswered questions, such as, was Ed Davis careless, thereby contributing to his own accident? Was the crane operator negligent? Or did the equipment malfunction?"

"But look how reluctant Mr. Davis was in even coming to you for help. The accident was months ago, and only now has his wife been able to persuade him to seek legal advice to see if they have a case."

Rosemary had a point, Sheila thought, leaning back to gaze out her window at the late-afternoon sun pouring its July heat relentlessly downward. Ed Davis came across as a quiet man, a man of simple tastes, honest and diligent. Except there was an underlying bitterness to his words, which, if his story checked out, was understandable.

A construction worker with over twenty years' experience, he'd been working on a downtown site where a large office building would go up. In the early stages of clearing ground, the operator of a large crane had dumped a huge load of dirt and debris off target, hitting two workers. The one man had been only mildly injured, but Ed had been trapped in such a way as to paralyze him from the waist down for life.

Tompkins Construction employed the crane operator and claimed that the two workers were in an area clearly marked as off limits and were hit due to their own carelessness. Ed's version differed radically. He insisted that the demolition operator lost control, zigzagged in its path, swayed many feet from the dumping ground and hit them in a so-called safe zone. Unfortunately the other worker had had his back to the machine and hadn't seen it coming. There'd been no other witnesses.

The company officials held firm in their beliefs, and the insurance company had a standard fellow-employee exclusion clause that disallowed payoffs due to on-the-job worker carelessness. Caught between a rock and a hard place, Dottie Davis told Sheila she'd been at the end of her rope when she'd come to her seeking legal assistance. Sheila found Dottie's impassioned pleas moving, but after some seven weeks of being in her own practice she was more cautious in forming her opinions.

"Mrs. Davis certainly feels they have a case," Sheila said. "But is she so adamant because of sudden financial need or because she really believes her husband was in the right? I probably sound a shade cynical saying that, but the thought crossed my mind."

Rosemary nodded. "Mine, too. And Ed said that Tompkins Construction has offered him a desk job, but he refused it. What do you make of that?"

Sheila toyed with her pen, her eyes on the file open in front of her. "Pride, maybe. A rugged man who's worked outdoors all his life and who doesn't feel he could adjust to a desk job and to paperwork. Or..."

"Or someone who thinks if he got a large settlement he wouldn't have to ever work again," Rosemary finished for her.

Glancing up, Sheila smiled. "You're getting as cynical as I am."

"Honey, when you've been involved with the law as long as I have, and you witness firsthand some of the rotten things people are capable of doing to one another, you'll suspect your own mother's motives."

"I certainly hope not. But the fact remains, Ed Davis no longer has the use of his legs, and someone's certainly responsible for that. But who? And why'd the Davises wait so long to seek help? This case is cold, the depositions from other workers and from the mechanics who checked the bulldozer over are six months old. I don't understand."

Standing, Rosemary placed her notes on Sheila's desk. "You going to run this by Tony, see what he thinks?"

Her chin resting on her hand, Sheila looked up at the older woman. "Rosie, I really don't consult with Tony on *all* my cases."

"Oh, honey," the secretary said, quickly apologetic, "I didn't mean to imply you couldn't do it alone. Sometimes it's just nice to talk about your work with someone who understands, that's all I meant."

Sheila's smile was forgiving. "Yes, it is. But since the Brewster conviction he's busy working on that appeal. Plus there's the Thornton mess. I'd say he's got a lot to occupy his mind."

"That's true. But you both work too hard. Spending time together relaxing, even if it's discussing your cases, is good for both of you."

Leaning back and crossing her legs, Sheila fought a smile. "Listen, you matchmaker you, I see ulterior motives here."

Rosemary tried a nonchalant shrug but couldn't quite carry it off. "Well, maybe, but I can see that you two are good for each other. Tony's more relaxed lately, and he smiles easily and often. Did you know, Tuesday he came in with just a sport coat over his shirt, no tie? I'd begun to think, except when he did yard work, that he even slept in one."

Sheila joined her in a chuckle. No, she thought mischievously, he doesn't sleep in a tie. Or anything else, either. In short order he'd abandoned the pajama bottoms he'd worn when she'd first met him. "So you think I've loosened him up a little?"

"Definitely. And he's good for you, too."

"You're sounding more like Dolly Levi every minute," Sheila said with a tolerant shake of her head. "How exactly is he good for me, wise lady?"

"Being in love definitely agrees with you, my dear," Rosemary said with a smug, satisfied expression. Reaching over, she picked up Sheila's left hand, her eyes on the small finger where a short, rounded nail replaced the previous jagged edge. "I see that your nerves have improved, too," she added, grinning.

"Don't you have some typing to do?" Sheila asked, snatching back her hand. But a faint blush colored her cheeks.

The ringing of the phone saved Rosemary from having to answer. With a wave and a chuckle, she left as Sheila spoke into the receiver. Recognizing her mother's voice, she felt a spread of warmth.

"It seems I have to make an appointment these days to talk with my own daughter," Carmella North said in her soft voice.

"I have been a little busy. It's so good to hear from you, Mom."

"You don't spend much time home evenings, either. Don't the courthouses in the big city close around five, too?"

"Oh, you know how it is, the paperwork gets done after hours. How are you? And how's Dad?"

"We're both fine. We *are* going to see you this weekend, aren't we? For the anniversary get-together?"

Was that *this* weekend? Sheila thought. Of course she'd go. She'd been planning all along to make the trip up north, but time had slipped by her.

"Your father will be so disappointed if you can't make it," Carmella went on.

Sheila chuckled. Always, when either of her parents called to ask her to visit, they told her that the other one would be dreadfully upset if she couldn't find the time. She wondered if they conferred on their strategy or did it spontaneously. Nevertheless, it seldom failed to work.

"Certainly I'm coming," Sheila said, her busy mind at work. "Uh, Mom, I wonder if I could bring someone with me?" The moment the words were out, she wondered at the wisdom of her impulsive request. Would Tony want to go? Would her parents make a big thing of it?

"Of course, darling."

Her mother hesitated a fraction too long. Sheila'd been gone four years now and had never before asked to bring a friend home. Sheila knew her mother's mind was working this idea over.

"Anyone special?" she added.

Before she realized it, Sheila's little finger was caught between her teeth. Exasperated with her own weakness, she settled her hand in her lap and made herself relax. Somehow she felt like a teenager again. "His name's Tony Adams, and he's the attorney who owns the building where I rent my office. I...I think you'll like him."

"By all means, bring him along," Carmella answered "Will you be coming Friday evening or Saturday morning?"

"Probably Saturday noonish, but I'll call you before we leave. Everyone else okay?"

They talked for a few more minutes about Sheila' brothers and sister and their families, but she scarcely wa able to follow the conversation. Her thoughts were al ready on Tony, on being away with him for the whol weekend, on her old turf. Would he like her family, th chaos and confusion? Would he, who'd always lived in big city, like the quiet lakeside town? Would he even agre to go with her?

Hanging up with her mother, Sheila sighed deeply an walked over to the window. Automatically her gaze wen to the parking area, and she saw that Tony's car wasn't there yet. He'd been working hard lately. Losing the Brewster decision had been a real blow to him, despite the fact that he still wasn't convinced of his client's innocence. The Thornton heirs were coming out of the woodwork, each nastier than the last. And his father'd been pressuring him to team up with him on several cases that Tony'd so far resisted. Yes, he could definitely use a weekend away. Perhaps they could wait to return on Monday, drive leisurely homeward, just be together. The thought certainly held a lot of appeal to her. Now if only Tony would feel the same.

Her eye caught a movement, and she saw Jed hurrying to his car. Glancing up, he gave her a quick wave, that she returned with a big smile. Since moving into her office, she'd come to know Jed even more and to like him even better. And his wife, Tanya, was every bit as nice. Just last week, she and Tony had spent a very pleasant evening with them and their two-year-old son, Matthew, at their home in suburban Grosse Pointe Woods. Relaxed and genuinely enjoying himself, Tony had taken their chubby little towhead on innumerable piggyback rides all over their spacious backyard while Jed had stoked the barbecue.

Over grilled steaks, corn on the cob and chilled wine, they'd talked and laughed and enjoyed. Sheila smiled, remembering the look of love on Jed's face as he'd hugged his wife to his side and spoke of their second child, due in two months. You see, Tony, she thought, shaking her head at his obtuseness, there *are* happy marriages, people truly in love. You just have to look around you. Did he honestly not see, or did he not *want* to see?

Returning to her desk, Sheila closed the Davis file and slipped it into her briefcase. She'd promised herself, when she'd first realized she loved Tony, that she'd go slowly with him, give him time to learn to care. She believed he did care, more each day. Now she needed to give him time to trust his feelings, to learn to believe that they could have a good life together. Snapping her case closed, Sheila sighed again. She was definitely not cut out for the waiting game.

She'd gotten past the infatuations of her youth, worked her way past a few meaningful relationships in her early twenties, but she'd never been in love before. But when she'd finally fallen, she'd fallen like the proverbial ton of bricks. She loved Tony Adams deeply, thoroughly, lastingly. Yes, she'd wait for him to come around. She had little choice in the matter.

Leaving her office and moving down the stairs, she headed for Tony's desk. It was already past six, and the building was deserted, but she knew that Tony always came back here, even after a long day in court, before going home. Humming, she scribbled a quick note, stuck it into an envelope and left it propped on his desk where he couldn't miss it.

On her way to her car, Sheila smiled. Though she'd decided to wait for Tony to make the next move, she'd also decided that reluctant lovers sometimes needed a little nudge.

He was hot, weary and feeling the beginnings of a headache. Loosening his tie, Tony let himself into his office and dropped his briefcase beside his desk. Rubbing the tension from the back of his neck, he wished he had a tall cold drink. Preferably a vodka and tonic with a huge chunk of lime, lots of cubes. He'd built a small bar behind cabinet doors across the room, but he didn't feel like sitting and drinking alone. Besides, he had the mail to read and some notes to go over and . . .

He recognized the handwriting on the pale blue envelope propped on his ashtray in the center of his desk. Quickly he tore it open. His face moved into a grin as he read what Sheila had written:

I'm waiting for you...
unarmed...
uninhibited...
undressed.

He no longer felt the heat of his fatigue. The headache had disappeared, too. Grabbing his keys, he decided all he felt was impatient...to be with Sheila.

In less than twenty minutes, minus coat and tie, he was bounding up the stairs to her carriage-house apartment, definitely ready to put the people and problems of his workday world on the back burner. Tonight he wanted to be just a man, a man coming to visit the woman he cared about.

At his ring, Sheila opened the door wearing a green satin robe, her special scent and a seductive smile. "What took you so long?" she asked, her voice husky.

Tony leaned against the doorframe as his deep gray eyes slowly traveled down and then up the length of her, admiring the way the soft fabric hugged her curves. "You lied to me," he said at last, his eyes meeting hers.

"Did I? How so?"

From behind his back, he whipped out her note. "It says here 'undressed.'"

Reaching down, she flashed open the folds of her robe, momentarily exposing a length of leg and thigh that clearly indicated she wore nothing underneath. Rewrapping and belting herself more tightly, she pulled him inside. "I thought you'd never get here," she whispered. Without further delay, she molded to him and offered her mouth.

He took, tasted and gloried in her. The kiss was long, deep and thoroughly enjoyable. Tony moved to bury his face in her hair, his hands sliding down her satiny back. He opened his eyes and saw dim lights, a bottle of wine chilling, snacks waiting. He pulled back to look at her.

"If I didn't know better, I'd say this looks like a seduction scene," he said.

She winked at him flirtatiously. "You always were bright."

Releasing her, he strolled to the coffee table. Caviar, chopped eggs and onions on crackers. A bowl of chilled shrimp with sauce. He popped one in his mouth and chewed appreciatively. "The good stuff, I see. The lady's pulled out all the stops." Examining the wine label, he smiled. "A good year. Plan to muddle my mind with alcohol, do you? Weaken my resistance?"

She moved to him, running her fingers along the buttons of his shirtfront, undoing as she went. "What resistance?" she asked as she felt his heartbeat escalate. He still carried the rumpled package of cigarettes. Would he ever have the confidence to let go of his crutch? she wondered.

"I know I had some resistance when I came in here," he answered as her busy fingers moved inside his shirt. The friction of her hands slowly rubbing and tangling in the hair of his chest spread heat swiftly everywhere she touched. He sucked in a heavy breath. "Then again, maybe I'll have to plead no contest."

Sheila moved closer, her lips placing a long, lingering kiss on the pulse throbbing in his throat. "It's a wise attorney who knows when the cards are stacked against him." She was hungry for him, her blood already heating, but she wanted to draw it out, to assume the unfamiliar role of seductress.

His arms slid around her and tightened as he tried to lower them both to the couch, but she resisted his efforts and slipped from his grasp. "Why don't you open the wine, and I'll get the glasses?"

Sighing his momentary defeat, Tony sat down and unwrapped the cork. He didn't know what game she was playing, but he was thoroughly enjoying it. "You really think we need a drink? I feel a little light-headed already." With hands that weren't quite steady, he removed the cork.

Returning with the glasses, she sat next to him and held them out as he poured. "I thought wine would relax you after a hard day, make you amenable to any and all suggestions."

Setting down the bottle, he turned toward her, his smile wicked. "Never let it be said I don't take suggestions well. What'd you have in mind?"

"You'll see." Smiling into his eyes, she clinked her glass against his and took a sip. Cool, tart and bubbly. Exactly the way she felt. She set their glasses on the table as his arm stretched out along the back of the couch. A light shiver raced down her spine as the backs of his fingers traced a gentle path along her cheek. Reaching up, she touched his forehead. "For starters, I'd like to remove these frown lines before they become permanent, take away the tension that put them there."

"Mmm, I think you're pretty good at relieving my tensions."

"One step at a time, counselor. Turn around and let me work a little magic on your neck and shoulders."

How could her hands be both gentle and strong at the same time? Tony wondered. She kneaded the tensely bunched muscles and cords, and he felt himself almost purring like Emma, who'd come to nestle alongside him. Reaching to take another long sip of wine, he let his head hang loose as Sheila continued her ministrations, an occasional grunt of satisfaction escaping his lips.

He was relaxing, inch by inch, Sheila thought. No time like the present to plunge right in. "I was wondering how you'd feel about a short trip. My folks are celebrating their fortieth wedding anniversary. I'm driving up for the weekend."

His voice was low and lazy. "Are you asking me to go with you?"

"Yes."

"When do we leave?"

Sheila released a nervous breath. She hadn't realized how much she'd wanted Tony to go with her until just that moment. "Early Saturday morning."

"Another weekend morning of sleep you're going to rob me of." He'd felt the change in her hands on his flesh, had sensed her tension, followed by her pleasure at his acceptance. So she wanted to take him home to her family. He'd jumped at her invitation, the thought of several days away with her holding much appeal. The family was another matter.

Was it their approval she was seeking? he wondered. The very thought brought hints of possible permanency into their relationship. He'd known she'd get around to this one day. He felt the trap closing in on him, with no easy answers available. He didn't want to lose Sheila, yet he didn't want marriage and all it signified. What was the solution he asked himself.

Emma curled up more comfortably in his lap and stretched her neck up to meet his touch. Tony stroked the cat lazily, shifting his eyes to the table where the goldfish was still surprisingly alive and well in his bowl. "Who's going to watch your menagerie while you're gone?"

"Emma will take care of Jonah," Sheila answered with maddening certainty.

"I can't believe Emma hasn't feasted on Jonah yet," he murmured, her hands making him drowsy.

"Emma's of sterling character. She's Jonah's protector, not his enemy."

Her fingers were up in his hair now, and suddenly he felt his body begin to awaken. "I'm impressed with your persuasive abilities. Just how did you manage to get this sense of responsibility across to Emma?"

The freedom to touch him as she wished was deeply pleasurable but was exacting its toll from her, Sheila decided as she felt a racing warmth flood through her. Touching a little made her want to touch more. But she'd promised herself she'd go slowly tonight. With a shuddering breath she brought her mind back to their conversation.

"I told her Jonah was vulnerable, that he needed her and trusted her so she couldn't possibly betray that trust by chewing on his fins. And I promised her all the tuna she could eat if she'd keep her paws out of the fishbowl."

He made his voice register shock. "Bribery? You?"

Slowly she wound her arms about him, her breasts, already fuller, rubbing against him through the thin material of his shirt. "Sure. Anything it takes."

The first taste of desire whipped through him like a stormy wind as he turned around to face her, his eyes darkening. "Anything?"

She nodded. "Within reason."

"Since I've met you I seem to have abandoned reason."

"Good. I think too much reason can cloud your thinking."

He stared at her, this beautiful, fascinating woman, this astoundingly captivating female who had him trapped in her emotional net as surely as Jonah was trapped in his bowl. He hadn't known she could do that to him, that any woman could. But she wasn't just any woman. She was Sheila, his woman.

With a soft moan he pulled her to him, closing his eyes, burying his face in the fragrance of her thick hair. He felt weak, lost. "Lady, you have me totally imprisoned against my will. Even a writ of habeas corpus won't get me out of this one."

Sheila pulled back from him to bring her gold-flecked gaze up to meet his eyes. "Against your will?"

"Once upon a time it was. I plead guilty on that one. But somewhere along the way, things changed. Why is it I didn't see it coming?"

"Maybe you didn't want to see. But I did, almost from the start." She brought her hands up to lovingly frame his face, her eyes dark and heavy with growing desire. "I saw a beautiful man—" she dragged one hand through his hair "—with curly hair that wouldn't stay put." Her finger brushed past his eyes. "And mysterious silver eyes that told more about what he was thinking than his mouth." She smiled and dropped her gaze to his lips, tracing the fullness with her thumb. "And such a mouth. The first time you kissed me, I was lost. Hours, days later, when I thought of that kiss, I still trembled. I'd never tasted excitement like that before."

Her words had mesmerized him and chased away his control. Almost roughly he pulled her to him, his mouth covering hers in a kiss savage with need.

For a long moment she teased him by responding, then pulled away to stand and pick up her glass. No, there would be no quick satisfaction or even lazy loving tonight. Tonight she wanted to make him feel, to make him need, to make him desperate for her. Chest heaving, she drained her wineglass and held it out for more. "Don't let's let this go to waste. Have some more."

It wasn't wine he wanted more of. With shaky hands he filled her glass and topped off his own. Willing himself to slow down, he took a long drink. Unused to cat-and-mouse games, he was beginning to lose patience. "If you wanted to untense me, it's not working."

"Sometimes tension can be useful," Sheila answered with a low laugh, a little giddy from the quick rush of wine and her newfound power over him. Moving to sit again beside him, but not too close, her hands went to his shirt buttons, freeing the rest. She felt the thud of his heart under her fingertips. "So strong," she whispered, her eyes on the hard cord of chest muscles. Easing his shirt from him, she ran shaky hands along his shoulders. "Yet often so very gentle. An exciting combination, strength and gentleness. Irresistible."

Almost trembling as he tried to hold on to his control, Tony kept his eyes steady on hers, unwilling to let her see too much, yet unable to hide his need for her. "Do you find me irresistible, Sheila?" he asked, his hands skimming the folds of her robe at the neckline. Sliding slowly lower, he let the backs of his fingers linger over the soft swell of her breasts, feel the fullness, the hardening tips reaching out for his touch.

"Yes." She swayed closer, her eyes growing heavy. "Oh, yes."

"I have a simple solution for that," he said, pulling her to her feet, then lowering them both into the plush softness of the carpet. "Stop resisting." His patience gone, his hunger unreasonable, he claimed her mouth to still any further protests as his rushing hands rid himself of the rest of his clothes. Finished, he pulled her into a hard embrace, tightening his arms about her, plunging his tongue into the warmth of her welcoming mouth.

No longer fighting him or herself, her head swimming, Sheila returned his kiss avidly. Passion played with her, an old friend now, one that Tony brought forth from her so effortlessly. He eased her gown from her, but she never felt the chill of loss. His hot hands seemed everywhere at once, followed closely by his greedy mouth. She closed her mind and just let herself feel as he sprinkled tiny love bites in a downward journey, leading them both halfway to madness. She was incredibly aroused, and her head thrashed as a torrent of heat spread up her body from his touch.

He found places to pleasure her that she hadn't known existed, his mouth and tongue and hands taking her past reason, her body moving with him and against him, with a mind of its own. Again she moaned his name as his intimate invasion catapulted her into a world of dark, pulsing desire.

So beautiful, she was so beautiful, Tony thought as he moved up to gaze at her flushed cheeks, her hair damp around her face, her eyes filled with sensual satisfaction. She'd teased and taunted and had her way, and now he would have his as his own needs could no longer be stilled. Thrusting into her, he felt her sigh a welcome as she closed around him, her arms pulling him to her. Head spinning, his mind filled with her scent and flavors, he drove them both at a terrifying speed, higher and faster than anything that had gone before. He felt her gasp into his mouth just before he lost control and brought them both to a shuddering finish.

How long he lay atop her and inside her, Tony was uncertain. Perhaps only moments, perhaps many minutes. The haze from his mind lifted slowly, his face buried in the warmth of her neck, her arms resting lightly about him. He could feel lingering flickers of passion filter to him from deep within her. Impossible that in all his experiences he'd never reached such heights before. Impossible to believe this small, fragile woman could shatter him so...impossible.

He made as if to ease his weight from her, but her small hands tightened at his back. "Don't move away, please, not yet. It feels so good, and I don't want it to end."

She wasn't a bit afraid to be honest. She humbled him. Lifting his head, he eased up so he could look at her. Her eyes were shiny, her fair skin pink with the residue of passion. Gently he brushed the damp hair from her face and smiled into her eyes. The look held and deepened. He saw so much there. Dare he believe it? Tony wondered.

Trapped. He was trapped, lost inside her warm brown eyes. He knew suddenly that there'd be no escaping it. Did he even want to?

Sheila hardly dared breathe as she saw the smile leave his face. He stared at her, looking for something, needing to find more. Not knowing exactly how to help him, she let all the love she felt for him shine from her eyes. And she waited.

"I love you," he said finally. Trembling, his mouth claimed hers desperately, his eyes tightly shut.

Stunned, she returned his kiss as tears slid from beneath her closed lids. Oh, God, had she heard right? Easing back from her, she saw a slow smile form on his face.

"Surprised you again, didn't I?" he asked, his voice stronger now.

"Oh, yes. Yes, you surely did." A million questions bubbled inside her, but an irrational fear kept her silent for a change.

"You made me do it, you know."

She took a deep breath, trying to steady her world. "Made you do what?"

"Made me fall in love with you. I didn't want to, and I'm still not sure it's best. But I close my eyes and you're there. I open them and I wish you were there. I go somewhere alone and I wish you were with me. I see something beautiful or funny and I wish I could share it with you. It drives me crazy, yet nothing else has changed. I could still hurt you—"

"Shhh," she whispered, shaking her head. "I don't want to hear all that right now. I'll take my chances."

He smiled down at her, a look of wonder on his face. "Sheila, Sheila. Other women I've known—"

Quickly she put a finger to his lips. "I *certainly* don't want to hear about other women you've known right now."

Kissing her finger, he curled her hand in his. "I think you might want to hear this. Other women I've known were never quite right, never enough. I never wanted to spend so much time with them, to listen to them, to watch them smile, to take them home with me or wake up beside them the next morning. They didn't make me laugh at myself or put me at ease or keep me up nights thinking about them. They simply weren't you." He watched another tear track down her soft cheek. "Why are you crying?"

"Say it again, please."

His mouth was whisper-close. "I love you, Sheila, and it scares the hell out of me."

"I've never loved before, either. Don't you think I'm scared?" she asked, touching his face, enjoying the scratchy growth she found on his chin. Deep inside her, she felt him grow and move. She smiled at him, knowing he felt it, too.

"Here we are, on the floor again," Tony said. "I move for a change of venue. How about shifting to the bed?"

Sheila shook her head. "I don't care *where*, I just care with whom. The first day I met you, I remember thinking that still waters ran deep inside you. I was *so* right."

Responding to the first tug of desire, he began to move, aware of her body reawakening. "Are you sorry?"

"No. Infinitely grateful." She pulled his head down to meet her kiss.

Chapter Eleven

I always thought a man who drove a Mercedes was dignified, aloof and a bit of a bore," Sheila said as the plush red car hummed along the highway on Saturday morning, heading toward her parents' home.

"Did you?" Tony asked, tossing her a quick sideways glance. "And now that you've spent two hours watching me drive one, do you still feel that way?"

Angling around in her seat toward him, she considered the question. "Dignified? I don't think you're old enough for that one. Aloof? Hardly ever, except maybe in the courtroom. A bore? Never. You see, you're definitely not the Mercedes type."

The early-morning sun reflected off the hood as Tony repositioned the air-conditioning vents to more fully cool them. They'd started off at eight, stopped for a leisurely breakfast about nine and planned to reach the Tawas house before noon, filling the pleasant hours in between with the easy conversation they never seemed to run short of. Tony felt the week's tensions already melting away. He found his eyes drifting over to the person who was the major reason for his relaxed mood, and a smile formed on his face unconsciously.

"So what type am I, then?" he asked, his gaze skimming over her cotton slacks and matching top. He loved her in kelly green. Actually, he hadn't found a color he didn't love her in. Perhaps that was because he loved her. And if that knowledge had surprised her, it still had him stunned. "A Maserati, you think? Or maybe a BMW?"

She shook her head. "No, both too stuffy." She reached to trail her fingers across the red-and-white rugby shirt he wore along with white denims. She'd recently gifted him with the shirt and been pleased when he'd shown up this morning wearing it. Wrinkling her brow thoughtfully, she suddenly smiled. "I've got it. A Corvette Stingray, older model, lovingly preserved, lightly souped up. Perfect!"

"So that's how you see me—interesting. And, should I ever run across such a find, what color do you prefer, madam?"

"Mmm, sunshine yellow, I think. To bring out the gold highlights in your hair."

"I had no idea one was supposed to match one's car to one's hair," he said with a teasing smile. "You're a font of trivia, counselor. Let's see now, you've updated my wardrobe, enticed me into street dancing and public necking and suggested my car choices are a bit stodgy. Anything else you want to change about me?"

You bet there is, Sheila thought. Like a wedding band on the third finger, left hand. But she didn't think he was ready to hear it just yet! Reaching over to kiss his cheek, she shifted and moved to his ear, her warm tongue sliding inside and sending an obvious message to his brain. "Everything else about you is absolutely perfect," she whispered.

His hand tightening on the wheel as he fought a sensual reaction, Tony reached to scoot her closer to him. "Come over here, but behave unless you want me to stop this dignified car and ravish you by the side of the road."

"Not a bad thought. I've never been ravished in a Mercedes."

"I think you'd find it more comfortable than a Corvette. That stick shift can be hazardous."

Snuggling close, she rested her hand on his warm thigh, enjoying the feel of his powerful muscles under her fingers. "It sounds as though you're speaking from experience. Maneuvered around a few stick shifts in your shady past, have you?"

"A few. I haven't *always* driven a Mercedes." He felt her fingers lightly caressing, the effect making him shift uncomfortably. "Lady, we'd better change the subject or we won't make it there before nightfall. Why don't you tell me a little about your family so I'll be somewhat prepared?"

"Whatever you say. I've already told you about my father. A wonderful man, but then I'm slightly prejudiced."

"Yes, he builds houses."

"Now he does. He started out as a bricklayer. I hope you'll be suitably impressed with the house. He built it, literally brick by brick."

"As a man who works hard just to hammer a nail in straight, I'm impressed already, and I haven't even seen the building yet."

"Oh, it's a wonderful house. It's trimmed in white wood, and all of the windows have these great shutters that Dad built by hand—he dabbles in carpentry, too—and a red roof. It sits on kind of a hill, and the lawn slopes down to the lake where there's a long dock for fishing and swimming and anchoring small boats. There're several weeping willows planted along the shoreline. There are six bedrooms and an enormous den with a Michigan field-stone fireplace, naturally. My mother's kitchen is huge, but it's the coziest room in the house.''

Tony heard the love in her voice more than the words she was saying. He wondered if he'd find her family as accepting as she did. He wondered, too, how many men she'd taken home for inspection and how he'd stack up against them. "Your mother spends a lot of time in the kitchen?" he asked, trying to remember the last time his own mother had fixed him a meal. The memory wouldn't surface.

"Oh, my, yes. And not just Italian cooking. My mother has magic hands when it comes to food. I imagine she's in there right now, baking and stirring up a storm.''

"Unlike her daughter, who's never cooked me a meal yet,'' he teased, speeding up as he passed a camper wheezing uphill in the right lane.

"I've tried, but every time you come over for dinner we get sidetracked and forget to eat," she told him pointedly.

"Mmm, and such nice sidetracking," he replied, covering her hand on his leg with his own. "Does the rest of your family live close by?''

"All within a radius of ten miles. My sister Mandy—I think I mentioned she's a nurse—is married to Jim, who sells insurance, and they have three children. My brother Louis is the oldest, and his wife Gina is really neat. They were high-school sweethearts, and now Louis works in my father's company. They have two children and they're expecting another one around Christmas. Then there's Angelo, who's two years older than me and a terrible tease. He's got a law practice in town and his wife's name is Nancy. They've been married six years and already have our children.''

Tony sighed and rolled his eyes. "Nine nephews and nieces. Don't they have television in Tawas or some other form of recreation?''

Sheila laughed. "Nine and a half. My family likes children."

"That's safe to say. I'll never remember all their names."

She hugged his arm to her. "Sure you will. They're all distinct individuals, you'll see. And I'll help you." She turned to look at him. "Are you worried about meeting them?"

"Nah, piece of cake." Only would it be? Tony asked himself. Another difference between them—children. He wasn't used to being around children, much less nine at a time. He liked children, but it was one thing to spend an evening playing with Jed and Tanya's son and quite another to spend a weekend with nine unfamiliar children in an unfamiliar setting.

Despite her relocation to a big city, Sheila was small-town through and through, whereas he was urban sophistication and hustle and bustle. You could be alone in the crowds, if you so chose. You could disappear or party every night. Or lose yourself in your work. You could be safe, secluded, anonymous. Tony preferred it that way. Where did a wife, kiddies and a picket fence fit in with his life-style? It didn't.

Raised amid broken dreams, a multitude of hypocrisies and shattered illusions, he wanted no part of a permanent relationship that could possibly turn out badly. Yet he wanted Sheila. How could he reconcile those two disparate desires? Tony wondered, frowning.

He'd been quiet too long, Sheila thought. Was he regretting his decision to accompany her? Was he fearful her family would overwhelm him, perhaps make demands on him? Or was he simply not secure enough in his feelings for her to want to go public with them? Perhaps she could lighten the mood. She squeezed his arm. "Do you want me to pin name tags on everyone so you won't get confused?"

She'd thought he'd smile, but he didn't. Instead he maneuvered the car off onto the right-hand shoulder and shifted into park. Swiftly he gathered her to him and lowered his lips to hers. His mouth was hard on hers, without patience, as if his need for her angered him.

The predator in him frightened her momentarily while it excited her inexplicably. But, as always, the tenderness she sensed underneath his harsh demand drew her with a certainty that rocked her. He seemed to be fighting demons inside himself she couldn't begin to identify. Seeking to soothe the turbulence in him, she ran a hand up past his collar to rub the nape of his neck, her fingers moving to tangle in his thick hair. Instantly he gentled, his mouth softening on hers, lingering there, kissing away the confusion.

Slowly he lifted his head to look at her, his eyes warm again. "Thank you, Sheily. I needed that. Sometimes I forget."

She caressed his cheek, wanting to understand. "Forget what?"

"Forget that others aren't important, not your family or mine. What's important is you and me and what we feel for each other."

Was he trying to convince her or himself? Sheila wondered. "Yes, it is. Don't ever forget it again."

He returned to her lips, needing her kiss, as if it were a lifeline. It was true: He didn't want the tags that went along with Sheila North—marriage, commitment, forever. Not because he didn't believe in her but because he didn't believe in those things. Yet why was it that when he was with her it was increasingly difficult to remember that? Moving his tongue inside the responsive warmth of her mouth, he deepened the kiss.

Lost in each other, they didn't hear the tap on the window at first. When it became more insistent, they parted in surprise, turning toward the sound. The state police officer peered through Tony's window at them, his arm stretched out onto the roof of the car. His raised brows questioned silently.

Tony lowered the window sheepishly. "Yes, officer?" he asked, trying with difficulty to look dignified.

"Aren't you two a little old to be necking by the side of the road in broad daylight?" the gray-haired, stocky lawman asked, his gaze skimming over their nice clothes, the expensive car, and then returning to meet their embarrassed eyes.

"Uh, we were just..."

"Yes, I know what you were just doing," he answered, taking out a small pad and pen. Using the pad to point to a sign not ten feet in front of them, he took a step back. "What does that sign say, son?"

Tony cleared his throat before reading aloud. "Emergency parking only."

"Uh-huh." He looked at the two of them meaningfully. "Was it an emergency?"

Clearly uncomfortable, Tony shifted in his seat while Sheila bent her head, her hand at her mouth catching a giggle threatening to escape. Neither said a word.

The officer slapped his pad onto his open palm and gave them a broad smile. "She's mighty pretty, son. I think, given the opportunity, I'd consider it an emergency, too." He winked at them. "Have a good trip." Whistling, he turned back to his car, which was idling behind them.

Shifting into gear before the man could change his mind, Tony eased the car back onto the highway. Shaking his head at Sheila's unbridled laughter, he turned to look at her. "Think it's funny, do you? I haven't felt like that since I was sixteen."

"How do you think you'd have felt if we'd moved to the ravishing part just before he showed up?" she asked, remembering the look of shock on Tony's face at finding himself caught red-handed.

"We wouldn't have gone that far," he insisted, picking up speed. He wanted to get as much distance between him and the smilingly tolerant policeman as possible. "I have more control than that."

It was Sheila's turn to raise her brows in surprise. The opportunity was too good to pass up. Moving closer, she tugged his shirt loose and insinuated her hand inside, touching warm flesh. "Really?" she asked innocently, her fingers playfully tugging at the hair on his chest.

He squirmed away from her touch. "Sheila! Do you want me to drive into a tree?"

Reinstating her fingers, she nuzzled his cheek as well. "There aren't any trees on the highway, Tony. What were you saying about your marvelous self-control?"

Squaring his shoulders firmly despite her ministrations, he shot her a stubborn look. "I am in perfect control, so you needn't test me."

Sliding lower, her hand inched into the danger zone. "Is that a fact?" she asked sweetly as she heard him suck in a deep gulp of air. Glancing out the front window, she saw there was very little traffic on the divided highway, which was fortunate since Tony was suddenly steering somewhat crookedly. With perfect precision her hand closed over him as her mouth moved to his ear.

"Okay, okay," he gasped, quickly removing her hand and placing it firmly back on his thigh, keeping it there with his own. "You win. I guess I failed the test."

Chuckling, she eased back to snuggle against his arm. "I'd say you passed with flying colors, counselor."

"You're a maddening woman, you know that?" he asked, looking down at her with reluctant appreciation. Always, how good she made him feel. How did she know the right things to say to get him responding, laughing, feeling great? He was not an easy man, and he knew it. How did she do it?

"Is that a complaint I hear?"

"More like admiration. And love. So much love."

Her face was in his neck, her lips on his throat. "Oh, counselor. Your arguments are eloquent, no question about it."

"Are you sure we have to go to your parents' today? How about I find us a nice country inn and we—"

Pulling back, she laughed lightly. "And disappoint those two nice people? We can't. But there are all those bedrooms just waiting to be filled. I'm sure we can work something out."

"In the home of your childhood? Sheila, I'm shocked."

"Mmm, I'm sure." She glanced through the windshield. "The next exit's ours. Get ready, counselor. You're about to be scrutinized."

And scrutinized he was, by all the Norths and their offspring, from the oldest to the youngest, through a welcome scene and a tour of the family home. The big brick house was filled with tantalizing kitchen aromas, a cacophony of sounds, innumerable children and an assortment of bustling adults who seemed to take it all in stride.

A dark-eyed grandchild pounded "Chopsticks" out on an old piano while the ball game droned from a forgotten radio. Sheila's father and her brother, Louis, noisily hammered in place a new wooden railing on the back porch. Carmella North stuffed sugar cookies into each grateful little child's hand that passed her, over their mothers' protests, stating her spoiling rights as a grandmother. Almost immediately Angelo cornered Tony for a discussion on practicing law in a big city versus a small town. Mandy, her sister, declared Tony to be "quite a hunk" and dragged Sheila off to hear "all about him." Sheila's eyes strayed frequently to Tony, wondering how he was viewing the chaos and confusion, and to her utter delight she saw he was enjoying himself immensely.

The family took to him just as readily. His initial reticence slid from him in short order as the kids crawled all over him with the friendliness that was second nature to them. And, to Sheila's amazement, he gave the younger ones piggyback rides, read a solemn fairy tale to a round-eyed three-year-old and her older sister and joined in an impromptu baseball game with the oldest kids and Angelo. It was all she could do to keep her mouth from dropping open as she watched dignified Tony Adams sliding into second base, dust-covered and grinning in triumph as the ump ruled him safe. Would wonders never cease?

Seeing the hope in her mother's eyes as she watched her youngest daughter hand-in-hand with Tony, Sheila swallowed a lump. It was as if Carmella had asked aloud, "Is he the one?" She'd already been through the third degree with Mandy, whose "you look happy, *really* happy, sis" had been intended to make her open up more than it had. Sheila held back, though, from both of them and from the gentle questions she'd noticed in her brothers' eyes and the quiet concern in her father's voice. Too soon, dear family, she thought. We've a ways to go yet.

After a boisterous luncheon served on picnic tables outside, everyone scampered to the lake for swimming, the children swinging on a big rubber tire hanging from a sturdy tree and jumping into the water with yelps of pleasure. The older ones looked after the little toddlers, and the grown-ups chatted with the familiar ease of people who are comfortable with one another. Try as he would, Tony couldn't pick up on the slightest undercurrent of animosity between them. The fact surprised and puzzled him.

Other things surprised him, too. Despite the noise and the number of people—he'd counted eighteen bobbing heads in the lake at one time—there was a peacefulness, a serenity he wouldn't have suspected. Was it the lazy summer day with the sun shining brightly and just a suggestion of a breeze on the glasslike perfection of the blue lake?

Was it the huge willow trees, their long weaving green arms
fanning and swaying, almost dipping to the grassy slopes?
Was it the musical sounds of the birds coaxed to join them
by Sheila's mother, who'd set up feeding stations and little houses with perches all over one section of the wide
yard for them? Or was it the big red-brick house with its
perky white shutters looking down at them from the top of
the hill, waiting to welcome their return? Tony didn't know
what it was, but though he'd traveled a great deal, he
hadn't experienced this measure of tranquility so quickly
anywhere else. And the obvious love and warm acceptance...it puzzled him.

Seeing Sheila in the surroundings of her youth surprised him, though it shouldn't have, he decided, watching her. She was such a natural person, so full of life and
fun and laughter, secure in the love of her family. He felt
a pang of envy for anyone who'd grown up in this atmosphere. How did they maintain it, year after year?

Taking a breather up on the lawn, he sat on one of the
wooden benches Mr. North had made and watched Sheila.
She played with the children in the water, tossing them
around and ducking their dark little heads, and the years
slipped away from her. She might have been a teenager
again, teased and chased by her brother Angelo, arm in
arm sharing confidences with her sister Mandy, spontaneously hugging her shorter, dark-haired mother with the
kind eyes, joining her tall, slender father at the end of the
dock as he sat quietly fishing and smoking his pipe. Wishing he had a cigarette, Tony watched and studied and
compared the scene with remembered snatches from his
childhood, and the memory saddened him.

"She's something, our Sheila, isn't she?" Angelo said,
coming over to join Tony, towel-drying his dark, curly
hair.

Tony had taken an immediate liking to the big, soft-
spoken man. And he hadn't missed Angelo's serious

brown eyes quietly following Sheila and him much of the afternoon. Recognizing the protective instincts of the older brother, Tony had figured that Angelo would find time to speak to him of things other than the law before the weekend was over.

"Yes, she certainly is," Tony agreed, watching Sheila as she laughingly wrinkled her nose at the wiggling worm she was trying to hook on to the end of her five-year-old nephew's fishing pole. "I don't know where she gets her energy from. She can run all day full-steam-ahead on less than six hours sleep...amazing."

Wrapping the towel around his neck, Angelo stretched out his legs and leaned back comfortably. "She's always been like that," he said. "Used to drive me crazy when we were kids. Even on Saturday mornings she'd come and wake me, often when it was still dark out, always with some project she wanted me to go in on with her, some surprise she was planning for someone, some new idea she'd dreamed up. She's a hard person to refuse."

"I've noticed that," Tony said, turning to study this brother who was the closest to Sheila. "It's as if for her there aren't enough hours in the day to complete all she wants to do. I run on a slower clock."

"Me, too," Angelo said, nodding. "Part of it's probably metabolism, but with Sheila most of that rushing to embrace life head-on is because of Shirley."

"Shirley?"

Angelo stretched his muscled arms along the back of the bench, his eyes on the sky overhead. "Yes, Shirley, Sheila's first real friend. Sheila was always mature beyond her years, and so older kids were drawn to her. The summer she was twelve, a family moved in up the road and they had an only child, a daughter named Shirley who was seventeen. Sheila and Shirley became fast friends, together always, fishing in a little rowboat, swimming, bicycling, movies—inseparable."

Angelo ran a hand through his damp hair, warming to his story. "Shirley was very talented. She could draw anyone's likeness in a matter of moments, serious or caricature. She did landscapes in chalk, cartoons in pencil, ink sketches, all of it. She had one more year of high school to finish and then she was going on to art school. Sheila can't draw worth a bean, like most of us, and she really admired Shirley. Plus they had this great friendship. Shirley was at our house all the time, probably because she was an only child. Our whole family thought she had a marvelous future in store for her."

"What happened?" Tony asked, listening intently. As an attorney, he knew how much a person's past affected their present outlook on life. As a man in love, he knew he wanted to understand Sheila.

"Well, one afternoon, driving home, Shirley and her father were hit head-on by a car out of control. Shirley died instantly. Her father lasted a week in a coma before he died. The mother was gone within a year, more from a broken heart than anything specific. It was a real tragedy, and it took Sheila a long time to get over the loss of her friend. But one day she came to me—remember she was only twelve—and she told me she'd decided you have to live every day as if it were your last because it really might be. It was her first brush with death, but she understood perfectly. And she said that she'd have to live twice as well as the next person, have twice as much fun, experience everything doubly. Once for herself and once for her friend Shirley, who would never have the chance."

Tony leaned back, his gaze drifting to the horizon where the blue lake merged with a cloudless sky. "That's quite a story," he said, his gaze finding Sheila, who was sitting on the side of the dock with her young nephew in her lap, helping him hold the pole in the water. "She often does seem to be having twice as much fun as the other people in the room."

"Yeah, she's stuck to it, all right. But then you may also have seen that trait in her. Tenacity. When she sees something she wants, she grabs hold and never lets go."

Haven't I just? Tony thought with an inward smile. "I have noticed that, yes."

Angelo turned to him, his look direct. "You care for her." It was more a statement than a question.

Tony swung his eyes to Sheila's brother. "Yes. Very much," he told him honestly. "Do you approve?"

Standing, Angelo smiled down at him. "I'm a good attorney, Tony, but I can't measure a man and his motives in one afternoon. And I stopped approving or disapproving of Sheila's friends more than ten years ago. In this family we trust each other's judgment, and Sheila's is on target more often than most. If she cares for you, that's good enough for me and the rest of us."

A small voice calling "Daddy" caught Angelo's attention. He waved to his son, who was standing at the water's edge strapped into his bright orange water wings. "I've got to go help Nancy with the kids. See you later."

"Right. Uh, Angelo?" The soft-spoken, dark-haired man turned to look at Tony over his shoulder. "Thanks." With a grin and a wave, he jogged toward the lake.

So she'd known she didn't need their approval, Tony thought, glancing up at the late-afternoon sky. Then why had she wanted him to come meet her family? Could it be that she wanted him to approve of them, knowing he wasn't exactly thrilled with his own family? Watching her with them, so much a part of them, he knew that though he might not return often, return she would, for she needed their love and support.

Then basically we're talking a package deal here, aren't we? Tony asked himself, stretching his arms along the back of the bench. Love me, love my family. He did love Sheila. From what he'd seen in the last six hours, her family was

very special, just as she'd indicated. But he'd always
steered clear of families. And now there was this.

This was not a family who would look with favor on him
and Sheila living together without benefit of clergy. She
might not need their approval, but could she handle their
disapproval, even if unspoken? Probably not. Back to
that—marriage, children, the whole forever scene. He
frowned, his troubled gaze taking in Sheila's relatives as
they lazed away a Saturday afternoon. Could he handle
becoming a part of this, fit in, believe it would work out?
Part of him yearned deeply for just that. Yearned for
something solid of his own, such as this big house on the
lake, instead of the picture-perfection of his impersonal
apartment. And someone to build it with and for. But another
part of him was scared to death.

He saw Sheila walking toward him hand in hand with a
grinning little boy who carried a pole, a tiny fish still
squirming on the end. A smile forming, he stood up to go
meet them. Time enough to think about his concerns later.

"You were right," Tony said, his arm sliding around
Sheila and drawing her close up against him as they
strolled in the moonlight. "Your mother's one hell of a
cook. I'm absolutely stuffed. And that anniversary cake—
super!"

"Mmm, it was good, wasn't it?" She stretched her arm
along his back, needing the closeness. Amid the clamor
and confusion, she'd noticed that Tony'd been unusually
quiet. Especially when Mandy sat down at the piano and
played "The Anniversary Waltz" and her parents, with
hesitant steps and love-filled eyes, danced a couple of turns
around the floor. She'd give a lot to know what he was
thinking about now, she thought, but she decided to let
him proceed at his own pace. To rush him would be a mistake.
Her father, sensing they needed a little time alone

had suggested they go for a walk before turning in, and she'd grabbed at the chance.

"So where are these trees your father wanted you to show me, and what's so special about them?"

"You'll see. They're just over that next small hill." She looked up at his eyes, unreadable in the dim light. "I know my family can be a little overwhelming, especially on a first visit. Are you sorry you came?"

He squeezed her to him and smiled. "No. I'm glad I came. Your family's wonderful, almost too good to be true."

Sheila felt pleased and hopeful. "I have a feeling they like you, too."

"Oh, they're so loyal they probably like every man you bring up here to meet them."

She came to a stop as they rounded the bend and faced him. "I've never brought anyone home before," she told him softly.

"No one?" His voice registered genuine surprise.

She shook her head. "Not a single soul." Turning, she pointed to four shade trees lined up in a row at the edge of their property. Three were of average size, full and healthy. The fourth was tall and stately, clearly the best of the bunch. "Those are the trees my father mentioned."

"What's their significance?"

"My father remembered an old saying about the search for happiness, and he had all four of us plant our own tree when we were six years old. I'm the youngest, so my tree's the newest. Mine is the end one, the biggest and the tallest. No one can understand why it's passed up the others."

He turned her in his arms, his hands resting lightly on her back, his face close to hers. "What saying about happiness?"

"Oh, you've probably heard it. In search of happiness, try three things. Write a book, plant a tree, have a child.

Dad felt we should do all three. Only Angelo's managed to squeeze them all in now that he's finally finished this book on law he's been working on for several years.''

Her eyes were dark and mysterious in the moonlight. He moved to brush a strand of hair from her face, leaving his hand on her cheek. ''And how are you doing on the list?''

She shrugged. ''I'm not sure I could write a book. As you see, I've planted a tree, and it's going crazy.''

''And the child? Would you like to have a child, Sheily?'' he asked, his voice low and husky. Where had that question come from? Tony wondered. He didn't know. He only knew he needed this woman's warmth, her caring touch, her comforting presence. Perhaps it was time to take a few risks. Could the consequences be worse than what he'd feel if she moved out of his life?

His use of her special childhood name at this exact moment was nearly her undoing. ''Yes,'' she whispered.

''With me?''

''Yes.''

''I'd like that, too.'' His mouth closed over hers, and he swallowed a soft sob from deep inside her throat.

Chapter Twelve

August is usually a grueling month in lower Michigan, hot, sticky and humid. And it had been a grueling day, Sheila thought as she climbed into her Volkswagen in the parking lot under the state courthouse. Long and grueling and frustrating.

She drove north on Jefferson, heading for her office, driving automatically, lost in thought. Since that idyllic weekend up north when she and Tony had visited her family, she'd hardly had a moment's free time. Days she'd spent preparing the Davis personal-injury case, evenings wrapped in Tony's arms and nights tossing and turning, unable to solve either dilemma to her satisfaction.

She honked crossly at a big Buick that tried to cut her off, and stepped firmly on the gas, pulling past it. She was definitely tired of being pushed around.

This recent case and its many ramifications chased around in her brain until she could feel the familiar beginnings of a headache. It simply wasn't like her to let her work muddle her mind, causing her to lose her usual sunny outlook on life. But something didn't set right with the Davis case and she couldn't put her finger on just what it was.

She'd painstakingly interviewed all parties again, taking fresh depositions from everyone, going over details searching for that elusive something. Jake Malloy, the crane operator who'd caused the injury, had to be the key. Sheila was certain. But everyone from the president of the firm, Dennis Tompkins, down to the men who worked with Jake swore to his spotless previous record, his sixteen years of experience in his job, his sterling character. Yet he never met her eyes squarely when she talked with him, and his hands twitched with nerves. Was he hiding something or just tired of all the questions? Sighing, Sheila wished she knew.

The thick summer air swirled around her head as she drove, and she wished she'd taken the time to put the top up. But she was plain too tired to bother and too annoyed to care much how she looked right now. She had to get a few things from her desk yet tonight, and she hoped everyone would be gone. Small talk was the last thing she needed. A miracle was what she needed.

Tompkins Construction had filed a motion for dismissal due to insufficient evidence. She had to attend the hearing tomorrow with her response to show cause why the case against the firm shouldn't be dismissed. Maybe she'd feel better if she wasn't up against such big guns, Sheila thought. The legal firm representing the construction and demolition company was Taylor and Tompkins, well known members of the good-old-boys' club of which Tony's father was most likely president and founder. They were wealthy, powerful men who stuck together through thick and thin. And Sam Tompkins, senior member of the law firm of Taylor and Tompkins, just happened to be the brother of Dennis Tompkins, who owned the company.

Ah, yes, a fine network of friends. How could she and Ed Davis win against such odds?

And now there was this new possibility to consider. Tompkins Construction had offered Ed a desk job guaranteed for life, plus a cash settlement. Having carefully gone over the package, however, Sheila and the Davises felt that they couldn't comfortably manage on the projected income. There were too many accumulated bills, future medical costs and other expenses. So what else *could* she do for Ed Davis? Sheila wondered frowning.

After going over every aspect of the accident and every inch of the site with the foreman and the man who'd been injured at the same time as Ed, Sheila was convinced that the crane operator was at fault. Either he had indeed miscalculated or his machine had malfunctioned. Proving it was quite another thing, however, she thought as she swung into her parking space.

Glancing over, she noticed Tony's car and the senator's. If Tony had been the only one in, perhaps she'd have gone to him, just to talk, to be held a moment, to take from his giving warmth. But she didn't want to encounter the senator, who'd been cool and disdainful of her since she'd shown the world that his pal, J. D. Tremaine, was less than honorable. It was odd how he blamed her instead of the man who'd have resorted to perjury to get his way. She could never understand a man like Maxwell T. Adams.

And if the truth be known, Sheila thought as she rubbed her damp forehead, she was having a little trouble understanding his son these days. Tony had, although somewhat reluctantly, admitted he loved her, desired her, wanted to be with her. He'd been warmly accepted by her family, and in turn he seemed pleased with them. He'd even, for God's sake, asked her if she'd like to have his baby. And that, Sheila thought with a deep, painful breath, had been that.

There was never further mention of the intimacy they'd shared up in Tawas, the closeness she knew they both had felt, the future they both had glimpsed—a future together. In the weeks since, they'd seen each other almost daily, had talked and laughed together, had made love countless times. But the talk had been superficial, the laughter a bit strained, the lovemaking a shade desperate. What did he want from her? she asked herself for perhaps the hundredth time. A forever affair? To put her life on hold while he took his good old time figuring out his feelings? A guaranteed successful marriage, free from problems and pain?

Getting out of the car, Sheila slammed the door harder than she'd intended. Not just the Davis case but also her topsy-turvy life with Tony was making her testy and quick-tempered, and she hated it. All this introspection was doing nothing for her but strengthening her headache and weakening her defenses. She'd get the papers she needed and drive home, she decided, to her small apartment, her sympathetic cat and her single bed. Maybe she'd buy a huge bag of chocolate-covered raisins and eat herself silly. An ache in the stomach was preferable to an ache in her heart.

As she walked quietly past the first-floor stairway leading down to the kitchen, the loud voices from below stopped her in her tracks. In the old building the angry argumentative sounds carried clearly to her ears. Glancing toward the open door to Rosemary's office, she wondered if the secretary was still in. Curious, she stood listening as she recognized the speakers.

"I tell you, I don't think she'll do it," Tony said, his voice firm.

"And I'm telling you she will. She's a smart lady, even if she hasn't always acted in her own best interest." The senator's voice was louder, overriding Tony's in tone.

"She's her own person, Dad. She showed Jim Tremaine up to be dishonest, and you know it. I've never understood your blind loyalty to a man who's a crooked wheeler-dealer."

A sound followed, as if someone had pounded a fist on the kitchen counter, startling Sheila. Quietly she set down her purse and briefcase and leaned closer to the stairwell railing.

"And I don't understand your naiveté. You've been in law for ten years. Do you think every one of your clients was lily white and the opposition's were all black? Grow up, son. I'm loyal to Jim Tremaine because we go back a long way. We understand each other. Sometimes, in business and in law, it's prudent to look the other way. I thought I taught you that a long time ago."

"I don't learn some lessons well, I guess. I defended Brewster to the best of my abilities, and he got convicted anyway. Although I'm not certain of his innocence, I can't be sure he's guilty, either. The man's entitled to a defense, and I gave him one—a damn good one. But if he'd confessed, if I'd *known* he was guilty, that would have been a whole different ball game. That's the way *I* operate. You don't care if they're innocent or guilty. If they're a friend, in your eyes they're clean. Which of us is wrong?"

The senator's voice was quieter, thoughtful. "Maybe neither of us. In our own way, we do what we think is right. I say loyalty to your friends is paramount. I've lived that way all my life, and I'll stand by that premise. Tony, everyone operates under shades of gray. Dennis Tompkins has a good construction company with a clean record. He provides work for hundreds of people. Do you feel that one incident is reason to close him down?"

Sheila's ears perked up. Tompkins? Her case. They were talking about her case. She angled her head, trying not to miss a word.

Tony's voice sounded exasperated. "Dad, we're talking about a man who's lost the use of his legs permanently. He can no longer work or support his family or hold his head high."

"Tompkins has offered Davis a lifetime desk job. And, on top of that, a cash settlement. That's what I'm trying to tell you. Sheila has to listen to reason. The dismissal hearing is tomorrow. She must convince Davis to withdraw the charges and accept Tompkins's offer. He and his family will be taken care of for the rest of their lives. What could be simpler?"

"What about justice?" Tony asked quietly. "A wrong was committed here somewhere. Are you so certain that Tompkins Construction, by their negligence, isn't guilty?"

"Justice is an abstraction we can't afford to worry about right now."

A low sound came from deep in Tony's throat. "How much would you be willing to take for the use of your legs, Dad?"

Something slammed even harder, on the table this time, a book, maybe. Sheila flinched, then resumed her listening pose.

"Don't get melodramatic with me, Tony," the senator said, louder again. "Sam and Dennis are just as sorry about that man being disabled as Sheila is. But what's done is done. The decent thing to do is compensate him for his loss, not bankrupt a company and humiliate the owner in court for what was clearly an accident. The Tompkinses are doing the decent thing with this very generous offer. Believe me, he wouldn't even get that if it weren't for—"

The senator stopped himself, as if fearful he'd already said too much. "Well, let's just say everyone will be a lot better off if Davis just takes the money and forgets everything else. Sam's been damned good to me. I owe him and I mean to come through for him. Sheila needs to be told what she has to do. She won't regret cooperating with a law firm with the clout of Taylor and Tompkins. They could direct a lot of business her way.''

"I'll be *very* interested to hear how Sheila responds to your requests, Dad.'' Tony's voice, nearer the doorway now, held an odd note, one Sheila couldn't pinpoint. Concern? Sarcasm?

Before either man could come out of the kitchen and spot her eavesdropping at the top of the stairs, Sheila quickly picked up her things and noiselessly made her way up the steps and into her office. Wearily she walked to the window and leaned against the frame. Not the slightest breeze stirred the leafy branches of the big maple tree. A small wren cocked his head warily at her from the precarious safety of a tiny twig. She felt a little like that wren right now, Sheila thought. Just a small thing out on a limb with no one by her side.

So the senator was up to his usual tricks, championing still another dear old friend. It didn't surprise her. In the back of her mind, since she'd learned that he was a friend of Sam and Dennis Tompkins, she'd almost been expecting it. The idea was for his pals to win, according to the senator. It didn't matter how. The end results would justify the means. And here she was, cramping his style again.

Movement in the backyard caught her eye, and she looked down. Briefcase in hand, Tony walked with long strides to his Mercedes. He had to notice her car parked right next to his, had to know she was in the building. Yet he didn't glance at her Volkswagen or up at her window. Why was he leaving in such a hurry? Why hadn't he come to see her, if only for a moment? A late appointment? Had his conversation with his father gotten hot and heavy after she'd moved upstairs out of hearing range?

Turning from the window, she went to her desk. She didn't have time right now to ponder Tony and his odd behavior. She had to get together the papers she'd come for and leave before the good senator cornered her. That was one scene she didn't feel up to right now.

In short order Sheila finished and snapped shut her briefcase, and was about to lock her desk drawer when she heard two sharp knocks on her door. Too late, she thought. Damn! Not waiting for her permission to enter, the senator opened the door and walked in, wearing that politician's smile she'd come to recognize. It was the one he wore when he wanted something from someone. Sheila braced herself.

"Sheila, my dear. I'm glad I caught you," he said, his voice silken and smooth, meant to charm the birds from the trees.

Not this little brown wren, Sheila thought, sitting down and sending a cool look his way. "Senator," she said, leaning back, waiting, hoping her eyes didn't betray her intense dislike for this manipulative man.

Fussing with the knot of his tie, he sat down opposite her and crossed his long legs. "I haven't seen you lately. How are you?"

Let's get on with this, she thought, her annoyance changing quickly to anger. "Fine."

"Good, good. Well, I met a friend of mine just a little over an hour ago. Sam Tompkins, a hell of a fine man. He's one of the attorneys in your Davis case."

"Yes," Sheila said quietly. She wasn't going to make this easier for him.

His cold blue eyes told her he knew it. "It looks like luck's in your corner again, Sheila, and you won't have to go to court and face Sam. He's got thirty years of court-room experience behind him, you know. Not too many attorneys can beat him." Sheila's gaze never wavered from his face. Maxwell T. Adams narrowed his eyes in a look of irritation—clearly he thought she wasn't smart enough to learn the rules and play the game... *his* game.

Clearing his throat noisily, the senator put on his winning smile. "I take it you've seen the Tompkins offer to Davis. Most generous, wouldn't you say?"

"Yes, I've seen it."

"Then all this is probably unnecessary. I imagine you've already talked with him, advised him to accept it. It'll set Ed Davis up for life without a worry in the world. Isn't that good news?"

Sheila tightened her hands on the arms of her chair, hoping the contact would steady her nerves. "I have discussed the offer with Ed and Dottie Davis. All three of us agree it's less than adequate—for his loss and for his future needs. The man was making very good money. After payment of his medical bills, he'll be receiving a little over half of his former income. You call that good news?"

The senator's smile moved a little off center. "Well, naturally, office jobs don't pay as well as high-risk contruction work. Perhaps I could talk Tompkins into a slight wage increase."

"In return for withdrawing the charges, I presume?" she asked, never taking her eyes from his.

"Well, yes, of course. No one gets something for nothing, you know." He chuckled and rubbed his manicured hands together. "And you'd be compensated, too, Sheila. Taylor and Tompkins is a most prestigious law firm. They won't forget this favor. They'll direct more business your way than you can handle. Dozens of young attorneys would snap up this golden opportunity. You'll be on your way."

Sheila closed her eyes a moment, too angry to trust her voice. It was not even veiled this time. This was an out-and-out, specific bribe.

"Tony told me you were a smart lady," he went on, shoring up his argument, "one who could be counted on to make the right decision."

At the mention of Tony, Sheila's eyes snapped open. "Tony said that?"

"Absolutely."

Frowning, Sheila went over in her mind what she'd overheard and what the senator was telling her. She recalled Tony saying early in the conversation that he didn't think she'd do it. That was before she'd known who they were discussing. Had he moved from that conviction to calling her "a smart lady who could be counted on to make the right decision" after she'd come upstairs? The last thing she'd heard Tony tell his father was that he'd be interested in hearing what Sheila'd have to say to him. Just how had he meant those words? And why had he left so hurriedly—to avoid her? Could she have misjudged him so?

"I just finished talking with Tony a few minutes ago," the senator said, sensing victory in her long silence. "He's got plans for you, young lady. Big plans. Together, two smart lawyers with good connections could go far in this town. What do you say?"

Sheila rubbed her forehead wearily. "So this is how the big boys play, right, Senator? If you can't lick 'em, you buy 'em. Or bribe them. Neat and tidy."

The senior Mr. Adams's face turned ugly as anger moved into it. "Now look here, Sheila. I'd be careful whom I accuse of bribery if I were you."

"No, *you* look here, Senator. What else do you call Tompkins's offer to direct business to an attorney he doesn't know in return for a favor, if not bribery? Mr. Davis won't accept your good friend's generous offer, and neither will I. You may feel free to tell him that."

Standing, she slung her purse strap over her shoulder, picked up her briefcase and headed for the door. Suddenly she turned to face him, her eyes finally registering fury. "I thought I smelled something rotten in this case. Whenever one of your *dear friends* is involved with the law, a permeating odor is sure to follow. You can give Mr. Tompkins another message. Tomorrow morning I'm moving for a postponement of the dismissal hearing. Then I'm going to the district attorney's office and requesting a full-scale investigation into Tompkins Construction's operations. This little can of worms you opened up, Senator, is going to pop right back into your face.''

The senator's face turned red while his eyes went icy blue. ''I wouldn't make a hasty decision I might regret, if I were you,'' he warned. ''Think of Tony, your future together.''

Her eyes took on a sadness the senator was too angry to notice. ''I don't believe my future's with Tony, though I do thank both of you for that juicy carrot you dangled in front of me. I guess you both thought I was not only young and inexperienced but stupid as well. It seems there's more to heredity than I'd counted on.''

Turning on her heel, Sheila left the room without a backward glance and hurried down the stairs, her vision blurring with a sudden rush of tears. She had to get away from here, from the senator, from the truth about Tony. She wouldn't cry now. There'd be plenty of time for tears when she was safely home.

Even though it was evening, waves of heat shimmered off the hood of the Mercedes as Tony drove along the crosstown expressway, heading for the east-side exit that would take him to Sheila's. He'd almost been late for his meeting with Mrs. Thornton after that disturbing conversation with his father in the office kitchen. And then it had taken forever to get some necessary information out of his client, having caught her in a maddeningly talkative mood. He pressed down a bit more on the accelerator, anxious to see Sheila, to hear what she'd said to the senator, to hold her again.

His father was not happy with him, but for a change Tony didn't mind. He knew he was right, that the senator would never get Sheila to agree to take Tompkins's payoff. He smiled at the thought of how fiery her dark eyes had probably gotten when she'd realized the senator was at it again. Not even the promise of plenty of referrals from a prestigious law firm would make Sheila compromise her ideals, and his father could not see that in her. Perhaps it was a case of a man who gazed into the face of integrity but couldn't recognize it, since he was hardly conversant with that particular quality.

Tony sighed as he slowed the car and eased it onto the exit ramp. He'd tried everything he could to dissuade his father from even approaching her, knowing that Sheila already thought the senator walked a mighty fine line between truth and corruption. This would surely put him over the edge in her mind. And in his own. Shenanigans like these, which his father had tried to pull time and again—never mind that he often hadn't gotten away with them because he and Jed had stepped in—were what had caused severe differences between father and son before the senator had moved to Washington.

He should never have agreed to let him rejoin the firm, Tony thought, turning north on Jefferson Avenue. Like a fool, he'd harbored the unspoken hope that his father had changed. No such luck. He was back again and worse than ever. He'd have to talk with Jed, and somehow they'd have to separate themselves from the senator. Sheila would stop him this time, of that Tony was certain, but who would the next time? And there most assuredly would be a next time.

No, too much risk here. Once the word got around, he and Jed and their practice would be in jeopardy; the reputation that they'd both worked so hard to keep clean and honorable would become tainted by association. The senator had to go, and it wasn't going to be pleasant. Sheila would agree with him, make the necessary change easier. Sheila made everything easier.

Sheila. Tony dragged an impatient hand through his hair. He could hardly wait to get to her place, to listen to a blow-by-blow account of her conversation with the senator, watch her get fired up all over again in the telling. Then, when she was calm, he would enjoy working her up again, this time in passion rather than anger. He felt his muscles tighten at the thought as he pulled in alongside her convertible and shut off the motor.

When the door had not opened after his second series of knocks, Tony looked around from the small landing at the top of the stairs, wondering if perhaps Sheila hadn't gone for a walk. He knocked again, frowning. At last he heard the chain slide back and began to smile as the door slowly opened. The smile abruptly left his face.

She stood there in a short white terry-cloth robe tightly knotted at her waist, her face paler than he'd ever seen it, her eyes red-rimmed.

"Sheila, what is it?" Tony asked, walking inside and pushing the door closed. He reached for her, but she evaded his touch, shoving her hands into her pockets. Barefoot, she made her way over to a wing-backed chair and, pulling her legs under her, sat down, her eyes not meeting his. Had his father upset her, or was something else wrong? "Sheila," he said, moving closer and sitting down anxiously on the edge of the couch, "tell me. What happened?"

Slowly she raised empty eyes to his face. "Why'd you come, Tony?" she asked, wishing he'd just let it drop, at last for tonight. She'd driven home blindly, not sure how she managed to arrive in one piece. She'd whipped off her clothes and taken a long, cleansing shower, but it hadn't helped, nor had the tears that she'd been unable to halt. Why did he have to show up and make her go through it all again?

"Why?" he asked, genuinely puzzled. "Did my father talk with you after I left? Is that what's upset you? I tried to tell him you wouldn't go for the idea."

Yes, she remembered he had said something like that—at first. Before the senator had coaxed him over to the other side. A weary sigh escaped from her. "How hard did you try, Tony?"

He frowned. The senator was not known for his finesse when he got his dander up, and most likely Sheila had raised his hackles with her refusal to cooperate. Well, Tony'd warned him she wouldn't take his suggestion lying down. Still, why should that have her looking defeated and vulnerable? "Sheila, he's not *all* bad, you know. He just has misplaced loyalties."

"So did Benedict Arnold." She watched him turn pale, but she was too hurt, too angry deep inside to stop now. "Misplaced loyalties, a character that's easily corruptible and totally without conscience. Have I left out anything?"

Tony ran a heavy hand across his tired face. Damn, but he should have canceled his appointment with Mrs. Thornton and stayed. He knew the senator could be pushy, even brutal, but he'd never thought he'd try it on Sheila since he knew how Tony felt about her. Or did he? "I know how it must seem to you."

"Do you?"

Tony stood and began to pace restlessly around the small room. How did two people who cared about each other get so sidetracked over other issues? he asked himself. "Personally, if it'll help explain things, I haven't agreed with most of the senator's decisions or opinions since I was nine years old. I've tolerated him because he's my father and—"

"I see you both have a strong loyalty streak. Admirable." Her voice was low, tinged with sarcasm.

His temper frayed, Tony stopped in front of her, his hands forming tight balls that he slammed onto his hips. "Now look here, Sheila, I—"

"No!" she fairly shouted, jumping to her feet, her eyes blazing up at him. "I'm not going to be lectured to by another exceedingly loyal, slightly corrupted Adams today, thank you. I've already had one lesson on how to get ahead in the world according to the Adams doctrine, and let me tell you, it stinks to high heaven."

Anger rose in him as her words sunk in. "Slightly corrupted? Are you lumping me in that category? What the hell's going on here?"

She didn't back down an inch. "Did you tell your father I was a smart lady, one who would make the *right* decisions?"

Tony thought a moment. He had said something exactly like that. And why not? It was the truth. "Yes. What's wrong with that?"

"Did you also happen to mention that probably, for a small, insignificant bribe of more law business sent my way than I could possibly handle, I would undoubtedly play ball? Doesn't every man have his price in the Adams rule book? And every woman?"

His mouth a thin, white line, Tony stood his ground. "Is that what he told you? And you believe that that's what I think of you?"

"How the hell do I know *what* to believe? I don't hear you denying anything."

Silently he stared at her. She was upset, that was all. He'd find out from his father what had been said and take care of it. Someone had to take control of the situation, and Sheila was obviously overreacting.

Sheila ground her teeth as Tony's calm attitude infuriated her further. Why didn't he scream denials at her, yell explanations to her, tell her it wasn't so and make the pain go away? "Still in control, aren't you, Tony?" She wiped at a tear that had escaped. "You're obsessed with never allowing yourself to lose control, and you don't, do you? No, sir, not the great Tony Adams. He stands there and offers no explanations. He wants me to laugh off the bribery offers, forget what I heard, betray my client and believe he had nothing to do with it out of blind loyalty."

It was Sheila's turn to pace and she did so, her bare feet slapping onto the floor, each step hitting hard and strong, her fury reaching all parts of her trembling body. "Well, I'm afraid *my* loyalty doesn't run as deep as the Adamses'. I won't adjust my morals to suit yours. I can't go along with wrongdoing, even if it involves...involves someone I love." Her voice caught on a sob and, running out of steam, she leaned against the window frame.

She didn't believe him, Tony thought. He'd lost her. How much could she love him if, after one conversation with his father, she could believe he was guilty? No matter what the senator had said, all he could do was cast doubts. But it appeared she was not strong enough to fight those doubts. She'd immediately jumped to the conclusion that he had sold her out by siding with his father. Why couldn't she have trusted him?

Wearily he walked to her. "Is that what you think, that I betrayed you?" His voice sounded old to his ears.

She turned back to him, the anger gone, replaced by sadness. Reaching up to touch the package of cigarettes in his shirt pocket, she met his eyes. "I'm like these cigarettes to you, Tony. Something you love but need to control. Something you'd like to give up, but you're not quite able to. You can't seem to commit to not smoking, so you keep them at the ready. You're afraid to make a commitment to me, too, yet you want undying loyalty from me offered in total blind faith. You're afraid loving me will make you lose control over yourself, that *I'll* take control of you, like a bad, addictive habit."

She dropped her hand, shaking her head. "I can understand your ambivalence with your father. I even understand your loyalties to him. But I can't understand a man who says he loves a woman but is afraid to commit himself to her, no matter the cost. I thought you would in time, but it seems you can't. Perhaps it's best we found out now."

How had they come to this? Tony asked himself. Perhaps it was best they found out now. Sheila wanted too much, and he couldn't deliver. Feeling as though he needed time to sort out his feelings, Tony turned and wordlessly walked out the door, closing it quietly behind him.

Her hand pressed to her mouth to keep from crying out to stop him, Sheila stood at the window, watching Tony hurry down the steps to his car. She knew he cared for her, but he was torn by divided loyalties. Had he sold her out, or had it just appeared that way? If not, why hadn't he spoken up?

While she had grown up in a household with a lot of family fights, she knew Tony hated confrontations of a personal nature. But she couldn't understand how, as a grown man, he wouldn't speak up for what he believed in no matter the cost, wouldn't defend himself to her, wouldn't take her in his arms and let her know he was strongly against his father's corrupt bribery attempt. But he hadn't.

Lowering her head, Sheila felt the tears begin again. How had she let herself fall in love with a man who would sit on the fence the rest of his life, unable to commit to either side?

Chapter Thirteen

Jed Blair watched a gold-green maple leaf flutter to the ground in his backyard and shook his dark head. "Damn if it doesn't feel like fall's in the air, and it's only the Labor Day weekend," he commented as he poked around in the coals of his barbecue.

Stretched out on the redwood lounge, Tony nodded. "You know Michigan. Turn around and the weather changes."

"No kidding, it's definitely chilly out here," Jed added with a frown.

Yes, it was, Tony thought, and it didn't have as much to do with the weather as it did with the cool welcome he'd received from his best friend when he'd arrived an hour ago... definitely not friendly.

Jed had popped his head into Tony's office door Friday, issuing an invitation from his wife Tanya for Monday's cookout. Tony had watched Jed struggling with his desire to mention whatever was bothering him. Thoug he'd known exactly what that was, Tony hadn't offered to help him. Finally Jed had shrugged and told him to bring a date if he wanted to, then had turned and walked out.

Tony swung his gaze out onto the rolling green lawn, his eyes landing on the row of tall poplars along the back of Jed's lot. Odd, but he'd been here countless times and he'd never before noticed that one tree at the far end was a good two feet taller than all the others. He did remember that Jed had planted all the new saplings at the same time. One tall tree...like Sheila's tree. Sighing, Tony raised his arms above his head and closed his eyes.

Two weeks ago, when Jed had first noticed the coolness between Tony and Sheila in the office, he'd tried to talk with his good buddy about it. Tony'd given him sketchy information, but that hadn't begun to satisfy his nosy though well-intentioned friend. Tony was fairly certain Jed had tried to get Sheila to open up but had struck out there, too.

Maybe Jed had even taken a whack at grilling Rosemary, but he should have known that wouldn't work. Rosemary was loyal to Tony to a fault. He wasn't sure how much of his heated words with the senator Rosemary had overheard that day. She'd never mentioned it to him, but he'd been oddly unquestioning, giving him a tight-lipped silence. He preferred that to Jed's insistent badgering, which he thought would undoubtedly soon rear its ugly head again today.

He'd made a mistake, Tony thought, that was all, and was damn hard to admit—and even harder to explain. He'd allowed himself to drop his guard, to get really close to Sheila, to fall in love. The rosy glow that accompanied those warm feelings had him almost ready to believe he wanted marriage, the little cottage, the kiddies, the whole package. And maybe he had for a short time. But that was just the problem. He'd seen far too many people go for it and have it last only a short time. And then divorce would come, the end of forever, broken promises, broken hearts. What was the point?

For a moment there, out on Sheila's folks' hill, holding her in his arms, he'd felt there'd be nothing more wonderful than to have a baby with Sheila, to put his hand on her and feel his child move inside her. Even now the thought left him breathless. But it wasn't fair to bring a baby into the world whose parents might grow disenchanted with one another and split. Or, perhaps worse still, they'd remain chained together by guilt, unable to hide their antagonism toward each other from that little person. He would ache every day if a child of his had to suffer that agony.

It was far better to break it off before things got that far along. He'd tried, but he simply wasn't marriage material. Sheila'd found him out. She'd been right that night in her apartment when she'd accused him of not wanting to relinquish control. He still didn't. If commitment to her and to their life together meant giving up his control over himself, he wanted no part of it. Maybe that was wrong but that was how he felt.

His mother had let herself love, given another control over her, and look where it'd gotten her. Even the senator, with his many marriages, had handed someone else control, if only for a little while. Freedom from some of his ex-wives had cost him dearly—money, property, peace of mind.

Sure, he was annoyed that Sheila had believed he might have betrayed her. Actually, he was more hurt than annoyed. But he could understand it. The senator presented a good case. He had no right to expect undying loyalty from someone he hadn't committed himself to. Only he almost had...for a moment there. Idly he wondered if putting all these problems aside, it could have worked between them. Now he would never know.

He did know that Sheila'd gotten her postponement of the Davis case, based on new evidence to follow. She'd pr the D.A.'s investigator on to Tompkins Construction as she'd threatened the senator she would. And Tony'd heard they were checking old records, new records, everything. He had no doubt that a sly old fox like Dennis Tompkins, aided and abetted by his attorney brother, had probably covered his tracks well, if in fact there were tracks to cover. And there probably were, or why else had they been so anxious to have Davis drop the matter? But the senator insisted that Tompkins would win, and he was furious with Sheila.

He was also furious with his son, because Tony had since asked him to move and set up his own practice elsewhere. Oddly, there'd been no scene. Tony had told him he was well aware of his insinuations to Sheila about his own feelings on the matter. He'd also warned the senator that he himself was doing some behind-the-scenes nosing-around on the Davis case for Sheila. And if he found what he suspected, he would have no qualms about turning them all in.

The senator hadn't retaliated, but there'd been cold, hard fury in his pale blue eyes as he'd listened, then told Tony he'd move out as soon as he decided where he would relocate. And he'd not spoken a word to him since, communicating a few terse messages through Jed or Rosemary. And that suited Tony just fine.

Tired of his own musings, Tony sat up, running a hand through his windblown hair, watching Jed arrange the glowing charcoal pieces into a good-sized pile. Why couldn't he be more like Jed? he wondered.

Here was an intense, intelligent man who'd jumped feet first into commitment and seemed never to have regretted a day of it. His wife, Tanya, small and fair, was the core of his existence. Towheaded Matthew, whom Tony had to admit was adorable, ran a close second. And now there was tiny, black-haired Marguerite, only two weeks old. More commitment, more responsibilities, more giving up of control over his life. How did Jed manage to do it and seem *happy*, truly happy?

"Guess that's as good as they get," Jed said, turning from the coals, and sitting down opposite Tony. "You want another beer?"

Tony shook his head, picking up the one he'd forgotten, and took a long swallow.

"The women should be out soon, and Matt'll be up from his nap," Jed said, his deep-set eyes on his friend. He gestured toward the patio door, which led into the kitchen. "What made you take up with Gail again?"

Setting down the bottle, Tony took his time answering. Gail Whitney was quite tall, well stacked, a bright and lovely redhead. She was also an architect in Sandy's company, determinedly single and terrific in the sack. They'd gone out together occasionally before he'd met Sheila, and when Jed's invitation had come along he'd thought it was time he got back into the mainstream of the dating scene. Then why was it that Jed's obvious disapproval bothered him?

"You said to bring a date," Tony answered carefully, not wanting to fuel the fire he felt simmering in Jed's casual question.

Taking a sip of his beer, Jed regarded Tony. "Right, I did. And Sheila was busy this weekend?" He raised his voice at the end, turning the comment into a question that demanded an answer. He was pushing, he knew. But someone had to.

"I wouldn't know," Tony answered evenly, his eyes on the late-afternoon clouds slowly gliding around a pale blue sky. Here it comes, he told himself. Brace yourself.

"And don't care?"

"Right."

"Dammit, Tony."

"Dammit, Jed, what do you want from me?"

"Nothing!"

"Good."

"Hell!" Jed jumped up and marched to the end of his wide patio and leaned against the pillar there, his very stance belligerent. It took him less than a full minute to cool down. This would get them nowhere. He turned and went back, resuming his seat, trying to put a reasonable look on his face.

"We've known each other too long to get hot over this," Jed said, his voice sincere.

Tony let out a shaky breath. "At least we agree on one thing."

Jed ran a hand along the back of his neck, honestly puzzled. "We used to be able to talk with one another." Lifting his eyes, he zeroed in. "Talk to me. Tell me what's wrong."

"What do you mean wrong? Sheila and I just weren't right for each other."

"Did you lie to me, Tony, back when I asked if you were stringing her along? Did you?"

Tony slowly shook his head. "No. I loved her then, and I still do. She's the one that wanted me out of her life."

"Why?"

Leaning back, Tony swallowed. Here was the hard part. "She thinks I'm like the senator, easily corrupted, ready to look the other way to win a case."

Jed waited a long moment, then shook his head. "That can't be. Nobody knows you better than me—*nobody*. You wouldn't do that."

Tony allowed himself a small smile. Actually, by now he was fairly certain Sheila had discovered the truth, that he hadn't switched sides and sold her out. But she hadn't come to him, and he knew why. There were things wrong between them still that had nothing to do with the senator or law cases. "I'm glad you feel that way. But then you've known the senator half your life. Sheila's only known him a couple of months."

"There has to be more to this."

He'd known that Jed's incisive lawyer's mind would eventually zero in on it. "She feels I can't handle commitment, that I always have to be in charge."

Jed's eyes bored into his. "Is she right?"

"Yeah, I guess so." Tony stood, moving restlessly about the patio. Suddenly he swung to face his friend. "Jed, how do you do it? How did you somehow *know* it would work out with you and Tanya? How can you bring children into this world knowing how badly they could be hurt if things don't work out with you two?"

Jed stood and walked over to face his friend, knowing the anguish hidden beneath his words was rooted in Tony's past. "It *will* work out. And as for the kids, don't you see, Tony? They're my commitment to forever. Long after I'm gone, those children—and their children after them— they'll make it all worthwhile. Tanya and them, they're my reason to get up in the morning. Without them, I wouldn't be the same. Oh, I'd function, but I wouldn't really be alive. I'd drift, aimless, without any real purpose."

Tony could see Jed meant what he said. Could Tony believe him? "But, Jed, you give up so much. You don't have control of your life anymore. If you want to work late you've got to worry about them and how they'll handle that. If you want to vacation in the Bahamas and it's bad for the kids, you don't go. If you want to move to California and Tanya doesn't, you don't."

"Yeah, I agree. Marriage has made me a lot less selfish." He watched that sink in. "It's not so bad, Tony, thinking of someone else first. Try it. If you love that someone, you'd be surprised how painless it is. Actually, it gives you enormous pleasure."

Tony sat down heavily. He remembered how Sheila had coaxed him to Belle Isle canoeing when he'd had his doubts, had dragged him to a ball game he hadn't really wanted to attend, had taken him up north to her family when he'd been fearful they'd pressure him. And he'd enjoyed all of it. He'd taken enormous pleasure in *her* pleasure, thereby ensuring his own. Maybe if he . . .

"We're ready to put the hamburgers on, Jed," Tanya said from the doorway. "Are the coals hot enough?"

With a glance at Tony, Jed stood and went to his wife. At least he'd given him a lot to think about. He could only hope it had been enough. "You bet," he told Tanya.

Gail Whitney, wearing a bright blue jumpsuit that fit her like a glove, came out onto the patio and sat down on the end of Tony's lounge chair. "You're looking awfully serious. You okay?"

Later—he'd think about all this later. "Sure," he said, leaning forward with a smile. Gail was a nice person. She didn't deserve his moodiness. "Anything I can do?"

"We've got things under control," she said, smiling as she saw him make the effort.

Control. There was that word again, back to haunt him even in small, insignificant ways.

Just then two-year-old Matt Blair, clad in denim overalls, yellow shirt and a Detroit Tigers baseball cap, came barrelling out the door and hurled himself into Tony's arms. "Uncle Tony!"

"Hey, champ, how're you doing?" Tony asked, smiling down into the youngster's laughing eyes. So full of love and trust. Could Jed be right? he wondered as he hugged the squirming bundle of energy to him.

Late Wednesday afternoon, Sheila finished the last notation, put away the file, took off her glasses and rubbed the bridge of her nose. She felt utterly drained, an all-too-familiar feeling lately. The last few weeks had been difficult. Maybe, once the Davis case was over, she'd take some time off and stay with her folks for a few days. She badly needed to recoup.

At the end of the week she had an appointment with the
D.A.'s office to go over the new evidence she'd acquired.
It was coming along, but so far was surprisingly sparse.
One reason was that due to the efforts of Dennis and Sam
Tompkins, those two grand old buddies of the senator,
some of the company records were either unaccountably
"lost" or looked suspiciously as if they had been altered.

There had to be a major cover-up somewhere, Sheila
thought as she gathered her things, for Tompkins to offer
her a bribe for talking Ed Davis into dropping the suit
against him. Of course, a verbal offer issued through the
senator—a third party—consisting of promised referrals,
was a mighty hard thing to prove. Maybe, with threats of
perjury hanging over their heads, some of the construction workers, who all just conveniently happened to be
elsewhere at the time of the accident, might recall glimps-
ing a thing or two. Fear of imprisonment and fines were
often wonderful jolts to the old memory.

Sighing, she wished fervently that this case was over and
done with. She was finding it increasingly difficult to share
an office building with Tony and the senator. Rosemary
had told her the senator was leaving, but she hadn't seen
it happen yet. They'd passed each other frequently in icy
silence. But it was Tony's presence that disturbed her
more.

Tony. She'd been rash in judging him so quickly, so
harshly, she now knew. The next day at the office, she'd
listened to Rosemary rant and rave about the nerve of the
senator threatening to bribe Sheila even after Tony had
warned him repeatedly that she wouldn't go for it. The
secretary had been in her office and had heard the heated
voices from the basement kitchen even after Sheila'd gone
upstairs. When Rosemary'd asked her outright if the senator had dangled referrals in front of her in return for her
getting the case dropped, she'd answered truthfully. What
she hadn't told her—or anyone—was that the senator had

lied to her, had implied that Tony had agreed with him. And she'd believed him.

Placing the files in her briefcase and shutting it, Sheila shook her head sadly. She'd been wrong, and she was ashamed of not having had more faith in Tony. Well, she'd learned her lesson the hard way. But then he didn't want her love anymore, anyhow. She hadn't been wrong about that part. Tony would never commit himself to a future with anyone, and she wasn't the kind of person who could settle for less.

She hadn't looked for love, but it had found her, inevitably, quickly, irrevocably. Contentment had made her mellow, lazy, soft. Defenses down, independence tucked aside, she'd opened the door to her heart, and he'd gradually but firmly eased inside.

He'd fought her all the way. From the start, she'd known he wanted no part of the things she needed—love, commitment, marriage and a family. He'd desired her, cared for her in his own way, she was certain. But she'd made the colossal mistake of the novice lover: she'd thought he'd change, come around, choose his love for her over his fears. It was proving to be a costly error in judgment...and one she'd have to live with now.

Looking around, she decided she had all the papers she needed for tonight. Turning off her lamp, she headed for the door. She'd get a good night's rest, for tomorrow was an important day for her client. Locking up, she gave a bitter laugh. A good night's sleep. She hadn't had one since...since Tony'd left.

Having spent the afternoon catching up on his paperwork, Tony came out of his office to give Rosemary some typing. But she wasn't at her desk. She was standing outside the anteroom talking in a low voice to Sheila, whose back was to him. Despite his best intentions, he stood staring. Sheila.

She was wearing the same navy suit she'd worn the first day he'd seen her in the courthouse, with a buttercup-yellow blouse, her hair just touching her shoulders . . . that beautiful hair that made him want to slide his hands into its softness. He remembered how it smelled—like a May day in the country, like wildflowers, like no one else.

He should go out to her, take her off somewhere like the day they'd played hooky in Greektown, talk it out. He should make her see that if two people loved each other there was nothing they couldn't talk away. He should get the hell out of here before he made a fool of himself. Tossing his papers onto Rosemary's desk, Tony turned and walked back into his office.

It would have to be up to him, he knew, to make the first move. She wasn't being stubborn. She knew she needed things he seemed unable to give her. Was he being stubborn in his unwillingness to change, or was he more a realist than she? After Monday night, he wasn't sure.

Swiveling his chair to stare unseeingly out his back window, he thought about the day and evening he and Gail had spent with Jed and Tanya and their children. Despite Jed's needling about Sheila, it had been a pleasant time. Driving Gail home, he'd decided to stop thinking so much, to lighten up, to have some fun without demands. He meant to wind up in Gail's bed. Only it hadn't worked out that way.

At her place, she'd asked him in for coffee although they'd both known it was just a preliminary. They'd dated before, and each knew the rules of the game. An evening together usually meant a lovely dinner, some laughs and good sex. Why was it then that sitting on the couch kissing her hadn't done a thing for him? When she'd stood and taken his hand, ready to lead him into her bedroom, he'd frozen, unable to move.

It hadn't been easy voicing a feeble explanation, that he'd been working hard and was undoubtedly overtired, which had sounded a shade false to his own ears. Gail was a good sport and had taken it well, though a shadow had moved into her eyes. He'd hated to disappoint her, but it couldn't be helped. It wouldn't have been fair to make love to her and all the while be thinking of Sheila.

Running a hand through his already tousled hair, Tony groaned aloud. Always before, when he'd been wound up tighter than a drum, a warm, willing body like Gail's for a few hours had made him feel on top of the world. Since breaking up with Sheila, he wanted to go back to those times, back to the days when lighthearted friendships with the opposite sex were enough. Casual affairs were safe. Everyone knew the score, no one got hurt, and nobody spoke of forever.

That was the way he wanted to live, not like his father, getting married every couple of years, promising each woman what she wanted to hear, then breaking his promise and her heart. Tony knew better. If you don't make promises, you don't have to worry about breaking them. Why was it then that, try as he had, he couldn't seem to get pleasure from those relationships anymore?

Sheila. It was her fault, for messing up his head with her dreams that couldn't possibly come true, with her talk of babies, with her vision of him as her dragon-slayer. Had she really lost her belief in him, or had she only pretended in an effort to get the real issue out in the open? And the real issue was his problem. Was he strong enough to commit himself to her, come what may, forever and ever? He wished he knew the answer. He—

"Well, big brother, so this is how you spend your work days," Sandy said, strolling through his open door and sliding into a chair opposite his desk as he slowly swiveled to face her.

Tony smiled at her outfit, which consisted of sneakers, designer jeans and a Mickey Mouse sweatshirt from Disneyland. "I see you're all dressed up. Where're you headed?"

"Actually, I've been gone all day. I was on my way home, but I thought I'd stop in. Haven't seen you in over a month. And I've got big news."

"What might that be?" Tony asked.

"Tim and I bought a house today!"

"A house? What for? Your apartment's great and close to everything."

Sandy slumped lower in her chair and shook her heavy hair back. "The apartment's been fine, but it's different now that we're going to be married. I want space, more room, a yard big enough for a swing set and a—"

"A swing set? Are you... I mean..."

Sandy laughed gleefully. "Tony, you're adorable. No, I'm not pregnant. Not yet. But I plan to be. I want two, maybe three children, and that means swings and bikes, a place to play ball and—"

Tony leaned forward, frowning. "Three children? Are you sure? That's so much responsibility."

Sandy shrugged it off. "So's being an architect. Or an attorney, for that matter. Neither of us has ever been afraid of responsibility, have we?" When he didn't answer, Sandy's eyes narrowed thoughtfully. "Have we, Tony?"

Sitting back, Tony toyed with his pen, his eyes not meeting hers. "So where is this great house with the yard?"

Sandy hesitated, studying her brother. "On the west side. Tim grew up over there and he loves the country atmosphere."

Tony's frown returned. "But you grew up on the *east* side," he emphasized. "Why'd you give in to him? What kind of a marriage is that going to be, with him calling all the shots, running your life?"

Giving herself a moment, Sandy settled herself more comfortably in the chair. "Funny, I never thought of it

Tim running my life or calling the shots. He likes the west side, so we went looking at homes over there. We found one we *both* like. It's got a basement Tim can tinker in and a kitchen I can be happy in. I call that compromise, each trying to bend a little for the other. How do you see it?''

Tony tossed down the pen and shook his head. "It doesn't matter."

Sandy sat up straighter, her eyes on his face. "It *does* matter. Tell me."

He hesitated a long moment. "All right. You're letting him control you. You like the east side, he likes the west side, so you move to the west side. And that's just the beginning."

Rising, she walked around to his side of the desk and leaned against the edge, looking at him. His troubled skittish eyes would not meet hers. His hands were unsteady and fidgety. "It doesn't matter to me where we live as long as Tim and I are together. Tony, when you love someone you do give up a certain amount of control, but that doesn't mean you *are* controlled. Each of you give to the other, and it's not a question of power but of union. You make decisions together, the two of you against the world. Sometimes you win, sometimes the other person, sometimes you each compromise a little. But it's for the all-round good of both of you. That's not a defeat—that's a victory."

Tony looked up at her at last. "I don't know, Sandy. You make it sound so simple.

"It is simple, Tony. Not necessarily easy at first, but truly simple." Reaching over, she touched his cheek with affection. "Why don't you give it a try? Jump in. The water's fine."

Taking her hand, he squeezed it, his eyes thoughtful. "I'll think about it."

Sandy glanced at her watch and straightened. "Are you through for the day? Maybe you and Sheila'd like to come over tonight? We could order a pizza, talk a little."

At the mention of Sheila his brow knitted.

"Thanks, but I can't. Dad's moving out today, the van's on its way, and I want to be around for that."

"Moving out? Whose idea was that, yours?"

Scooting back his chair, Tony stood. "Yes, and I want to make sure he gets everything that's his so he can't come back to us about anything."

Shaking her head and sliding her arm around his back as he walked her to the door, Sandy sighed. "I know how hard it's been for you, having him around. For a while there, I was really worried that he was influencing you."

He stopped them both abruptly, and stared at her.

"Oh, not in your work ethics. But face it, Tony, all those random affairs you've had have been more like Dad's lifestyle than you cared to admit. In trying so hard to *avoid* being like him, you were *becoming* like him, even though you didn't see it. The only difference was that you didn't marry the women. But you still loved them and left them. You were both running from commitment. No guts and certainly no glory."

She turned and smiled up at his still-frowning face. "But that's all behind you. Now there's Sheila, and let me tell you, Tony, she has made a tremendous difference in you. You're warmer, kinder, more spontaneous...."

"Oh, come now—"

"It's true. Sheila took one look at you and fell in love, enthusiastically, unashamedly, wildly in love. More or less the way Tim did with me. And then they took us by the hand and taught us how to love in return. They freed us. We weren't very good prospects, either of us, with our background. But it didn't stop them, and we should be damned grateful." She glanced out the doorway. "Sa where is Sheila? It's been so long since I've seen her. Is she upstairs?"

"Uhh, no. She had to go out earlier."

Hand on the door, she glanced back at him. "You sure you and she can't make it over tonight after Dad moves out?"

Tony shook his head. Then, surprising them both, he leaned down and kissed Sandy's cheek. "Not this time. Thanks for stopping in, Sandy. I've . . . I've missed you."

She gave him a quick, hard hug. "Me, too. See you soon. And hug Sheila for me, will you?"

Nodding, he watched her wave to Rosemary and disappear through the archway. Slowly Tony walked back to his desk.

Sandy's words echoed in his head. *It's not a question of power but of union. Giving up some control doesn't mean you are controlled. In trying to avoid being like Dad, you were becoming just like him, only you didn't see it. . . .*

And then Jed's strong words. *They're my reason for getting up in the morning. Without them, I'd drift, aimless, without any real purpose. . . . Yeah, marriage has made me a lot less selfish.*

Tony stroked his chin thoughtfully. Could they be right?

Chapter Fourteen

On Friday morning Sheila sat in the small reception room outside the district attorney's office, waiting to see Ted Wilson, one of his assistants. She was a bit early for her ten-o'clock appointment, so she leaned back in her chair, crossed her legs and mentally went over the contents of the file she'd be presenting to Ted. A frown appeared on her forehead as she acknowledged that she didn't have much. Something had to break for them, and soon, or Tompkins Construction would win and poor Ed Davis wouldn't have many options left open to him.

At the sound of the hallway door opening, Sheila looked up. A uniformed officer of the court walked in and approached the receptionist's desk. Glancing at the door to Ted Wilson's office, Sheila rubbed her forehead and wished he'd finish with whoever was in there and get her. This waiting was nerve-racking and—

"Miss North?"

She looked up at the tall young officer standing by her chair. "Yes?"

He was holding a large manila envelope, which he handed to her. "This is for you."

Accepting the envelope, she turned it over, looking at both sides. Nothing on it but her typed name. "Thank you," she told him.

He smiled and walked back to talk with the receptionist. Puzzled, Sheila opened the envelope. After a few moments of glancing through the contents, she leaned forward eagerly to examine the documents more closely.

It was an old personnel file on Jake Malloy, the crane operator for Tompkins Construction, dating back to when he'd joined the firm. Someone had circled with red ink three separate notations by the manager about a drinking problem, tardiness, carelessness. This differed considerably from the sheet she'd seen, which had to have been altered. If he knew of this, and he surely must have, how could Sam have taken the chance and not disclosed this information to her as opposing counsel? Sheila wondered.

Next there was a copy of a police report on a drinking and brawling incident involving Jake Malloy, a report less than two years old. How could this be? She'd gone in person to police headquarters and had been told that Jake Malloy had no police record...interesting. Who had sent this?

The third sheet was a photo copy of a note from Dennis Tompkins to his attorney brother, Sam. In no uncertain terms, it outlined the payoff amounts to two named workers who'd seen the accident and had known of Jake's record and condition on the morning of the accident. The money involved was substantial. It would have to be for suppression of evidence.

The next document was a copy of a birth certificate. It showed Jake Malloy to be Dennis Tompkins's nephew, his sister's son. And Sam's nephew as well. It was starting to make sense. Blood was still thicker than water, Sheila thought. But to risk a legal career seemed above and beyond even family favors. Had they been that certain that they'd never be caught? Or perhaps even more certain that Sheila North would play ball with Senator Adams persuading her.

Her heart hammering with renewed hope, Sheila took a deep breath. Of course, she'd have to check the authenticity of the documents. But if they were real, Ed Davis had indeed told the truth. The implications contained in these papers were clear. Evidently Jake Malloy, with a history of a drinking problem, had been under the influence operating the crane that morning. Judgment impaired, he'd miscalculated, hurting one worker and permanently injuring Ed. He was guilty of gross negligence, and Tompkins Construction was liable because they'd allowed him to continue in a hazardous job when they knew about his record. With these papers, if they were real, the assistant district attorney could get to the truth.

And there was no clue as to who'd sent this damning evidence to her. Again Sheila examined the envelope, front and back. As she did so, a small sheet of white paper fell to the floor. Picking it up, she recognized the bold handwriting and read it quickly.

"You once told me a story about a young man who told the woman he loved that they belonged together and that if she believed in him enough, if they met dragons on their travels, he would slay them for her. I just slew my first dragon. If you still believe in me, won't you be my wife and come help me slay any other dragons we may meet? I love you, and together I know now that we can make it."

A smile lighting her face, Sheila stuffed the papers back

into the envelope and quickly walked to the young officer who was still in conversation with the receptionist. "Who gave you this?"

"A man in the hall asked me to deliver it to Miss North who had an appointment in this office. Is something wrong?"

"No, I think something's very right. Was he tall, with curly brown hair and gray eyes?" she asked, moving toward the door.

"I'm not sure about the color of his eyes, but the rest is right. "Oh, I almost forgot. He did something strange."

Pausing with her hand on the doorknob, Sheila turned back. "What's that?"

Reaching into his pocket, the officer pulled out a small, rumpled package. "He told me to mention to you that he gave me this pack of cigarettes because he had no further use for them. Now why would he do that? I don't even smoke."

Blinking back a sudden rush of tears, Sheila smiled broadly. "Only one reason. A beautiful reason." Turning, she rushed out the door.

But as she stepped into the hallway and looked toward the elevators, she saw a tall man with dark hair in a brown suit step in and the silent doors slide shut. Damn! Glancing at her watch, she wondered if she could catch him in the lobby.

"Miss North," the receptionist called to her from the door, "Mr. Wilson will see you now."

With a longing look toward the elevators, Sheila turned back. It was better this way. She'd go in and explain the situation to Ted and then find Tony. She understood. She had to make the next move by going to him, to prove to him she believed in him. And she did. She'd never really stopped.

With a confident smile, she walked toward Ted Wilson's office.

The meeting, though productive, had seemed interminable. Ted Wilson was making a few calls, and she was to check back with him later. Rushing to the phones, she'd learned from Rosemary that Tony wasn't in, that he was home not feeling well. Smiling, Sheila hurried to her car. Not feeling well, hmmm? Perhaps she had the perfect cure for what ailed Mr. Tony Adams.

The drive took forever in hot, congested noontime traffic. Arriving at last, Sheila impatiently slammed the door and all but ran inside Tony's building and into the elevators. Standing in the hallway in front of his door, suddenly she got cold feet. What if the grand reconciliation scene she'd envisioned on the way over backfired somehow? No, she mustn't think like that, she told herself. They had too much between them to give up on their relationship. Taking a deep breath, she pressed the bell.

Tony opened the door and saw Sheila standing there, saw that heart-stoppingly familiar smile he'd thought he'd never see aimed at him again, noticed the tears shining in those beautiful brown eyes. He opened his arms, and she ran into them. At last, at last, he held her as if he'd never let her go. His mouth closed over hers and shut out the world.

With him again, she was with him again where she belonged. Sheila's arms went around him, her heart pounding, her pulse racing. She'd been right after all. Love could make the difference. She tasted love and hope as his lips ground their message into hers. Never would she let him go again. Never.

Finally he pulled back, and she felt her feet touch the floor once more. Blinking away her grateful tears, she looked up at him. The moment of truth had arrived, and though she was frightened, she was ready for it.

"Tony, I was wrong." She turned aside nervously, filled with emotion. "I did believe in you, but when your father talked with me, I . . . I . . ."

He moved in front of her, placing his hands on her upper arms, forcing her to face him. "You jumped to conclusions again, counselor. Based on hearsay. Shame on you."

She nodded. "Yes, I did, I'm ashamed to admit. A bad habit of mine, worse than biting my nails." She reached to pat his empty shirt pocket. "I see you're better at kicking your bad habits than I am."

"Some of them, and I'm working on the others. You were right about the cigarettes. I somehow tied it into losing control if I went back to smoking." Leading them over to the couch, Tony pulled her down beside him, taking hold of her hand. "I don't know if I can make you understand. I was reluctant to let any control over myself slip out of my hands because I felt that, little by little, all of it would disappear. And I thought that if we made a commitment to each other, something would go wrong and we'd both be disappointed."

Sheila raised a hand to caress his cheek. Dark circles under his eyes matched the ones under her own. They'd both agonized over this. "I do understand. You thought through sheer willpower that you could control everything in your life."

He nodded, feeling that she did see. "And I could, most everything, anyhow. Except my feelings for you. From the first day I saw you, feelings more powerful than I'd ever known took over, and control went out the window."

"But, Tony, is that such a bad thing? Nobody in love has total control of themselves."

"I know that now." He reached up and ran his hand down her cheek, then curved it around her chin, his eyes warm on hers. "I've done a lot of thinking. And I've talked with Sandy. And Jed. I fell in love with you, but I don't think I realized all that loving entailed. It's no longer a question of one, but of two. It's not a question of who's the strongest, but how much stronger we can be together.

I wasn't used to thinking in terms of two. Now I think it's the sweetest number I know."

Sheila cocked a mischievous eye at him. "I don't know. I kind of like three, perhaps four."

Her tone was teasing, but he knew her statement had a serious question hidden inside. He thought of Jed and his two little reasons for getting up in the morning. Tony's smile had his heart in it. "Yes, three, four, maybe more, if they'll all turn out to be like their mother."

"Mmm," Sheila said, moving closer and sliding her arms around him, "I think the boys might want to be a mite taller." She trailed one hand into his hair. "And I would like the girls to have your wonderful, curly hair." Leaning forward, she placed a kiss on his eyes. "And gray eyes are so much more interesting than plain brown ones. No, I want them to look like their father."

Tony cuddled her closer. "Maybe we could compromise. I understand that's what sharing a life together's all about."

"By golly, I think he's got it!"

Smiling and settling back, he gazed deeply into her eyes. "Lady, you turned my whole world around. Do you know, do you even suspect how much I love you, Sheily?"

Sheila's heart felt ready to burst. The words she'd been longing to hear, said not reluctantly but with conviction and joy, were finally coming from him, and she could scarcely believe her ears. "As much as I love you, I hope."

"More. Much more. You were raised with love, surrounded by it all your life, with a family that cares deeply for you. Your love is all the more important to me because I've never been loved before to the exclusion of all else. But please be patient with me, Sheila. I've a ways to go yet. Just have faith in me, and I'll slay all those dragons for you."

She gave him a quick kiss. "I do have faith in you, but from now on we slay dragons together. No more soloing

We're a team, remember? And you may have to be patient with me, too. I promise to try not to jump to conclusions so readily, to judge too quickly, but occasionally I may backslide. You'll have to bring me up short, remind me how very fallible I am."

"You're practically perfect." He reached for her small finger and then noticed that several others were also well chewed. "Uh-oh. Speaking of backsliding..."

"It's a wonder I have any nails left. Without you, I just go to pot."

"Then I guess I'd better stick around. How soon will you marry me?"

"As soon as my nails grow in. I can't walk down the aisle with hands that look like this."

He leaned his face in, kissing her warm, fragrant neck. "You can wear gloves. No one will notice. Soon, lady. We've wasted too much time already."

"When you make up your mind, you really move." Slowly she felt the heat spreading as his hands wandered to the buttons of her blouse and his mouth continued its busy work. "I'd love to continue this, but I checked with Rosemary and she said you'd called in sick. Are you sure physical activity of a strenuous nature isn't harmful to your health?"

"Abstinence is harmful to my health. I could hardly wait until you looked over that material, handed it in to the D.A. and found your way over here."

She moved back, stilling his hands. "Pretty sure of yourself, weren't you? In the excitement of being with you again, I almost forgot to thank you. How did you find all that information?"

"I'd been looking into the Davis case on my own since our parting of the ways that day. I had a hunch something was going on. The other day I helped Dad move out of the building, and we sat down and had a long talk." Tony sighed deeply, remembering his father's reactions. "When

I told him what I'd discovered, I think he aged five years before my eyes. Oh, I know he's not an innocent, but I honestly believe he didn't know how far Sam and Dennis had gone. He simply never checked it out. And they were so sure he'd come through and help them cover up.''

Tony shook his head sadly as he squeezed her hand. "The senator's a stubborn man, but his life hasn't been all that easy. I never thought how difficult his early years were because of a forced marriage to a woman he didn't love. It doesn't excuse what he's let himself become, but I suppose it helps me understand him a little. He wasn't as lucky as I am. I found you and your love.''

"I'm glad you at least talked with him. Maybe one day—''

"I don't hold too much hope that we'll ever be friends, but at least perhaps I can stop blaming him entirely.'' He nuzzled her cheek. "So my findings helped?''

"Enormously. Ted's checking it out right now.'' Sheila squirmed to look at her watch. "I told him I'd call him back in an hour.'' She gave him a quick kiss. "Don't lose your place. I'll make that call and be right back.''

Tony knew how important it was for Sheila to win the case for the Davises. Though he wanted her desperately, he could afford to be patient a little longer. He had forever with her now, and the thought held a world of appeal to him. Giving her an encouraging smile, he leaned back on the couch. "Go get 'em, tiger. I'll be waiting for you.''

*　*　*　*　*

*. . . and now an exciting short story
from Silhouette Books.*

*

HEATHER GRAHAM POZZESSERE
Shadows on the Nile

CHAPTER ONE

Alex could tell that the woman was very nervous. Her fingers were wound tightly about the arm rests, and she had been staring straight ahead since the flight began. Who was she? Why was she flying alone? Why to Egypt? She was a small woman, fine-boned, with classical features and porcelain skin. Her hair was golden blond, and she had blue-gray eyes that were slightly tilted at the corners, giving her a sensual and exotic appeal.

And she smelled divine. He had been sitting there, glancing through the flight magazine, and her scent had reached him, filling him like something rushing through his bloodstream, and before he had looked at her he had known that she would be beautiful.

John was frowning at him. His gaze clearly said that this was not the time for Alex to become interested in a woman. Alex lowered his head, grinning. Nuts to John. He was the one who had made the reservations so late that there was already another passenger between them in their row. Alex couldn't have remained silent anyway; he was certain that he could ease the flight for her. Besides, he had to know her name, had to see if her eyes would turn silver when she smiled. Even though he should, he couldn't ignore her.

"Alex," John said warningly.

Maybe John was wrong, Alex thought. Maybe this was precisely the right time for him to get involved. A woman would be the perfect shield, in case anyone was interested in his business in Cairo.

The two men should have been sitting next to each other, Jillian decided. She didn't know why she had wound up sandwiched between the two of them, but she couldn't do a thing about it. Frankly, she was far too nervous to do much of anything.

"It's really not so bad," a voice said sympathetically. It came from her right. It was the younger of the two men, the one next to the window. "How about a drink? That might help."

Jillian took a deep, steadying breath, then managed to answer. "Yes . . . please. Thank you."

His fingers curled over hers. Long, very strong fingers, nicely tanned. She had noticed him when she had taken her seat—he was difficult not to notice. There was an arresting quality about him. He had a certain look: high powered, confident, self-reliant. He was medium tall and medium built, with shoulders that nicely filled out his suit jacket, dark brown eyes, and sandy hair that seemed to defy any effort at combing it. And he had a wonderful voice, deep and compelling. It broke through her fear and actually soothed her. Or perhaps it was the warmth of his hand over hers that did it.

"Your first trip to Egypt?" he asked. She managed a brief nod, but was saved from having to comment when the stewardess came by. Her companion ordered her white wine, then began to converse with her quite normally, as if unaware that her fear of flying had nearly rendered her speechless. He asked her what she did for a living, and she heard herself tell him that she was a music teacher at a junior college. He responded easily to everything she said, his voice warm and concerned each time he asked another question. She didn't think; she simply an

wered him, because flying had become easier the moment he touched her. She even told him that she was a
widow, that her husband had been killed in a car accident
four years ago, and that she was here now to fulfill a long-
held dream, because she had always longed to see the pyramids, the Nile and all the ancient wonders Egypt held.

She had loved her husband, Alex thought, watching as
pain briefly darkened her eyes. Her voice held a thread of
sadness when she mentioned her husband's name. Out of
nowhere, he wondered how it would feel to be loved by
such a woman.

Alex noticed that even John was listening, commenting
on things now and then. How interesting, Alex thought,
looking across at his friend and associate.

The stewardess came with the wine. Alex took it for her,
chatting casually with the woman as he paid. Charmer,
Jillian thought ruefully. She flushed, realizing that it was
his charm that had led her to tell him so much about her
life.

Her fingers trembled when she took the wineglass. "I'm
sorry," she murmured. "I don't really like to fly."

Alex—he had introduced himself as Alex, but without
telling her his last name—laughed and said that was the
understatement of the year. He pointed out the window to
the clear blue sky—an omen of good things to come, he
said—then assured her that the airline had an excellent
safety record. His friend, the older man with the haggard,
world-weary face, eventually introduced himself as John.
He joked and tried to reassure her, too, and eventually
their efforts paid off. Once she felt a little calmer, she offered to move, so they could converse without her in the
way.

Alex tightened his fingers around hers, and she felt the
startling warmth in his eyes. His gaze was appreciative and
casual, without being insulting. She felt a rush of sweet
heat swirl within her, and she realized with surprise that it

was excitement, that she was enjoying his company the way
a woman enjoyed the company of a man who attracted
her. She had thought she would never feel that way again.

"I wouldn't move for all the gold in ancient Egypt," he
said with a grin, "and I doubt that John would, either."
He touched her cheek. "I might lose track of you, and
don't even know your name."

"Jillian," she said, meeting his eyes. "Jillian Jacoby."

He repeated her name softly, as if to commit it to memory, then went on to talk about Cairo, the pyramids at
Giza, the Valley of the Kings, and the beauty of the night
when the sun set over the desert in a riot of blazing red.

And then the plane was landing. To her amazement, the
flight had ended. Once she was on solid ground again, Jillian realized that Alex knew all sorts of things about her
while she didn't know a thing about him or John—not
even their full names.

They went through customs together. Jillian was immediately fascinated, in love with the colorful atmosphere of Cairo, and not at all dismayed by the waiting and
the bureaucracy. When they finally reached the street she
fell head over heels in love with the exotic land. The heat
shimmered in the air, and taxi drivers in long burnooses
lined up for fares. She could hear the soft singsong of the
language, and she was thrilled to realize that the dream she
had harbored for so long was finally coming true.

She didn't realize that two men had followed them from
the airport to the street. Alex, however, did. He saw the
men behind him, and his jaw tightened as he nodded
John to stay put and hurried after Jillian.

"Where are you staying?" he asked her.

"The Hilton," she told him, pleased at his interest.
Maybe her dream was going to turn out to have some unexpected aspects.

He whistled for a taxi. Then, as the driver opened the
door, Jillian looked up to find Alex staring at her. S

felt . . . something. A fleeting magic raced along her spine, as if she knew what he was about to do. Knew, and should have protested, but couldn't.

Alex slipped his arm around her. One hand fell to her waist, the other cupped her nape, and he kissed her. His mouth was hot, his touch firm, persuasive. She was filled with heat; she trembled . . . and then she broke away at last, staring at him, the look in her eyes more eloquent than any words. Confused, she turned away and stepped into the taxi. As soon as she was seated she turned to stare after him, but he was already gone, a part of the crowd.

She touched her lips as the taxi sped toward the heart of the city. She shouldn't have allowed the kiss; she barely knew him. But she couldn't forget him.

She was still thinking about him when she reached the Hilton. She checked in quickly, but she was too late to acquire a guide for the day. The manager suggested that she stop by the Kahil bazaar, not far from the hotel. She dropped her bags in her room, then took another taxi to the bazaar. Once again she was enchanted. She loved everything: the noise, the people, the donkey carts that blocked the narrow streets, the shops with their beaded entryways and beautiful wares in silver and stone, copper and brass. Old men smoking water pipes sat on mats drinking tea, while younger men shouted out their wares from stalls and doorways. Jillian began walking slowly, trying to take it all in. She was occasionally jostled, but she kept her hand on her purse and sidestepped quickly. She was just congratulating herself on her competence when she was suddenly dragged into an alley by two Arabs swaddled in burnooses.

"What—" she gasped, but then her voice suddenly fled. The alley was empty and shadowed, and night was coming. One man had a scar on his cheek, and held a long, curved knife; the other carried a switchblade.

"Where is it?" the first demanded.

"Where is what?" she asked frantically.

The one with the scar compressed his lips grimly. He set his knife against her cheek, then stroked the flat side down to her throat. She could feel the deadly coolness of the steel blade.

"Where is it? Tell me now!"

Her knees were trembling, and she tried to find the breath to speak. Suddenly she noticed a shadow emerging from the darkness behind her attackers. She gasped stunned, as the man drew nearer. It was Alex.

Alex . . . silent, stealthy, his features taut and grim. He heart seemed to stop. Had he come to her rescue? Or wa he allied with her attackers, there to threaten, even de stroy, her?

* * * * *

Watch for Chapter Two of SHADOWS ON THE NILE coming next month—only in Silhouette Intimate Moments.

Silhouette Special Edition

COMING NEXT MONTH

#415 TIME AFTER TIME—Billie Green
Airline executives Leah French and Paul Gregory had a cool,
professional relationship. Then the dreams began, dreams that
carried them out of time, to faraway lands and into each
other's arms.

#416 FOOLS RUSH IN—Ginna Gray
In tracing her missing twin, Erin Blaine's first find was dashing
Max Delany, her sister's supposed beloved. Dodging gunmen and
double-crossers, Max and Erin sought clues...and stumbled onto
unwanted desire.

#417 WHITE NIGHTS—Dee Norman
Whether racing down ski slopes or chasing the chills in a hot tub,
Jennifer Ericson couldn't seem to avoid hostile financier
Travis MacKay. Though he suspected her of pursuing him, she
was really only running from love.

#418 TORN ASUNDER—Celeste Hamilton
Years ago Alexa Thorpe, the boss's daughter, and Ty Duncan,
the laborer's son, fell in forbidden love, but family objections
and deceptions drove them apart. By tackling their history, could
they succeed in sharing a future?

#419 SUMMER RAIN—Lisa Jackson
Widowed Ainsley Hughes reluctantly brought her troubled son to
her father's ranch, only to find the Circle S failing...and aloof
Trent McCullough in charge. She'd once loved Trent's fire, but
could she trust his iciness now?

#420 LESSONS IN LOVING—Bay Matthews
Bachelor Mitch Bishop had much to learn about parenting, and
special ed teacher Jamie Carr was the perfect instructor. But in
the school of love, both adults faltered on their ABC's.

AVAILABLE THIS MONTH

In response
to last year's outstanding success,
Silhouette Brings You:

Silhouette
Christmas
Stories
1987

Specially chosen for you in a delightful volume celebrating the holiday season, four original romantic stories written by four of your favorite Silhouette authors.

Dixie Browning—*Henry the Ninth*
Ginna Gray—*Season of Miracles*
Linda Howard—*Bluebird Winter*
Diana Palmer—*The Humbug Man*

Each of these bestselling authors will enchant you with their unforgettable stories, exuding the magic of Christmas and the wonder of falling in love.

A heartwarming Christmas gift during the holiday season...indulge yourself and give this book to a special friend!

Available November 1987

XM87